PRAISE FOR

SONG OF BELONGING

"In the way that Willa Cather captures the soul of the prairie, Michelle St. Romain captures the soul of the sea—from the New Orleans bayous to the Pacific Ocean. The prose in the aptly titled *Song of Belonging* is lyrical and rhythmic. A double-timeline narrative with historical and contemporary stories, this book reminds us that if you take action, you can be part of saving our beautiful planet."

—Libby Gill, author of *Malibu Summer*

"*Song of Belonging* is a masterful exploration of connection—to nature, to our ancestors, to ourselves. The characters are revealed like slowly opening flowers, with layers of complexity unfolding through generations with heartbreaking beauty. This is storytelling at its finest: grounded yet transcendent, personal yet universal. A profound meditation on what it means to heed the call of both our lineage and our planet."

—Maressa Voss, author of *When Shadows Grow Tall*

"*Song of Belonging* is as lyrical as its title suggests, flowing rhythmically as it explores the links between people and place across generations. As human beings, we all share an innate need to connect and belong, and Michelle St. Romain pens a compelling journey of connection and identity across past and future, inspiring purpose, healing, and vital connection to the natural world."

—Pam Breaux, President and Chief Executive Officer,
National Assembly of State Arts Agencies

"Set along the rivers of Louisiana and the rocky California coast, *Song of Belonging* contains multitudes. A beautiful story of spiritual renewal and our connection to the past and the future, the natural world, and all the threads of the universe."

—Donnaldson Brown, author of *Because I Loved You*

"*Song of Belonging* by Michelle St. Romain is a well-crafted, gripping, and powerful story of deep grief, discovery, healing, belonging, and connections to the past and future, to our ancestors, and to the natural world. This complex, multigenerational novel featuring magical realism and a bit of romance is a must-read. . . . Highly recommended."

—*Readers' Favorite*, 5-star review

"*Song of Belonging* is a spellbinding novel in which voices of the past whisper secrets, love blooms in the present, and hope for the future is restored. Like ocean ripples washing over pebbles, Michelle St. Romain's lyrical prose enchants and captivates as it sings of love, longing, and hope for the future of our oceans and ourselves."

—Jennifer Roberts, author of
The Village Healer's Book of Cures

"A hauntingly beautiful debut, weaving past and present in a seamless story of love, loss, redemption, and belonging. Highly recommended."

—Ashley Sweeney, author of *The Irish Girl*

"Michelle Wilson's writing is exquisite, achieving a delicate balance between poetry and women's fiction. This enchanting story about family gifts and secrets that are revealed like the tide being pulled back by the moon will have you charmed from the very first page."

—Kaylie Newell, author of *The Moonshadow's Daughter*

"Intriguingly haunting dual story. Present-day Alice is tormented by visions from a mysterious maternal line of ancestral healers she cannot ignore, a power mirrored in her great-grandmother, Grace, who is drowning in grief after the tragic loss of her young daughter. As descendants of healing women who tend the waters, their lives unspool as potent, psychological journeys celebrating the profound wisdom of older women and the ancient trust required to embrace one's destiny. A must-read for readers intrigued by the revelations spiritual guidance curates for us when we're ready."

—Joan Fernandez, author of *Saving Vincent*

"Seamlessly weaving the past and the present, *Song of Belonging* creates a fully believable world where the voices of the grandmothers speak, magic happens, romance flourishes, and nature conquers. Readers will be enthralled all the way to the end with this compelling love story and with the struggle to save the planet by honoring the wisdom passed down through generations."

—Kathryn Williams, author of *Rhino Dreams*

"*Song of Belonging* takes the reader on a magical journey. The connections between ocean cultures—from Louisiana to California and from Hawaii to Ireland—create an evocative backdrop to Alice's story. She learns to be brave in the face of her destiny, leading her to find her inner compass as she unravels the stories of her grandmothers and others in her family."

—Laura Kealoha Yardley, author of *The Heart of Huna*

SONG OF BELONGING

a novel

MICHELLE ST. ROMAIN

SHE WRITES PRESS

Published in 2026 by
She Writes Press, an imprint of The Stable Book Group

32 Court Street, Suite 2109
Brooklyn, NY 11201
https://shewritespress.com
Library of Congress Control Number: 2025926949
ISBN: 979-8-89636-126-8
eISBN: 979-8-89636-127-5

Interior Designer: Tabitha Lahr
Interior illustrations: page v, page 53 turtle, and page 177 sea otter by Lindsey Cleworth art and design; all additional illustrations © Shutterstock.com

Printed in the United States

Also by Michelle St. Romain

Promised Fruit
(coauthored with Alma Rosa Alvarez)

Water's Edge
(coauthored with Alma Rosa Alvarez)

To my mother, grandmothers, aunts, and ancestors

To my family and those to come in future generations

Together, we are a constellation of stars
in this beautiful universe

Song of Belonging

Partial Family Tree (The Mother Line)

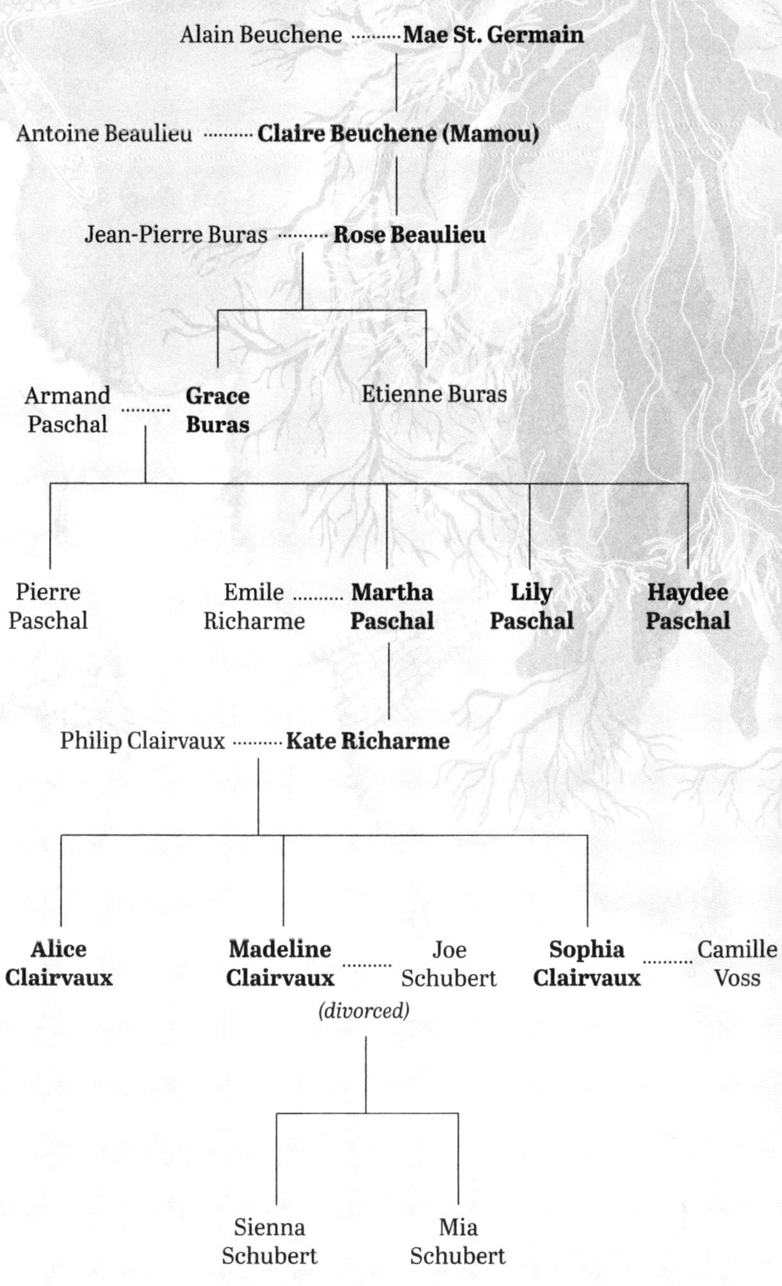

Our ancestors' memories live inside of us
lining the cells of our own perceptions

Our lives are mirrors of their loves
and jagged wounds
their longings and unsung joy

What are we to do
with this
blessed, weighted gift?

PROLOGUE

This story starts in the sea, in the shadowy depths where sounds are muffled by the weight of water hung heavy with salt and memories of those who came before. It begins with those who lived in the warm waters of the oceans and gulfs, when the ancient ones moved among the animals of the land and the creatures of the sea.

In this time, a woman lived in the ocean depths. She grew from the willowy, green seaweed and sang the songs of her ancestors. They came from the stars but stayed connected through the waves of sound and the folds of time, which opened through rituals known only to those who were able to access the hidden doorways with their thoughts.

She sang songs that brought the creatures of the ocean toward her, first the small ones that lived among the seaweed, the urchins and fish that could be cupped within her palms. Next came the dolphins and sea turtles, the monk seals and small sharks. Finally, the larger ones came, the whales which moved through warm waters only when the northern currents were too cold, and they followed the trail of small fish to the gateway of the Southern hemisphere. The sea beings moved toward her in the way birds change flight patterns in the sky, moved suddenly by invisible sound waves, the melody of her song ringing through their skins. They were pulled toward her songs, haunting melodies that caused the waves to move more forcefully toward the shore, with each note she released from her body.

She moved from the ocean depths, climbing onto a jagged rock, then swam toward the sandy shore of a nearby island. She stood still, listening, until the Eastern wind pushed her toward the center of the island. She found herself standing in a place she had never been, but which was completely familiar to her.

She did not know that in this moment sea turtles began to swim in from the ocean and walk toward the center of the island, shedding their shells, becoming women with long, slender legs and flowing hair the color of moss. Sea otters came next, small families moving together, the young ones following behind their mothers. The seals moved behind them, taking their place in a growing circle around the woman. The beings of the sea began to sing a haunting melody, a song she had forgotten, given to her by the ancient ones before she came into being in the ocean depths. The song spiraled around her, creating a wave-like barrier, protecting and holding her close.

She melted in this moment, her human skin becoming translucent, shimmering a radiant light that became a beam, pointing back to the stars, to the dark milky sky above her, endless in its depth. She did not know how far the light beam traveled or how far it reached. She did not know if it connected with anything other than the endless echoes of sky and space. When she felt herself becoming more translucent than even the crystal waterfalls on the cliffs around her, she breathed in a single gasp of air and held it, still and silent, until she dissolved into a pool of shimmering water in the sand.

One with the water now. Luminous. One with everything.

PART 1

Opening

CHAPTER 1—ALICE CLAIRVAUX

June 2019, Berkeley, California

The day started with a crash. That, and water spilling everywhere. Alice opened her eyes to the sound of her favorite glass on the dresser beside her bed smashing onto the wooden floor, shattering into pieces, the water it had contained soaking the cardboard box on the floor.

Isabella.

The cat, startled as Alice was by the crash, jumped from the nightstand onto the pillow, distancing herself from the mess she'd just made, her tail still swishing. Alice sat up in bed and swept the tabby into her arms.

"What did you do, Isabella?" She paused, rubbing the cat's head, allowing herself a moment to take in her surroundings. The next words came out softly. "You're confused here, aren't you?"

Alice looked around, taking in the line of unpacked boxes. Her new North Berkeley apartment was filled with the contents of her life, all stacked in neat piles of taped-up cardboard. She put Isabella down, carefully stepping over the shards of glass, and moved to the window, peering out onto the street. Wild flowers, roses, and lavender stalks lined the sidewalk, an explosion of bright colors leaning against the white picket fence surrounding her tiny yard.

She turned back and took in the scene before her. Light filtered into the apartment through the white lace curtains, shimmering on Isabella's gray and white fur, giving it a silver sheen like the minnows flickering in the gulf waters of her childhood.

"It's our first day in our new neighborhood, ma chérie. I know I've said this before, but this is a place I think we'll stay for a while. It's a beautiful Saturday. I'll clean up this mess, then what shall we do today?"

Her mind drifted toward the stack of research on her desk at work. Should she spend the day drafting the article on a new farm-to-table bistro that was opening in North Oakland? Her dream of writing for a national magazine was finally seeming possible and she had no intention of letting anything stop her from making that happen. For a moment, everything she had sacrificed for her career flashed before her—dating, relationships, even weekend trips with friends. All of it came behind work. And it was worth it. Yes, research this afternoon after unpacking boxes.

First thing this morning, though—clean up the broken glass, feed Isabella, and get some breakfast for herself. Grabbing the broom and dustpan from the bathroom, she swept up the shattered glass and dumped it in the trash can.

Caffeine next. She needed something to wake her up before taking on anything else. She found her old coffee pot quickly, packed in a box on the table, along with her favorite New Orleans brand coffee and chicory. As the deep brown grounds started brewing, filling her small apartment with the aroma that reminded her of every morning of childhood, she decided to dry off the box next to the bed and salvage what was inside.

This one contained everything she wanted to put on her new bookshelf. A few favorites were here: *Their Eyes Were Watching God* and *Bless Me, Ultima* next to Strunk and

White's manual. Just under those a few Louisiana classics, including Kate Chopin's *The Awakening* and an autographed cookbook and memoir by Paul Prudhomme which had been given to her great-uncle, left to Alice after he died.

Slipping her hands deeper into the box, her fingers touched something soft, worn, and slightly padded. Her great-grandmother's jewelry box, packed just below the books. It would be displayed on the bookshelf in her new apartment, she'd already decided. No longer would it stay hidden on a closet shelf, unopened, left to sit behind dusty boxes and other neglected items from her life. Time to have a more grown up look for her tiny home, beyond decorative blankets thrown over yard sale tables and bookshelves made of crates from thrift stores. The new bookshelf stood waiting in the corner, unadorned, ready for books and a few decorative items. The jewelry box would be perfect there.

Guilt crept over her as she stroked the box's faded green lid, thinking about how long she had kept it hidden away. Ten years had passed since she'd last opened it. Ten years since she'd left home for college and started life on her own. On her own terms. Determined to write for a living and make a difference in the world with her research and carefully chosen words.

Pausing, she let her fingers run over the faded jewelry box top, choosing almost on their own, it seemed, to click open the lid. She was surprised by the faint floral scent drifting up from its contents. Grandmere Grace's perfume continued to linger in these treasures from her life, decades after her passing: the tiny handmade doll, its hair made of crumbling moss from an oak tree, eyes from dried black-eyed peas. Below the doll was the packet of quilt squares in a patchwork of spring colors, a set of hair pins tucked inside, each one decorated with a hand-carved sea animal at the top. The turtle was her favorite, carved from forest green malachite.

The seal, whale, and bright yellow fish were carved from other semi-precious stones—moonstone, lapis lazuli, and citrine—creating a small rainbow of tropical colors. She remembered her great-grandmother wearing these two at a time to keep her silver-white hair back from her face.

Below these treasures she found the jewel-toned silk scarf wrapped around a smooth river rock, a spiral and tiny stars painted across it. The scarf had been her great-grandmother's and the stone had been wrapped in it when Alice received the jewelry box as a child. She picked up the stone, admiring the bright stars and spiral, and wrapped her palm around it. Warmth radiated through her hand—a gentle pulsing that took her by surprise. Curious, she held it for a few seconds before putting it down. Had that ever happened before?

She reached to the bottom of the jewelry box to find the note her great-grandmother had left her, folded neatly into a square on stationary with a large P at the top.

Grace Paschal had been a small woman, just over five feet tall, but a large presence in Alice's life. She had died when Alice was seven and the jewelry box remained as a reminder of their connection. The paper was pale yellow now, more than twenty years later, slightly translucent with the passing of years.

My dear Alice, ma chérie, I am leaving you this jewelry box as a gift so you know I will always be with you. I have watched you grow from a baby to a beautiful young girl and your life has a lot in store for you. I want you to remember that you have gifts that are meant to be shared with the world. You do not understand them now, but they will make themselves known to you and you must decide how to use them. These gifts have been passed to you from those who came before, and they have been shut down for too long. The world you will grow up in needs them to be re-opened now.

You are not alone, Alice. Be brave and follow what you hear in the silence. Go into nature when the world around you gets too loud. When you feel lost, turn to the natural world to heal and teach you, and give back to it whenever you can. It nurtures and supports us and without it, we are lost. We are the caretakers of it, my sweet Alice, remember that. It speaks to us if we listen. It has both wisdom to share and messages to help us know which way to turn when life is challenging.

Our family has always been connected to the natural world, but especially to the waters that surround and nurture us—the ocean and gulf, the rivers and bayous. We are protectors of it, and your gifts will lead you to your place in our family line.

Stay curious and pay attention to everything around you. This world is layered, and the veils between those layers are thinner than many would believe. As you grow up, I pray you will be brave enough to let yourself see what is truly before you.

When you are old enough to be on your own, take this jewelry box to the ocean and let it tell you secrets from those who came before. The stone is a gift from your grandmothers, and it carries a history of light and darkness. Let the spiral lead you to answers you seek about your life and help you understand the gifts you have been given. Use your gifts to protect what you love and create what you desire.

You will always find me when you visit the rivers and the ocean. So much life is below the surface of the waters, and there is much to understand for those who have eyes to see and ears to hear. You are loved beyond the sky and stars and sea.

I am always with you.

Je t'aime, Alice. Je t'aime.

Alice traced the lines of the last words with her finger. The sounds of her great-grandmother's lilting French, always mingled with English, sang in her ears.

Use your gifts to protect what you love and create what you desire.

What did she desire? The question pulled her out of thoughts of her grandmothers and back to her own life. She knew she wanted a successful writing career and at some point, marriage and a family. But the career had to be the focus now, taking all of her time as she worked to reach her goal.

The memory of receiving the box was fresh in her mind, even though over two decades had passed. The day after Great-Grandmere Grace died, Grandmere Martha had called her into the back bedroom of her house. Grandmere Grace had spent her last years there, cared for by her daughter. Grandmere Martha pulled the jewelry box down from a shelf and handed it to Alice, with words that remained a mystery. "Mamere wanted you to have this. I'm not sure why. She said she knew you would take good care of it."

Now, standing in her new apartment, she still wondered why it had been given to her. Several grandchildren and great-grandchildren lived close by, and Alice had been the one to receive it. She pulled from the bottom of the jewelry box a tiny card—not much larger than a stamp—the most curious of all the items in the box, blank with only the date June 21, 1934, written in her great-grandmother's hand.

Alice remembered standing in her grandmother's bedroom the first time she opened the jewelry box, surrounded by African violets and lace-covered antiques. When she clicked the lid open, a tingle had run up her spine. Was it fear she felt? She remembered thinking that only two days before, Grandmere Grace had been alive in the room, her breath perhaps still floating in the air, feeding the African violets. Sounds of family members drifted into the room from the parlor. Someone was in the kitchen cooking gumbo, the sweet, smoky aroma of crawfish wafting through the house, mingled with the heady scent of bouquets of flowers, all sent before Grandmere Grace's funeral.

Melting into those sensory memories, Alice held the letter and drifted into her childhood with its oak tables covered in linen doilies and the soft Southern lilt of her grandmothers' voices.

Coffee gurgling in the pot brought her back to the present. Berkeley, not New Orleans. Twenty-eight years old now, not a child, lost in between the worlds of the living and those who've passed on. Time to find her favorite coffee mug. Opening the box always created a sense of unease she couldn't shake—an uncertainty she couldn't quite name.

A familiar push and pull rose inside, an internal teetering she knew too well between wanting to push away anything she couldn't explain, followed by a pull to . . . what? Let herself be haunted by the past? By things she could never tell anyone about? Open to secrets about herself she'd closed up firmly when she'd left Louisiana, like the boxes taped-up all around her now?

No. The answer was clear, as always. Stand firmly in the present and keep a steady head. Coffee was the answer to help with that, and she found the cup she was looking for in the next box. Warm and soothing, the first sip went down easily. She moved to the window and looked out again at her new neighborhood.

"Isabella, I'm going to take a walk to check out the park. You keep an eye on things here." The last words came out almost inaudibly as she turned to face the cat. "It's time for me to take a trip to the ocean next weekend with the jewelry box, as Grandmere Grace wanted." *Check it off the list*, she thought. *Get rid of this weird feeling that's probably just guilt.*

Clothes lay in piles around her bed. She poked through a stack of t-shirts until she found the one she was looking for, deep blue with a turtle on the front. A gift from a friend who had recently visited Hawaii. Pulling it on over a pair of jean shorts, she headed out the door, coffee in hand. The bright colors of the scarf caught her attention and she slipped it around her neck before walking out into her new neighborhood.

Sprawling craftsman houses lined the street, steps leading up to wooden porches covered with flowering pots of petunias, zinnias, smiling-faced pansies. The heady scent of lavender overtook her as she walked past one yard, the purple flowers poking through the slats of a wooden fence in need of a new coat of paint. One house was flanked by two Meyer lemon trees, filled with tiny flowers. The sweet taste of lemonade came to mind, and she made a note to befriend the owners of this house.

She walked toward Live Oak Park, just around the corner from her apartment. As she turned right onto Walnut Street, the warmth of the early summer sun brought back memories of her childhood in New Orleans. Flowering jasmine mingled with abundant rose bushes—pale yellow, two-toned gold and pink—all reminding her of her grandmother's garden.

Maybe she would find a farmer's market at the park. Her refrigerator was close to empty, and her small potted herbs only gave her a little basil, mint, and chamomile to work with. Adding some lettuce and tomatoes would give her at least enough for a salad.

Children's laughter greeted her as she got closer. Instead of farmer's market stalls, she saw a playground with a small community theater nestled back from the street. A tree with shade would be a good place to sit, take in her new neighborhood, and finish her coffee. The grassy area near the theater was filled with children and their parents and she noticed a sign for a live performance later that day. OLIVER TWIST. TWO P.M.

Enjoying a play that afternoon tempted her for a moment, but unpacked boxes and work projects brought her back to her plan for the weekend. Get things done. Turn this week's articles in early, as usual.

A large oak tree, branches sprawling in all directions, created a canopy over a grassy area in front of her. Plopping down in the soft dirt at its base, she leaned into it, stretched out her legs, and pressed her back against the trunk. The jewelry box and its contents rose in her mind. June twenty-first, the date on the tiny card in the box, was only a week away.

She hadn't discovered the card until she was eighteen, packing to move away to Baton Rouge to begin her freshman year at Louisiana State University. She'd opened the jewelry box, rummaging through its contents as she decided what to take with her to school. She fumbled upon a slim pocket on the inside of the box and reached inside. The small card had been hidden there all those years. Intrigued by the sparseness of its message, only a date, she had wondered about what it meant before slipping it back into the tiny pocket, then placing the box back in the closet. She'd finally taken it from her childhood closet and brought it with her when she'd moved from Louisiana to California after college, but it had remained tucked away. Until now. It was beautiful and deserved a place of honor, this gift from her great-grandmother.

June twenty-first would fall on a Friday this year, just six days away. She would take the day off and go to the beach. Face the unease the jewelry box and its contents brought up the way she faced projects at work—with a sense of purpose. What her great-grandmother asked was simple, really, and there was no reason not to do it this year. Then put the box on the bookshelf, where it would stay, a simple reminder of her family at home.

"Hi."

A young girl's voice broke into her thoughts, jarring her back to the present. Light brown hair hung around the child's face, framing deep brown eyes. The girl smiled. A memory arose in Alice's mind and her body tensed, her breath caught in her chest.

"I love the trees," the child said, tipping her face up toward the leafy branches above. "Do you?"

Unsure how to respond, Alice sat up straighter, noticing the small, bare feet before her draped at the ankles by a long white cotton dress. Or was it a nightgown? A slight chill ran through Alice's body.

"Yes, I do love the trees," she said slowly.

"Oak trees are my favorite. The moss is like hair coming down from the branches. That's why I think the oaks are women. The acorns are their babies. I collect them."

A familiar tingle rose from the base of Alice's spine. The girl? Here, now? A breeze ruffled the leaves on the trees.

"Want to see the ones I've collected?"

Her tiny hands uncurled slowly to reveal six acorns nestled lightly in her palms.

"I'm giving them names. Isabelle, Pearl, Robbie, Benjamin, Rose, and Martha."

Martha, her grandmother's name. It was just a coincidence. Not a coincidence? Everything seemed to swim before Alice, the sounds of children playing nearby fading away. A light hum encircled them, creating a wave around their two bodies, the six acorns anchoring them, held in the center.

"What's your name? Are your parents nearby?" The question came out in a hoarse whisper, a squeak of a question, Alice's voice held in her throat.

Was she back, this time in the flesh, this child in the white nightgown? Because, yes, it was a nightgown. Was it only Alice's imagination that her face seemed to glow with an ethereal haze?

"My parents aren't here now, but that's OK. They know I just love being near the trees. The trees talk to me, like the acorns, but different. It's more like a song I hear from them. What does it sound like to you? The trees, I mean. What do they sound like to you?"

Tilting her head slightly, Alice wondered how to respond. What do the trees sound like? She took a deep breath to slow down the rapid heartbeat pounding in her chest.

"I'm not sure what the trees sound like to me. I like hearing the wind move through them, though. I like the sound of the leaves rattling. It reminds me of home, where I grew up."

"Near water, right? Where it's warm."

Alice leaned back against the body of the oak tree, anchoring herself, fear creeping through her body. How could this girl know it was warm where she grew up?

"Yes, it was warm where I grew up. I lived in New Orleans." She paused. "Water is everywhere in Louisiana. My neighborhood wasn't too close to water, but there is a lot of water all around the city."

"I know. And it's murky in some places. And in some places, you can't see what's underneath the top of the water. But that's what makes it interesting. At least that's what my mamma used to say."

The tingling in Alice's spine grew stronger, fear threatening to overtake her now.

"Where is your mother? Is she nearby?"

"Did you see the otter family in the creek behind the park? There's a mamma there and two babies. I love watching them swim and sometimes they come to shore and visit me. I've gotta go now, but you should visit them too." The little girl held out one acorn to Alice. "I'll leave Martha here for you, but take good care of her. She talks if you ask her questions. They don't all talk, but she does."

The girl leaned down and with one finger traced a spiral in the dirt, then placed the acorn in the center. She twirled in a circle once, twice, smiled one more time.

"And I love your scarf. The colors make me think of being in a magical place. Maybe I'll see you here again sometime." She ran off toward the community theater, getting lost in the small crowd of children and adults gathering near the door.

Alice sat stunned, staring at the spiral in the dirt, afraid to move.

Who was that child? She seemed so like the one from her childhood, with that nightgown, bare feet, long brown hair and haunting gaze. It had been years since she'd appeared. And now, here. Leaving a spiral in the dirt—like the one on the stone from the jewelry box—and an acorn named Martha.

Images flashed before Alice. Her childhood memories were punctuated with flashes of a girl in a white nightgown, appearing only occasionally but always leaving behind a lingering feeling of uncertainty about the lines between the worlds. Often more like visitations than just images, Alice had worked for years to shut them out, a popcorn trail of experiences that disturbed her sense of sanity. Her first memory of the girl's appearance still sent a shiver through her. Tall enough to see over the chairs in the kitchen but not over the table where they ate breakfast, Alice stood near the stove watching her mother scramble eggs, bacon crackling in the frying pan. Wearing her red and white gingham nightgown, she turned to the window looking out over the gardenias in their lush yard and saw a young girl standing in the grass. A girl or an apparition? Slightly taller than Alice and wearing a white gown, she mirrored Alice, both girls barefoot in their cotton nightgowns that let humidity breathe through. Loose brown hair cascading down their shoulders, brown eyes staring at each other like deer caught in headlights. The girl waved at Alice, smiled with her lips closed, one side curling up slightly to form a crescent moon shape, then . . . faded away. She didn't walk away. She vanished. Like a ghost.

Like the girl here at the park had just vanished.

Without thinking, Alice put her empty coffee mug into her backpack. Picking up the acorn, she rubbed her finger over the smooth surface. Oak trees, here in the park before her, at home in Louisiana. Moss hanging from branches above her. The doll in the jewelry box, hair made of moss, still intact after all these years. Swirling memories from childhood mingled with the sights before her, creating an unwelcome lightheadedness.

She stood up and walked toward the theater. She would find the little girl. Ask her more questions. Maybe she was dressed for a part in Oliver Twist, being theatrical, trying to get a response.

Alice approached the small theater crowded with families, but the child was not among them. Perhaps she was inside. But what if she wasn't? Better to leave her alone. Better to leave this whole thing and turn back to her plans for the day. Shake this off and set up her apartment.

She turned away from the theater, the oak trees, the child. Keep walking. Let the images go. Let the girl go. It was simply a strange encounter, throwing her off because she was slightly disoriented from the move across town. All Alice had to do was control her day just as she always had, focusing her attention on what was in front of her. Everything else would wash away.

A large church and school loomed before her as she crossed Henry Street. In the Spanish mission style, the off-white buildings were outlined with soft brown edges: pointed roof, window frames, large doors. She paused, remembering the Catholic churches of her childhood, and something quietly called to her from inside. Should she enter? Maybe being in the church would settle her thoughts. Needing comfort, she turned toward the tall building, her body pulled by an invisible tug, her feet pacing the steps up the white-washed walkway leading to the entrance. A wave of dizziness hit. She closed her eyes, steadying herself, then slowly opened the door, the sun's rays pouring into the church from behind her, creating a pathway of light on the marbled floor.

She poked her head around the doors, looking for signs of people inside. The pungent aroma of incense mingled with the sweet scent of candle wax. One more step and the door closed behind her with a quiet thud, then silence.

Familiar sights everywhere: white linen cloth layered over tables near the inner door, leading into the sanctuary. Weekly bulletins, a basket of mints. A tall vase overflowing with white lilies, fresh lavender. Without thinking, her body pulled by something she couldn't see, her feet moved forward, one step at a time, until the full church opened before her. Vaulted ceilings, rising high above the marbled floor. Stained glass windows filtering sunlight in shades of crimson, ocean blue, honeyed gold. Statues of saints standing on pedestals high above the pews. Watching. Quietly watching.

Alice's knees buckled and she reached out, placing her hand on the back of a pew to steady herself, then sat down. She closed her eyes, shutting out the light and statues and altar at the front of the church, her breath caught in her chest. The fear she had been pushing away crept more clearly to the surface.

The calm she sought escaped her, replaced instead with swirling lights, a kaleidoscope of colors dancing before her. The child's face emerging through the lights. "*Martha. Her name is Martha. She talks if you ask her questions.*"

Alice opened her eyes, her fingers gripped tightly to the pew. Her attention was pulled up to a stained-glass window behind the altar. A woman draped in a red cloak, right hand reaching out, one foot curled beneath her. Who was she? Mary, Jesus' mother, was always dressed in pale blue. Alice looked down and noticed the church bulletin in the pocket of the pew. St. Mary Magdalene Church, Berkeley.

Of course. Mary Magdalene. The woman who first saw Jesus at the tomb on Easter morning. Jesus' friend and confidant.

A teacher. A woman whose story was still largely hidden, silently looking at Alice from the stained-glass window above the altar.

She closed her eyes again and heard a faint hum—like the sound of buzzing bees. The sound melted away and images from the day arose, creating a mosaic with missing pieces.

Martha.

The gifted acorn was in her pocket now. She pulled it out and wrapped her palm around it, feeling its lightness. A tiny acorn that would—in the right circumstances—grow to become a large oak tree, another reminder of her childhood home, the bayous and land of Louisiana.

She opened her eyes. A new image appeared before her—was it real? Alice gripped the pew, but the polished wood offered no reassurance.

A small coffin in the aisle, pews filled with mourners draped in black. Sounds of muffled crying. Smells of sweat and tobacco. One woman's cries louder than the others, rising in volume until it pierced Alice's chest. Another swimming sensation, dizzying lightheadedness, then the image slowly faded away and the contours of the empty church came into focus.

Alice leaned back against the pew, panic rising. *What was that? There's no one here. Just me.* She looked around to make sure, closed her eyes again, willing away unbidden images. *Am I losing my mind? Are my grandmothers here? Am I supposed to do something?*

No, she told herself firmly. This was just fatigue. A week of packing and little sleep was leaving her vulnerable to delusions. *Shake it off,* she said quietly, immediately wondering again if anyone was nearby who might have heard her. She opened her eyes and looked around, placing her hand on her stomach, which roiled with confusion. *No one else is here.*

The silence of the church suddenly felt smothering. The walk home would wash this all away. A good lunch and a few hours spent unpacking would shift her out of whatever haze had been haunting her since she'd opened the jewelry box earlier.

She stood up, put the acorn in her pocket, and walked outside, the bright mid-day sunlight greeting her as the wooden door opened. Next Friday she'd drive to the ocean with the jewelry box. She would take it to the ocean as her great-grandmother asked—she could fulfill that simple request. Then whatever door had opened up in her mind when she turned the clasp on the jewelry box that morning would close back up.

She hoped.

CHAPTER 2—GRACE PASCHAL

July 1934, Richarme, Louisiana

The world split open the day you were born.

I mean that literally. Lightning struck our known world an hour after you were born, cracking open our small shotgun house with an electrical current that lit up your grandmother's eyes and sent the rifles hanging in the front room crashing to the floor.

We thought the world was ending. Or maybe beginning again, right there with your birth. You were in your father's arms and I was still lying on the bed, wet from sweat and salty from my own tears, still in awe at the miracle of seeing you before us.

My waters had broken open only hours before, and the wood floor was still soaked with that small sea inside of me, the one that had protected you for nine months. Your birth took hours, my body straining and moving with the waves that shook us both, my mother standing beside me through it all, whispering words of love to coax you forward and give me strength.

I closed my eyes before the final push that released your tiny body from mine. As you entered this world, the shining face of a woman appeared before me, radiant, rising from the sea, the water glimmering behind her like starlight. She reached out her arms as though to hand you to me, transporting you from one world to the next, and I was filled with a calmness that released my body from the pain of giving birth. I opened my eyes and saw you there, shiny and wet. You gave a small cry then settled into the world around you, taking it all in with eyes that shone out of your small face like messengers from another world.

Eyes wide open. That's what I kept saying. Her eyes are wide open, taking in her home, so new from whatever world is on the other side of the veil. She wants to see everything there is to see, I said. Then the world itself split open before I could even drink a cup of hot tea.

* * *

We named you Lily Mae. I love lilies and it was the month of May, and your name came to me the minute I looked into your eyes. I was named Grace because my grandmere sang the song "Amazing Grace" to my maman when I was born. Your daddy wanted to name you after his maman, but he'd named Martha and it was my turn. He loves family names, but I said if we name all our children after relatives, they won't be able to get out from under that weight and live their own lives. I couldn't save Martha from living with the ghosts of the Paschals on your daddy's side of the family, but I decided I would save you. Your middle name does come from one of your great-grandmothers, but your first name is all your own. I knew from the time I first felt you in my body that you had your own life to live, and we just had to give you the space and love to live it.

I wish you had lived long enough for us to see who you would have become. Seven years was not enough for the bright star of your spirit to live on this Earth.

* * *

The sky was dark when we buried you, the day starting and ending in a black drape of sorrow, the world closed up tight under the blanket of rain and storm clouds. That heavy veil hung over everything and I was glad of it. I didn't have to pretend to be walking among the living. My own heart and the world inside of me were shadowed and the sky above mirrored it. We'd had too short of a time to love you, and my body was weighted with grief too heavy to bear.

I was the first one awake that morning. I pulled myself out of bed before I even heard the rooster crow. When I walked into the kitchen, the first thing my eyes rested on was the quilt Mamou made so many years ago, folded on the chair where I'd put it the night before. I wanted to wrap you in it, Lily, before they buried you, but I knew when I saw it that I needed it for myself. You didn't need anything from us anymore. I picked it up, wrapped it around my shoulders, and slid down to the ground like a child myself, huddled and crying until your daddy walked in and found me.

He didn't say a word. He looked at me for a moment, his eyes brimming with tears, then turned and walked out to the front porch. Martha and Pierre got up soon after and I found a way to move my body enough to make their pancakes for breakfast. Martha asked what she should wear to your funeral and it was only then I realized she didn't have a single dress in good enough shape to honor you. I haven't been able to buy much new material for clothes for any of us with your daddy making less from fishing and shrimping these last few years.

In that moment, when I looked at Martha and saw her face, puckered up from grief she didn't know how to bear again—the second time she lost a sister in just a few short years—I realized that she needed me, and I didn't know if I had anything left to give her. I'm still haunted by that, knowing I may never be able to give Martha and Pierre what they need from me, with my heart broken into something I don't recognize anymore. They are only nine and eleven, Pierre now feeling that he has to take care of his younger sister. They are too young to lose their mother along with all the loss they've already experienced. Haydee's few months of life, ended with an illness the doctors couldn't cure, was more than enough to weigh us with grief. That moment in the kitchen I wondered if your passing had pulled us too deep to ever recover.

We all pulled out the best we had. Every one of us was in black, but I didn't want to see you off in such a dark color, Lily. Your spirit was too bright for that. I stopped in the front yard and cut a camellia and pinned it to my dress before we walked to the church. I wanted to see you off with flowers, bright and alive, reminding us of who you were and what you left behind.

We walked to Mary Magdalen Church and none of us said a word the whole way. You were already there, your small body held like a doll in a simple pine casket, waiting for us near the altar. When we reached the bridge over the Vermillion River, I stopped to take a breath before I could cross it. We all looked at the water, silent before it, the dark flow on top covering the strong undercurrents below the surface.

I thought of the little family of river otters you loved so much, the times you visited them to check on them—the way you always said you could hear the mamma talking to you, whispering things to you that no one else could hear or understand. You always wanted to protect them, take care of them. Thinking of the family of otters and that mother otter holding her babies was too much for me to bear in that moment, as we prepared to let you go forever.

I looked deep into the water, thinking of the coulees running off it, the bayous around us, all of it flowing into the Gulf of Mexico, and all of that water pulled me deeper into the grief that was already drowning me.

I had a sudden sense that your spirit flew by me, almost through me, really, catching me off guard. My head swirled and I had to stop myself from jumping into the current below, allowing it to pull me under forever. I didn't want to be part of this world anymore, not without you in it.

Pierre was behind me and saw me stop. He walked up and grabbed my hand, holding on to me, keeping me anchored to the planks of the bridge. Your daddy was behind us, holding Martha's hand, and for a moment we all stood there. Thunder broke across the sky, reminding us the rain was coming. The heat was so thick with humidity I felt as though I was walking through a swamp. Sweat drizzled down my back, but I didn't care. I was only thinking of you, of getting to the church where I knew I would have to say goodbye to you. I took one step and then another, my feet moving slowly down Josephine Street until we finally reached the church square.

Father Comeaux was waiting for us outside and asked if we wanted to visit you alone before the guests arrived. We had a few last minutes with you up near the altar before everyone came, and I found myself praying the Hail Mary over and over in my mind, a song that wouldn't stop. *Hail Mary, full of Grace, the Lord is with Thee.* My eyes were drawn to the stained-glass window of Mary Magdalen. The way the light came in, it seemed as though she was moving, reaching out to me. I saw you with her, Lily, behind her, held by Mother Mary, and it gave me some comfort.

I've prayed every day that the two Marys have been holding you, both Jesus's mother and the Mary who first saw him rise from his own death. I pray that Mamou and all the other grandmothers are with you. I must believe that they are. It's the only way I can get through this sorrow that covers everything around me.

My mamma arrived first, and your daddy's family came soon after. Cousins came from Jennings and Morgan City, even a few from Bunkie. Some of your daddy's coworkers came all cleaned up in Sunday clothes, but the salty smell of gulf waters clung to their bodies, reminding us again of the waters all around us. Everyone from church was there, clutching rosaries and looking down, because no one knew what to say to us. What could anyone say? No one really knew what had happened and we weren't ready to talk. Mystery and grief hung from the rafters like the moss lining the trees in Magdalen Square. No prayers or songs from the church choir could penetrate it, and that gave me some comfort. I wanted the whole world to know that all the light had left our home. I wanted everyone to feel that. And I felt it most of all when I saw the Benoit family sitting in one of the back pews.

Mrs. Benoit had her head down through the whole service and Mr. Benoit stared out the window, trying to get through it without looking at anyone. The boys had on their Sunday best, shoes shined and faces washed. I could barely look at them, my thoughts already jagged and pointed toward those boys. At the very end of the service, when we walked down the aisle behind your casket, I turned and looked at them. Neither of the boys would look at me, and they didn't come to the house that afternoon. Only Mrs. Benoit came, bringing a small bundt cake with icing. She put it on the table, offered me her condolences, and left without talking to anyone else. Father Comeaux was sitting with me and put his hand on mine as Antoinette walked out the door. I didn't know then what he was thinking, but I was comforted by it, his hand on mine, another anchor holding me to this Earth when I wasn't sure if my spirit had the strength to stay here.

Everyone brought food that day. Our table was covered with deviled eggs, rice dressing, fresh bread from Colombs Bakery, potato salad, even some sliced pork. None of us ate, but I was glad the food was there to feed the guests who came.

The house was bathed in the fragrance of flowers. Some people who've lost too many people say they hate the smell of flowers because it reminds them of funerals, with churches and living rooms filled up with blooms. The flowers brought me comfort. Something living—bright and colorful—was what we needed that day.

That evening, after everyone left, we walked back to the cemetery to visit your grave. Fresh dirt covered the place where they buried you. Your daddy stood next to me, hat in hand, unable to say a word. The muggy air after the rainstorms closed in on us, but the sweet smell of wet grass washed us clean, bringing a bright spot of life to our grief. For a moment I thought of honeysuckle, the way you loved the smell of it, and that one memory broke through the veil I'd wrapped around myself.

I dropped to my knees crying. The clouds opened, the heavy air around us filling with the short afternoon rains of summer. As the waters poured over us, I felt as if my own tears came down from the heavens. The sky itself was joining me—us—in grief. The thin lines of my body melted into Earth and sky and clouds, and I couldn't feel myself as anything other than part of the world of grief that held us all.

The rain stopped as quickly as it started, sun moving from behind a cloud, bringing light and a hint of blue sky. We were all drenched, our clothes soaked, our hair washed down on our faces. Your daddy reached a hand to me and pulled me to standing.

We had lilies and roses and put them there for you, and for Haydee too. Her tiny grave next to yours gave me some comfort, as though you could hold on to each other until it would be my time to join you both. I knew I shouldn't have had those thoughts, that Martha and Pierre still needed me, but I did. I did, Lily Mae. I couldn't imagine how I will continue to live this life without you in it.

On our walk back home, we heard a train pass by in the distance, probably bringing people over from Lafayette or maybe people headed for the gulf. The sound of the whistle and wheels clacking on the tracks reminded me that the world was going to keep moving, whether you were in it or not, and maybe this helped us keep putting one foot in front of the other, getting us home.

Your daddy sat out on the porch until late that night, listening to the wind in the trees and the occasional owl hooting from the woods. His heart is as broken as mine, and he doesn't have the ability to say what he's feeling, so I know this is going to keep us apart for a long time. Our memories of you when you were alive are what will keep us going.

The world opened when you were born and closed when you died and now you are everywhere, like the air wrapping around us after a thunderstorm, thick and pure and hanging with the deep scent of water from the heavens.

CHAPTER 3—ALICE

June 2019, Berkeley, California

Isabella's tail brushed against her bare arm, a gentle swish nudging her awake. Alice rolled over. The deep hues of water from her dream were mirrored in the bright green flickering of the cat's eyes. She rubbed Isabella's head.

"Food," she mumbled. "I know. Give me a minute."

She rolled onto the pillow, closed her eyes. Sinking into the soft hollow of the mattress, the dream returned slowly, pulling her back under into a hazy, wet world.

Water everywhere. Women with long, flowing hair. Gargled singing. The sense of needing to come up to breathe. Turtles swimming toward her from all directions, followed by seals, then sea otters, bodies slipping through the waves like dark-colored seaweed. Hundreds of them, beautiful creatures, starting tiny and growing larger as they approached. Light breaking through the ocean's surface above, illuminating everything until the water splintered into diamond-shaped fractals. A haunting melody ringing in her ears. Was it women singing?

Isabella's paw swatted her cheek gently. Alice opened her eyes again and willed herself into the world of her bedroom. Unsettled, she sat up. Frightened. What had happened yesterday? What doors were opened by her meeting with the little girl at the park?

This wasn't the first time the crack between the worlds seemed to break open in her mind, but it had never been like this. Memories throughout her childhood of seeing spirits from other worlds—or just her imagination?—crept into her thoughts. Of her parents and sisters telling her that she was just a dreamer, that she needed to get her head out of the clouds. Of feeling like she straddled the line between the physical reality everyone around her lived in and a world on the other side of a curtain that could open any time, revealing images that haunted and beckoned her. She'd tried to push it away and the experiences happened only rarely now. The girl hadn't appeared to her in years, other than occasionally in a dream. What was happening? An old familiar feeling of her life teetering on shifting sands between reality and a world she didn't know how to navigate held her frozen for a moment. What had opened yesterday when she'd opened the jewelry box?

Whatever it was, she had to close it. Keep her sanity, body, and mind planted firmly in the present world. Keep her mind on her career.

Focus there—work. There was plenty of it. Her desk was littered with research on the history of viticulture in California and notes she'd taken on her last trip to Petaluma for an article she was writing on the Ten Best Hidden Wineries in Sonoma Valley. Her small office at *Pacific Travel*, a regional magazine that covered special interest stories on the West Coast states, Alaska, and the Pacific islands, had one small window looking out at a coffee shop. A mid-afternoon espresso always gave her the extra brain push she needed to work until after six each evening, past when most of her coworkers left the office. The long days of research and carefully chosen words on the page kept her life ordered, a straight line of cultivated information. Daydreams and visions of small girls in nightgowns had no place here. She'd created order and safety from the images that haunted her childhood through work centered on writing pieces that entertained and informed. Simple. Straightforward. A step toward her goal of writing for a national publication.

She pulled herself up and moved into the day, grateful for the distraction work would bring.

* * *

The work week passed quickly. Alice peered out the window of her small kitchen, happy to have a Friday off and a three-day weekend. Outside, the sun shone brightly, the morning ripe with potential.

She started her coffee-making ritual, brewing coffee beans, boiling a small pan of milk. She loved drinking café au lait, the rich New Orleans brew everyone in her family drank, and she made it the same way her mother did. The simple steps in the ritual were comforting: one step at a time, one ingredient at a time, creating a perfectly layered drink.

Her attention was drawn this morning to the small patch of flowers and herbs she'd planted the evening before in a wooden flower box hanging from the ledge outside her kitchen window. She had just enough fresh basil to create a perfect cheese and tomato sandwich. If she hurried, she'd have enough time to stop at the market to buy fruit and still make it to the beach by midday.

* * *

The drive from Berkeley to the coast just north of San Francisco took her past one of her favorite spots: Mount Tamalpais. She loved it from the first time she visited. The name was said to have come from the name *tamal pajis,* given by the Miwok tribe that lived in this area for thousands of years. She had read that the name means *west hill,* and she thought of the mountain as the great hill protecting the West Coast area she called home, with Mount Tam as a sacred guardian of the waters. The mountain was also called The Sleeping Lady, its body curled in the pose of a woman lying down for a nap. When she stood at one of its peaks after a day of hiking, looking down at the water through low lying clouds, she felt as if heaven had opened a spot for her. Her memories of those days were magical, and she was grateful to drive below the mountain and bring to her senses the fresh smells of the oak and madrone trees that graced the hillsides.

She loved the stories she heard about the mountain, ones that spoke of mountain spirits and ancestors living among the clouds. What she most treasured, though, were her own experiences, days when she'd hiked through forest areas that opened into hidden groves of ancient fir and oak trees that led her to momentarily believe every story she'd ever heard. A memory came to her: walking on a quiet trail with two friends, sounds of eucalyptus clacking above. Suddenly, a gush of air—something almost solid—moved through her, chilling her to the bone. Stopping her breath. Had a spirit walked through her? That's what it felt like, but she didn't know. Words rang through her mind: *What happened? What do you want?* Another wave washed over her, running down her spine before sending her stomach into a slight lurch. She was temporarily disoriented, then intentionally focused on her feet connected to the ground beneath her and the grand beauty of the sky above. Her friends had continued walking, and she chose not to tell them what she'd felt.

She'd learned years before, from her earliest childhood memories, to keep these types of occurrences to herself, if for no other reason than that she could not explain them to herself, much less try to make sense of them to other people.

When she was honest with herself, they scared her. They pulled at her at the same time, curiosity battling with her fear until she inevitably closed it all down. Or tried to. A tenuous dance she'd had to learn to keep her sanity.

Today the sun shone brightly, blue sky above her seemingly endless. This was the kind of day when the Bay Area was showing off, and she still wondered about the unexpected set of circumstances that led her to call this beautiful area her home. She'd assumed she would always live in Louisiana, near her family. Coming from the French Acadian culture, she was part of a tribe of family members that included over thirty first cousins and more distant cousins than she could count. Most stayed in the South, and because she loved New Orleans, with its rich mix of culture and cobbled history that seemed to rise off the steamy streets of the French Quarter, she assumed she'd always live there. After she graduated from college, she stayed in Baton Rouge for a while working for *Louisiana Stories*, a state-wide magazine focused on history and culture. When a co-worker showed her the job opening in Berkeley at a much larger magazine, Alice jumped at the chance. Amazed when she actually landed the job, she made the move in a period of a few short months, with little time to process the change she was making.

On her first evening in the city, after landing at the nearby Oakland airport, she was taken by surprise at how immediately she felt at home. The thrum of the city, spicy smells of foods she'd never tried before, and the cool evening air enveloping her created a sense of peacefulness that surprised her.

A sign for the East Point trail and lookout on Mt. Tam came into view as she curved around a corner on Highway 1. She decided to turn off the main road and wind up to a trailhead. She hadn't hiked any of these trails for a while and felt a pull to feel her feet on the deep earth of the mountain. She could do a short hike and still make it to the coast by mid-afternoon.

She reached the trailhead parking lot and grabbed her backpack. The jewelry box caught her eye, partially covered by a beach towel. Opening the lid, she looked at the contents again. She had pored over them so many times over the years, inspecting each small detail of the handmade doll, gently stroking the mossy hair. She pulled the silk scarf out and brought it to her nose: the slightly musty, perfumed smell still clung to it. *Gardenias—that was the fragrance.* As she rubbed the soft silk to her face an image of her great-grandmother wearing the large floral print scarf popped into her mind.

Alice would wear the scarf today, in honor of Grandmere Grace. The soft silk, smooth against her skin, brought on a smile. *Thank you, Grandmere. For the scarf, the box, for everything you've left me.*

The trail was fairly empty. Only two other sets of hikers passed as she walked the narrow path through ancient trees, past meadows filled with golden poppies and brilliant blue lupines, and, finally, up to a crest that overlooked the Pacific Ocean.

This is what she longed for: a view of sapphire blue water stretching to the end of the horizon, mingled scents of salt water and pine trees, light breeze brushing against her skin. She slid down to the ground, sitting crossed-legged, leaning back on her hands with her face turned toward the sky. Eyes closed, the fresh air filled her, and she drifted into a relaxed state. There was something about this part of the mountain that always made her feel as if she had left human civilization far behind, entering the realm of the gods high above the world. She let herself drift until all she was aware of was the breeze on her arms and the sound of occasional birds in the trees. Her mind was blank as she melted into the natural world around her.

It came suddenly and without warning, the sense of something beside her. At first, only a lift in the breeze and the whiff of a strong perfume, out of place in this purely natural world.

Jolting awake she looked around, expecting to see someone nearby. Fear ran through her body—this was a deserted area of the mountain. She saw no one, which brought comfort, but then she wondered if someone was hiding behind the trees. The smell of perfume was strong and distinct. Reaching up to touch the scarf, she reminded herself that it carried a perfumed smell. *I must have had a whiff of it with a strong passing breeze. Everything's fine.*

The tightness that had entered her body was just starting to relax when she felt blinded by an image. Suddenly the line between the world in front of her and the one she was seeing blurred. She felt slightly nauseous. In between flashes of light, faint images arose, causing her chest to tighten. Two young boys holding shotguns, one pointing it toward her with his eye on the trigger. Sounds of whooping laughter. Then a shot rang out and a blaze of hot air shot by her, sending a jolt through her body.

Alice shivered. It was over. As quickly as it had come, the images disappeared and the sounds that had filled her ears and run through her consciousness dimmed and were replaced by the distant sound of the ocean.

She straightened her body, caught her breath, and stared blankly, eyes open wide. Willing herself to come back to the present, she sat perfectly still, as though a complete lack of movement might protect her from being overcome again by unbidden images and sounds. *One. Two. Three.* Be still and count slowly. Come back to this moment: soft grass, ocean breeze, smell of trees towering above. She counted, a practiced method of calming her pounding heart as she waited for the world around her to come back into focus. Deep breaths.

Eyes closed, her body still moved slightly in rhythm with receding waves of dizziness, dimming lights flashing behind her eyelids. Deep breath and tense muscles slowly relaxing, shoulders loosening as she reflexively brought her attention from her neck, down her spine, to the feel of the grass below the open palm of her left hand.

Familiar questions moved through Alice's mind: what was that? Why now? And, most of all, what am I supposed to do with it?

The gun in her face, pointed at her. The laughter pealing through her—as if it had an energy of its own, as frightening as the threat of the gun, slicing through her body. A wave of electricity rising from the base of her spine, breath caught in her throat. Fear leaving her frozen still. Icy. This was different from experiences in the past. Quite literally—more chilling.

She thought again of her early memories of experiencing things that set her apart from others, of seeing flashes of images that seemed to come out of the mist from another dimension, momentarily take form before her, then vanish as quickly as they came. A kindly face appearing behind someone, or a sense of a quiet presence standing nearby for a few seconds before it evaporated. She had learned to shake the experiences off and they rarely happened now that her life was filled with work and deadlines, but occasionally experiences still happened that startled her. More than once, she had sensed the presence of someone's grandmother or grandfather standing behind them, as though wanting to get her attention to share a piece of information with the person standing before her. She either ignored the images until they disappeared or, in the case of particularly persistent ones, willed them to go away with her mind. Mostly they complied. When they didn't, she was left wondering what she was meant to do with whatever had come to her.

This was what she felt now. Struck by how quickly it had happened, how sharp the gunshot sounded in her ears, how electric and alive the air near her arm felt as the sound of that shot rang out, she slowly stood up, trying to shake off the dizzy feeling that still lingered.

The young girl's face before her now.

Her name is Martha.

She talks if you ask her questions.

Alice shoved her hands into her pockets, knowing even as she did so that the acorn was not there. She needed something to touch, something of the natural world in front of her to let her know she was on solid ground. But she felt too dizzy to move, too uncertain to risk trying to take even one step forward.

The wave that had overtaken her had wiped out her sense of time, as though she had been pulled through an invisible curtain into a different dimension, then spit back out onto the mountain. Her hand again moved up to the scarf around her neck. The soft silkiness brought back her great-grandmother, her aunts, the women of her family.

Ma chérie, everything will be alright.

Relax, sweet Alice. We are always here.

Was someone talking to her? Was she alone?

Grandmere Grace, what's happening to me?

Wrapping her arms around her body for comfort, she turned and began walking back down the trail, focusing her eyes on the ground below her feet, anchoring her mind to the rhythmic movement of her body. One foot in front of the other.

* * *

The ocean was only a twenty-minute drive away, but the curves down the mountain required complete focus. Grasping the wheel, she fought off the fear of losing control for even a second and careening off a cliff. Breathtaking views of the coastline appeared, crystal blue water reaching far into the horizon. It was early afternoon, giving her hours to spend on the beach before nightfall.

As she drove, she cleared her mind with a favorite playlist, singing along with Jack Johnson and Tracy Chapman. When she finally pulled her car into a parking spot on the narrow street curving toward Stinson Beach, she forced herself to focus on the purpose of her visit, which was to finally bring the jewelry box to the ocean as the note in the box suggested. She felt relieved that the June heat was bringing her back fully to the experience of her body, beads of sweat running down her neck.

The thought of icy snowballs, a treat from her childhood visits to New Orleans, arose unexpectedly. Her mind meandered through memories of visiting her grandmother and great-grandmother when she was a girl, of family trips to the French Quarter, walks to the snowball stand on muggy days, the cool taste of the shaved ice, flavored with watermelon or spearmint.

Before she got out of the car, she stopped and looked again at the jewelry box. She was still wearing the scarf and decided to keep it on for the day. She put the box into her backpack, picked up her water bottle, and headed toward the water.

The blinding beauty of the shoreline melted her thoughts as she approached the beach. With fewer rocks than most of the Northern California coast, this stretch was a hidden sanctuary for people living in crowded Bay Area cities and a place she loved to visit. She'd heard of recent sightings of great white sharks, but she knew this rarely discouraged the die-hard surfers who saw themselves as creatures of the water, protected from predators. She took her shoes off and headed toward a deserted area on the beach, shielding her eyes from the sun, her shoes dangling by her side in her hand.

She spread out a blanket and sat down. No clear plan yet of what to do to honor her great-grandmother's wishes, she decided to relax in the sun for a while and pulled out the book she'd thrown into her backpack. *The Awakening,* by

Kate Chopin. Edna Pontellier—a woman living a secure but uninspired life in New Orleans in the 1800s who slowly awakened to deeper longings—seemed like a good story to read on a day of remembering her great-grandmother. Grandmere Grace didn't live in New Orleans until much later in her life, but Alice liked thinking of her as Edna's contemporary, both choosing to live their lives on their own terms, both with stories to tell before they died. The cover art of a woman with her back turned to the reader, as though she had a secret to share—or to learn herself—resonated with Alice. She pulled on her sunhat and settled in.

CHAPTER 4—GRACE

July 1934, Richarme, Louisiana

As I write this, only weeks from that day we buried you, I think about everything that came between your birth and the time you left us. From the beginning you showed us you were different, my sweet Lily. I couldn't quite say how, but it was always there, that something extra that seemed to be happening in your world. It seeped out of you in a way I could never put my finger on, swirling in the air around your body, moving like a hungry ghost that followed you wherever you went.

When you were a toddler, just starting to move around our little house, your hands wanted to touch everything around you. And not just touch things—you'd stay in one place for a few minutes, your hand resting on a lace doily my grandmother made or softly running your finger over a cut azalea in a vase as though you were in a trance. I'd see your eyes glaze over, like you were seeing something more than what any of the rest of us could see. Nobody else seemed to notice it, but I did. Maybe it was because I nursed you so long that you and I were like one person at times, two living bodies connected by your hunger and my love, and my love for you seemed to just get bigger and bigger all the time.

Now, I want you to know that I didn't just love you this way. I loved Martha and Pierre that way before you, and I loved little Haydee for the few months God let her stay with us on Earth. There was something different about you, though, Lily Mae. Sometimes you seemed as though you didn't belong in this world. You were a bright light wherever you went, your eyes and smile always working magic on those around you. And I loved how often you turned that magic toward me, your maman.

You seemed to want—no, to need—to be close to my body in a way that the others didn't. Martha and Pierre were ready to let go much sooner than you, and your need to stay connected to my body continued far past the nursing days. The way you would circle around me and play, making bigger and bigger circles as you explored the world around you, then come back to me just to touch me. It was like you needed to plug into me sometimes, and I loved it, really. I loved how it seemed that you needed me to keep you tethered to this world. And we both learned what a harsh world it could be. I always wanted to be the one you could hold onto as you saw how ugly people could be, how mean and hard-hearted. I always tried to be that for you, Lily Mae. I'm sorry for the ways I failed you. I'm so sorry.

* * *

Here's how it started. The first time other people saw that there was something special about you was a day just like the day you were born. It was raining, crazy crawl-under-the-bed kind of rain and thunder. I was cooking gumbo, shrimp and okra because you know we never eat meat on Fridays, even when it isn't Lent. The gumbo was bubbling on the stove with smells of shrimp swirling up out of the pot and I was searching the cupboard for the filé. Martha was helping me get bread and butter on the table and you were sitting in a chair, waiting for supper. All of a sudden one of those big thunder rolls started and you looked up at Martha and said, "Haydee's visiting us. I think she wants to tell Mamma something."

Martha stopped moving. I turned around and you looked over at me, your eyes with that far-off look you'd get. "Mamma, Haydee wants you to know she's happy now. When you hear the thunder and rain, she's visiting us. That's how we'll know she's here."

Martha dropped the butter dish onto the table. I couldn't tell if she was scared or happy, but I knew you were seeing something we weren't. It had been a year since Haydee had left us and we tried not to talk about her when you kids were around. Martha took Haydee's leaving extra hard, because she'd spent so much time helping me care for her. I was so sick, my body so torn up from that birth, that Martha became Haydee's second mother.

I wasn't sure how to respond to you. For a second, I wondered if I should say something to Haydee, but I looked over and saw your daddy standing at the door and I thought he was about to cry. I knew there was no way he would let either of you see him cry, so I said the first thing that came out of my mind. "I'm sure we'll have her with us a lot, then, since it rains all the time around here. Martha, can you help me get the lemonade?"

Martha went back to the kitchen and your daddy turned and went to our room. I went back to stirring the gumbo, sprinkling filé on top, my mind swirling in a haze. Smells of shrimp and sassafras spiraled around our kitchen like my thoughts, and when I turned and looked at you, it seemed you had forgotten all about what just happened and were simply waiting for me to serve you a hot bowl of love. We never talked about it again, but I always think of Haydee when it rains, especially when the thunder comes rolling through like a trumpet call from heaven. And now I think of you, Lily. You, too, are in the rain.

That evening we all walked to the river together. My grandmother, your great-grandmother Mamou, saw herself as a protector of the water and all the creatures that live in and around it. She'd go to the water when she needed an answer to something, looking out into the river or bayou or the gulf, wherever she was standing, and ask questions, waiting for the spirit of the water, I guess, to give her the answers she sought.

As we stood there that evening, I felt her presence with us. I stared out at the river and thought about how it wanders down to the gulf, and how that opens out to the ocean. Water connects us to people all over the world, lapping up on our shores then washing back out and traveling to other continents and islands and people. What does all that water carry? What was washing up on the banks of our river and what were we sending out in it that night, standing there, thinking and feeling so much from the day?

I thought about you and wondered if there were any other mammas in the world watching their daughters like I was watching you now, wondering about what they could see beyond this world, wondering how to protect them from the gifts they had, gifts that most people don't understand. Fear can make people mean, Lily, and that night at the water's edge, I sent a prayer up to the stars that you would be protected. I think Haydee was watching over us, one of the stars in that beautiful night sky.

* * *

I'm going to tell you a story, Lily Mae. This is one no one knows, about a time when I was a little girl growing up in Bunkie. That part of Louisiana was not much more than a corner of dirt and small houses, squared off by the slow-moving water of bayous and groves of trees protecting us from the rest of the world. Back then, we didn't even have an indoor toilet and there were very few stores, but because we didn't know any better, we were happy with how we lived.

Mostly happy, anyway. Daddy's anger flared up at unexpected times and we all knew the best thing to do was to go outside and find a big tree to hide behind. Mamma would take him into the back room and try to talk him down. We would wait until we heard her whistling a little song. That was the sign it was safe to go back inside. She never told us that and we never talked about it. We just knew, somehow, that her quiet whistle meant the anger had seeped out and her song was washing it away. He didn't get angry too often, but when he did, we knew to get out of the way. It was usually about something happening with the house or animals, which he loved as much as he loved us, I think.

You probably know your grandfather built our house with his own two hands. I don't know how much you remember him, since he died when you were so little, but he was a big man. His parents had come straight from France, not like my mamma's family who came down from Canada with all the other French people who decided to head south and start over. My daddy's family thought they were better than the French people who'd come from Canada, even though we're all related if you go far enough back. They seemed to think they had a stronger connection to the motherland, but that never made sense to me. Mamma's family seemed just as French as Daddy's—same food, same way of dancing every Saturday night away, under the moon in the grassy patch behind our house. Those were some of my best childhood memories. But that's not the story I want to tell right now.

The story I want to tell is about the time I, too, thought I had a special gift. I was only seven, old enough to be doing plenty of chores but not old enough to boss anyone around like my older brother—your Uncle Etienne—did. He and I were outside getting wood for the fire while Mamma was talking Daddy down. It was just before supper, when the songs of the frogs and crickets started to serenade everyone around into a little reverie. I walked over to the edge of the woods behind our house right near the bayou and for a minute I thought I saw something, a shadow of light, or a spirit. I stopped right where I was, holding an oak branch in my hand, frozen in place. I stayed that way for a few seconds, hoping to see what had just whirled in front of me, but nothing moved.

So I did. I took a few more steps into the brush and the trees and saw it again, a swirl of light that moved around a tree trunk, and this time it came with a little whisper, a *huussshhh* sound that disappeared into the woods with a barely visible trail behind it. Usually I was pretty timid and wouldn't take chances on things that might not be safe, but this time something moved me, pulled me, really, and I walked toward the tree where I saw that swirl of light and haze. I stood in front of it, holding the oak branch in my hand like a prayer stick, waiting for the tree to show me whatever secret it had hidden. And it did. One more time I saw this swirl of brightness around the tree. It was a big oak tree with lots of moss hanging down like an old woman's curly white hair, and the light puffed up around the trunk like a filmy white debutante dress, then dropped back down into the brown earth.

I held my breath and waited for it to happen again, but nothing moved. The trees just kept still, their leaves breathing in that woody air with me.

I thought I'd seen a spirit, Lily Mae. I decided that if I had, it was a good spirit because of how peaceful I felt, even after seeing something that didn't belong in the world I understood. When I realized it wasn't going to show itself to me again, I bowed to the tree—I know, that sounds silly, but it seemed the right thing to do—and turned around. I walked quietly back toward the house and found Etienne, who yelled at me to hurry and get more kindling for the fire. I decided right then that I wouldn't tell him or anyone else about what happened.

When I walked out of that clearing I felt like I was coming out of a magic world into the real one, and the real one suddenly seemed a little harsher to me. Somehow, I knew that what I saw was not meant to be spoken, that it was a secret that had decided to show itself just to me, so I decided to keep it safe. It became something I carried with me everywhere, a memory of that swirl of light I could pull out of my mind any time. It was a reminder that something magic and beautiful was just around the corner, behind the next tree, if I ever needed it. And we both know I did need it. We both did, you and me.

Sometimes, Lily Mae, I have wondered if that swirl of light I saw that day was you, your bright spirit just waiting for the time when you could come into this world and be my child. And I find myself looking for you now, behind the next tree, wondering if you'll show yourself to me again.

* * *

I have a lot of stories I want to tell you. Stories about the ones who came before us. Stories that might help us all make sense of what happened. So many stories—I should have told you all of them a long time ago. The truth was, I was afraid. I was afraid that if I ever said them out loud, then what I was starting to suspect might actually show itself to be true—that you had the gifts that run through our family. And that they would only be a danger to you.

It's a funny thing how our minds work, as though by ignoring a thing, we think can make it not be true. It's too late for things to change with you, but maybe if I let these stories come out of me, I can at least put them someplace outside of my own self. Since you've been gone, they've weighed on me like a dead burden, hanging right over the place where my heart beats. It's time I get them out of me, let them go. Maybe they will find you where you are, if you're listening. I do pray you're listening, even if you can't talk back to me.

Lily Mae

Maman, can you hear me?
I'm the sound you hear between the cool breaths of wind in fall, the little breaths of air in summer's sticky heat.
I'm with Haydee who comes in the thunder and rain and with Mamou whose spirit lives in the plants and trees around you.
It wasn't your fault, Maman.
It was never your fault.
How could you have known what was happening to me?
How could you have stopped me when the pull from the other side was so much stronger than anything on Earth?
Even you, Maman, couldn't have protected me. There are things that happen in all of our lives that no one can protect us from, no matter how much a person might want to try.
And I know you tried to protect me, Maman.
I know that.

CHAPTER 5—ALICE

June 2019, Berkeley, California

"Looks like you found a perfect spot on this beach."

Alice looked up, startled.

"Nice day for a good book, yes?"

She took in the lanky figure standing behind her. A mane of curly red hair, so thick it could be woven into a rug, its sheen almost unnatural. The bright afternoon sunlight radiating around his body. A luminous face: large, wide eyes the color of aquamarine, skin freckled from the sun, a closed-lip smile that gave a sense of a secret knowing. Or were his eyes the color of sea glass?

Her face softened into a smile as she closed her book.

"Yes. I've been reading for a while but was just thinking of going for a walk." She stopped herself from saying more, unnerved by his confident presence.

"I love walking this time of day. The water is its most beautiful when sunlight shines directly down." He paused. "I hope I'm not interrupting you. You're probably looking for a quiet afternoon. I was just struck by the beautiful colors of your scarf and decided to walk over. I can leave you to your book now."

Slight Irish accent. Could he be from Ireland? Alice smiled back and looked down at his feet. They were bare and solid on the sand. She found herself briefly thinking that those feet could walk anywhere. Feeling an odd sense of safety with this man, she looked back up, realizing she didn't want him to walk away just yet.

"Do you live here?" she asked.

"I live in the city. I grew up in the Bay Area, but I'm originally from Ireland, from County Cork. My family has always lived near the sea, though, so the ocean feels like home, wherever I am."

So he was from Ireland, land of crystal-clear water shining like emeralds, grassy cliffs soaring into the sky.

"I've never been to Ireland but have always wanted to visit. What do you do now?"

"Mostly I walk the beach." Alice waited for more, wondering if he was a surfer. His face broke into a wide smile overtaken by gorgeous teeth and eyes that lit up like the stars. "And sometimes I'm a cartographer. I like seeing where things go. Putting them in their rightful place. You?" Startled by his response, she smiled. Map maker. Made sense. His ancestors probably charted the night sky and northern oceans.

"I write for *Pacific Travel* magazine," she said, immediately thinking she shouldn't have told him where she worked. Too much information. Even as she thought this, she realized she was intrigued by him and wanted to keep talking. "I write stories about travel, mostly."

"I'm Ronan."

"Alice. Nice to meet you."

The remains of lunch lay on the blanket.

"Would you like a strawberry? They're fresh from the market."

"I love strawberries." He took one from the dish she held up and paused. "Would you like to join me on my walk? It's low tide, the time to see if treasures have washed up on the shore, after big waves have pulled things in from the ocean bottom. Only people who take the time to see what others can't see can find the best treasures."

"Um, I don't think so," she said quickly, a familiar need to guard herself rising. "I want to read a few more chapters."

"OK. Have a good afternoon with that book."

"Thanks. You too."

He gave her a small nod and walked toward the ocean. An immediate stab of regret rose as she wished she'd said yes. She watched him walk away, her eyes taking in his thin, muscular frame—*like a reed that lives close to the water.* His red hair swept his shoulders as he took long, graceful strides.

He left a trail of faint footsteps in the sand. With the sun lowering on the horizon the ocean glistened, light reflecting off the waves like diamonds. She wondered why he'd walked up to her.

Did you send him, Grandmere Grace?

Memories rushed in—of men she'd dated, pushed away, broken up with when they came too close, her mind swirling with their faces, parting words from her last boyfriend ringing in her ears. *You'll never let anyone near enough to love you, Alice. You'll always turn back to your work, but that won't be enough one day when you realize how alone you really are.*

Edward lasted only four months before she'd closed that door. Abruptly, with little explanation, as always. He'd stayed over on a night when she'd had a visitation from the little girl—this time only a fleeting image in her dreams—but it had ruffled her, waking her in the dark. She decided then that she couldn't let anyone get that close, at least as long as the dreams continued. What if she called out during the night, said something in her sleep, and he asked her about it? She could barely deal with it by herself and wasn't ready to think about talking with someone else about it. If she just kept pushing it away—dreams of the child, the images that came in a foggy haze when she let herself get too vulnerable—maybe it would eventually leave her. She'd read about people wishing they had the "gift" of being intuitive, of being able to see "ghosts"—but to her, this wasn't a gift. It was a curse.

She shook off the thoughts. Ronan was close to the shore, his lean figure—clad in green board shorts and a foamy white t-shirt—seeming part of the ocean scene.

Maybe I should take a walk too. Alice thought of the note in the box, the message from her great-grandmother which she did not fully understand. She realized that Ronan had just given her something else to think about, people "who see what others do not see." What did he see that others did not? Was she missing something just in front of her, on the sand? She decided to walk down and look for something to take with her, a treasure, perhaps, to add to the collection in her jewelry box.

Tucking the box in the crook of her arm, she walked toward the ocean. A faint sound of singing pulled her toward the shore. She looked around and saw no one close to the water except for Ronan. He was far enough away now that he was only a distant figure on the beach, a form of a man standing still against the vast sand and waves.

He was staring out to the ocean, just as she was, and she realized the voice she heard was his. The song floated through the air like a steady mist, with a familiar melody and lilting tones that melted her chest muscles. For a moment she had the sense that he was an ancestor, visiting her in the shape of a young man, and she stood silent watching him, listening to his haunting song. She couldn't fully hear the words, but the sounds carried, halting her.

Without realizing she was doing it she began to hum along with him. She didn't know how she knew the melody, but she found herself making gentle sounds in rhythm with his song. She suddenly realized where she'd heard it—it was the song that had been in her dream, the one that had woken her up. The haunting sounds gave rise to images of women with turtle shells on their backs, women with seal bodies, all with flowing hair similar to Ronan's. She closed her eyes, continued to hum the tune along with him.

Water, deep water. Women swimming to the shore from every direction. One woman standing on the shoreline facing out to sea, watching them coming ashore, singing a song that blended with the one Alice hummed. She heard Ronan's deep voice down the beach and opened her eyes to look over at him. He began to lower the sound of his melody, fading down to a barely audible sound, then stopping abruptly. Self-conscious, she stood for a moment staring at him. Without saying a word, he smiled at her, that wide, easy smile that had made her relax when they first spoke, then nodded his head slightly toward her and turned away, walking into the distance.

She stood breathless, wondering what had just happened. Both startled and strangely calm, she felt as though she had entered another world that was foreign but, this time, not frightening. Almost comforting.

An ocean breeze sent the tail of the scarf fluttering in the wind. The solid weight of the jewelry box in her arms anchored her, bringing her back to the present. She looked out toward the horizon. There were a few hours left before sundown, and she was not ready to go home. A few small hotels were just a short distance inland and she decided to stay the night. She could check into the hotel and come back to the ocean at sunset. For some reason she did not understand, she felt as if she was finally going to begin to understand the messages from her great-grandmother, the pull from the past that haunted her like a hungry ghost.

PART 2

Knowing

CHAPTER 6–GRACE

July 1934, Richarme, Louisiana

I'm going to start us back about one hundred years now, my sweet Lily. We're going back to your great-grandmother's time. My Grandmere Claire's family came from Canada when the French people there were kicked out or just left on their own, depending on who's telling the story. Her mother was Irish and her father was French. She was born a Beauchene—the name means "beautiful oak"—then she married your great-grandfather, Antoine Beaulieu. Everyone called her Mamou. Her name was like a title, one that set her as the matriarch for as long as she was living.

What I remember most about her was her hands, the way they gently curled up around whatever they were touching and held on both tightly and softly at the same time. Her hands seemed alive, as though they were a thing of their own, separate from the rest of her and empowered with a kind of magic that wasn't part of this world. When I was a little girl and we would visit her house, I'd always find a way to get her to touch me, to lay those hands on me and soothe whatever was on my mind or in my heart that day. I'd sidle up beside her and lean in close, snuggling my body next to hers, or I'd say that something on my body needed tending to, a small cut or bug bite, just so she'd reach over and touch me. And it was like a healing, like the hand of God coming down and through my grandmother's arm right to me, a little girl down in the bayous of Louisiana, one no one else would notice any more than they might notice a ladybug resting on a leaf. But when Mamou touched me, I was seen. My life seemed to mean something, at least in that moment.

My grandma had a healing touch, not just with her hands but with her mind, and the words she always knew to say just when someone needed them. She helped people's bodies heal, too. She grew plants in her yard that she used to make teas and poultices, and some she put in her cooking like secret ingredients that were meant to give what we ate a little something extra. We enjoyed it because it was some of the best food anywhere. Her kitchen always smelled delicious. Something always seemed to be cooking on her stove and if she wasn't stirring with her big wooden spoon, she was cutting up herbs or vegetables from her garden to put in the pot. She always said that you could tell a lot about a person by what they served on their dinner table. In her kitchen, food was another kind of medicine. She knew that healing comes in lots of forms. She taught us all that.

I was the youngest of her grandchildren, so that gave me a special place in the family. When we got together, she'd let me sit in her big lap while the others ran around outside, and as I got older, she'd let me work with her in the garden. I loved everything there, and it became my special place, the little patch of Earth that felt protected from the rest of the world. She'd tell me about the plants she was growing, and sometimes she'd tell me stories. She had a little patch of manglier that she grew, and once she told me how she'd learned about it when she was a little girl.

Before she started, she went into a kind of trance for a few seconds, like she was visiting someplace far away. I could see that the place she was visiting was not a happy one because of the way her mouth tightened up and her eyes got watery. She told me it all started when she was about seven years old and was walking along the banks of the river behind their house and saw something she'd never forget. The head was visible first, the smooth face of a deer with its eyes still wide open, but frozen, with a glazed look. The deer had been shot by a bow and arrow and left to die a painful death. People hunt for food, but this hunter had never come back to get the deer—just killed it in the most painful way possible, leaving it to suffer. The arrow was still in the deer's side, sticking out of it at an angle, with dried blood running down into the earth. Mamou was haunted by the face, the way the deer seemed to be looking at her, but she could see its sweet spirit was long gone from that body.

She realized in that moment she wanted to be a healer. She knew she couldn't stop people from doing cruel things, but she thought she could help stop some of the pain she saw in the world around her. She decided then to be a protector of the animals that lived in or near the water, the creatures of the river she loved so much and those that lived on its banks.

She looked down near the body of the deer and saw a smooth river rock, one that fit perfectly in her palm. She picked it up and took it home, and later she painted a spiral on it, surrounded by stars from the night sky. It became a part of her healing work, that stone, and she used it whenever she wanted to bring the power of her gifts to something that needed more than just prayers and herbs to heal it. Because of the promise she made to herself that day, the stone became something that helped her connect with the healing spirits of the Earth and our ancestors. For many years, it was her most important treasure.

She also saw a patch of manglier there beside the deer, with tiny white flowers poking up from the ground off the dark green leaves. She knew what it was because their neighbor used it for teas when anyone had a cold or runny nose. My grandma leaned down and picked some of it, cradled it in her hands, then left a little at the feet of the deer before she turned around and headed back home. She said that for the rest of her life, everything she did was in part for that deer, its suffering, and for all innocent creatures that suffer at the hands of cruelty and ignorance. She knew many people just ignored what they felt they couldn't fix in the world, especially if it was something that didn't affect them personally, but for her, there was no separation. When she saw suffering of any kind, she felt it as personal, and she lived her life in the service of healing it.

Because of what happened that day, manglier became the first plant she started working with, letting it teach her its magical powers. Mamou was another one she used, that beautiful plant spiked with red flowers. I always wondered if she got her name because she used the plant for healing people. She put that in teas too, sometimes with a little of my grandfather's home-grown whiskey, for when any of us girls got the monthly cramping. The first time she gave it to me felt like a ritual that brought me home into a quiet world she presided over, filled with secret prayers and healing herbs and the sweet scent of her love, dripping everywhere she went.

I learned recently that not everyone has these plants, manglier and mamou, like we do here in Louisiana. Turns out that they grow here for those of us who live in this part of the world, so we need to make sure we keep teaching the ones who come after us how to use them. I do wish I had told you a little more about them, Lily Mae. You were like Mamou and seemed to pick it up on your own. When you first told me that the plants talked to you, it was just a couple of years after Mamou died, and I wondered if she was whispering secrets into your ears. You swore it was the plants talking, though, and I didn't have any reason not to believe you because I knew what kind of magic runs through our family's veins.

Mamou told me that some of what she learned came from things her mamma taught her, so that's how I know the magic comes from way before us, running through from one to the next. It seems like it pops up and takes shape for some and not for others, choosing whoever in each generation has a big enough heart and enough bravery to use it.

When it showed itself in you, at first I was afraid for you. I wanted to get closer and help you learn how to use it, but we both know I failed in that. It's the greatest failure of my life, the thing I will most regret. I pray that writing these words will heal some of my broken heart and spirit, reach up to you wherever you are, and maybe save my soul a little. Maybe even do something beyond all of us, helping those to come in our family as I release some of my guilt and grief.

Since you've been gone, I haven't believed much in soul-saving in the way the Church teaches it. I can only hope that my soul might be saved by the fact that I'm still getting up each day, still trying to face the world with a little bit of love, even when it feels so hard to do.

* * *

Do you remember the quilt, Lily? The one Mamou gave to my mother, who gave it to me, and I gave it to you? I know I've told you this story before, but I'm going to tell it to you again, just to ease my spirit.

When I gave it to you, you were sick with a fever and nothing we tried seemed to ease it. I tried the manglier tea but you couldn't get it down. I put ice packs on you. Your grandma came and sang to you, her voice so beautiful I hoped it would pull you out of your haze. But nothing seemed to work. You were six years old, and your body was so small. You always seemed like your body was too little to hold your big spirit, Lily Mae, and when you were sick like that, I was afraid you might fly away forever and leave us. Your daddy was afraid too, so much so that he had to walk out of our house, saying that he was going hunting for dinner. I saw in his eyes the look of fear that was in my own heart that afternoon.

I went into our bedroom to get something from the dresser and saw the quilt draped over a chair. I was drawn to it, and suddenly I felt Mamou there, leading me over to pick it up. I knew she wanted it to go to you then. I brought it into your room, laying it over you gently. My mamma was afraid it would make you hotter, but I knew it would help you. I knew Mamou was going to help bring your fever down, that she was wrapping you up in all of her big love, pouring her healing powers right onto you through that quilt. When I laid it on you, your eyes opened for a few seconds and you gave me a weak smile. You said in such a quiet voice, "Merci, Maman. I'm going to rest now." I looked over at my mamma and neither of us knew what to say. You hadn't spoken all day, and for a minute I was afraid you were telling me that you really were going to leave us then.

But you didn't. You rested for a few hours, just like you said, and when you woke up around supper time, you asked for a cup of water. You still had a fever but your body didn't have the chills and shaking you'd had earlier. After that first cup of water you were able to get down a little soup, then a full cup of manglier tea, this time with honey. After you finished that you smiled with your lips sealed up, the way you'd smile when it looked like you had a secret you weren't going to tell the rest of us. You rolled over, wrapping the quilt up around your neck, and fell back asleep. Within an hour we could see the fever had broken because you woke up sweating. I gave you a bath, my baby girl, and when you came out of that tub, your eyes were lit up and I knew you were back with us. You told me you had been dreaming about a big forest with angels and plants that could talk. You said it was the best place you'd ever been.

You asked me if a place like that existed anywhere in the real world and I told you I didn't think so. I was wrong about that. Like so many other things I said and did, Lily Mae, I was wrong. But still you loved me through it all. You still loved me, and that night when you came back to us, I knew it was Mamou and the quilt that did it, brought you back to us so I could keep feeling all that love you had to give me and everyone else you knew in your short life.

CHAPTER 7–ALICE

June 2019, Berkeley, California

Alice drove a few miles inland to the hotel. Three things were on her mind: what she would do with the jewelry box that evening at the ocean, a coastal dinner of barbecued oysters and San Francisco sourdough, and a call to her sister.

It had been over a week since she'd talked with Madeline, when she'd called her about an article she was writing on the wine country. A professional chef, Madeline was three years older in age but often seemed a decade older in what she had done with her life. Madeline was the middle of the three girls in their family. Their older sister, Sophia, lived in New York with her wife and worked in the heirloom jewelry business.

Madeline was the only of the three to stay home in New Orleans. She married right out of college, had two children, purchased a house in the uptown section of New Orleans, and started a career as a caterer. Even though her marriage ended the year after her second child was born, she and her ex-husband remained friends, and now she owned her own catering business, one of the most sought after in the city. With a retirement account and a partially paid-off mortgage, she seemed miles away from where Alice felt she was in the life game.

Jealousy sometimes rose when Alice wondered if she'd ever feel settled anywhere. Brushing off those feelings with the thought that one day the right guy would finally come along—after she landed her big job—she never let herself think too long about the different trajectories her life could have taken.

Now, she just wanted to talk with her sister. The day had taken so many turns, a phone call with Madeline would help her mind settle.

"Hi, Alice," Madeline said.

"Hi, Maddie." Alice sat on the bed, hearing herself slip into the slight Southern accent that returned when she talked with family. It was almost like slipping into an old nightgown, weightless and comfortable, requiring no effort or thought. "I'm at the coast. I've had the wildest day. Do you have a minute?"

"A few. The kids are at Joe's tonight, but I have book club in an hour and I still need to get a dish together. We're just doing appetizers, but I thought I'd bring angels on horseback."

Alice's mouth watered, momentarily distracted from why she'd called. Marinated oysters wrapped in bacon. The smoky smell and briny flavor as they slid down the throat. A favorite appetizer, especially the ones her mom made.

"Sounds like a good dish to bring."

"Do you know how long Mom marinates the oysters in wine before she wraps them in the bacon? I have a bottle of white wine I opened a few nights ago and it's no good to drink now, so I thought I'd use it for this. I usually just wrap the oysters without marinating them, but Mom's were so good last Christmas when she served them, and she said it was the wine and garlic. I'd like to try it this way tonight and see how it turns out. I'm catering a party next weekend and this would be a great dish for it."

"I don't know, Madeline. I don't cook oysters much. I do plan to have some tonight for dinner though." Alice paused. "Hey, I've had kind of a weird day. Can I tell you about it?"

"I'd love to hear. I just have a few minutes now, but what's up?" The clang of a lid landing on a pot punctuated Madeline's words.

Alice paused. "I just met this guy on the beach, and . . . something happened."

"A new guy, huh? Someone you might be interested in for more than a couple of dates?"

"That's not what I meant. I'm not interested in him in that way. At least I don't think so. I just had a strange experience with him. He sang this song on the beach and I had this weird feeling that I'd heard it before, then . . . well . . ."

"Singing on the beach?"

"Yes. It sounded like an ancient song." *I sound crazy. What am I saying? This isn't even what I really called about.* "What I want to talk with you about is something different, though, something that happened to me today when I was sitting up on Mt. Tam. I had a weird image come to me, something with a shotgun. I don't know how to describe it."

"What do you mean, Alice? What kind of image? And what does this have to do with the guy you met? I need to go soon, but you're worrying me a bit. Are you OK?"

"I'm fine. And the guy and what I'm asking you about are two different things. At least I think they are. I just had another one of these things happen to me today that sometimes happens, you know, when I kind of see things—or feel things." Alice stopped. She had shared some of her experiences with her sister and Madeline had always listened quietly, never seeming to judge. But what did she really think? That was less clear.

"Oh, Alice, maybe you were just tired? Or maybe you heard someone near you on the mountain?"

Alice hated when her sister's voice got that tone that sounded like pity, or at least wistful sadness, as though Alice's experiences were related to an affliction that couldn't be cured.

"I'm really OK. Never mind. It's not important." Alice's voice drifted off, memories of childhood conversations about things she'd experienced arising in her mind. Dead end conversations ending with a silent stare that said, *"Don't talk about these things."*

"Are you sure?"

"Yes. Have fun with your book club tonight and just give me a call sometime when you can. I love you. I'm going to go get some oysters myself now. I hope you have fun with your friends tonight."

"Take care of yourself, Alice. You're worrying me a bit. Let me know what happens with the guy, if you see him again. Love you, sis. Talk to you soon."

"Good night." As Alice hung up, her hand reached up to her great-grandmother's scarf, still wrapped around her neck. Alone with her thoughts. Alone with her experiences, again. *It looks like it's just you and me, Grandmere Grace. Let's go to the ocean—Point Reyes beach tonight.*

Alice reached for the jewelry box and opened the lid. The smooth river rock caught her attention, the painted spiral glistening from rays of sunlight coming in through the window. She gently picked up the box and headed to her car.

* * *

Too anxious to eat, she headed right back to the ocean. As she walked onto the beach, a wide stretch of sand lay before her with the sun hanging low on the horizon across the sea, spreading light in dancing images across the water. She found a spot relatively secluded from other people and spread out a blanket. Sitting down cross-legged, she pulled out the jewelry box, opened it, and took a deep breath.

OK, Grandmere Grace. I'm here. I'm not entirely sure what I'm supposed to do, but I'm here. Alice hesitated. "Are you?"

she whispered quietly. She waited for a few seconds and closed her eyes. Nothing.

The scarf lay in the jewelry box where she'd placed it after her earlier trip to the beach. A thought curled its way into her mind: she'd been wearing the scarf the day she saw the young girl in the park. She'd also been wearing it earlier when she had the visions on Mt. Tam. Was the scarf bringing them on?

Reaching into the box, she picked the scarf up, looked at it closely, then put it back quickly. Of course not. It was just a scarf.

She closed her eyes again. Inviting in the images this time would help her control them, put them in order. That's what she needed to do. Taking a deep breath, she waited.

Nothing happened. No images. No messages from her grandmother.

The stone lay just beneath the scarf. She picked them both up, slid the scarf around her neck, and held the stone in her palm.

What am I to do? What's supposed to happen here?

Warmth pulsed through her hand, the stone seeming to be activated by her touch. A rush went up her spine followed by a sudden whiff of perfume, the same perfume she'd smelled on top of the mountain. She kept her eyes closed, waiting.

Grandmere?

And then something began to emerge behind her closed eyes, a scene rising through mist which slowly cleared. A small river, banks flanked with tall oak trees, moss hanging from the limbs in tangled webs. A young girl running down the path along the water, feet bare, loose hair swinging behind her back, mimicking the waves of the moss in the trees. The sound of a shotgun ringing out, the sharp haze of smoke hanging in the air. The acrid smell filled her nostrils, choking her momentarily. Stomach tight, nausea again. Fear. Almost panic.

What was this? Who was this girl? Was this her great-grandmother as a child?

The scenes faded away, leaving as swiftly as they'd welled up. Alice was vaguely aware of the rushing of the ocean before her, but it seemed to be louder than usual, as though the sounds before her were mixing with sounds coming from inside her mind. The roar of the waves rising from her mind came as a full-body experience, as though she was being swept into the ocean herself, engulfed by the water and suddenly going under, where everything was silent. Images of turtles appeared, swimming in the ocean and coming right up to her, one so close she could see deep into its eyes. Drowning into the pupils of this ancient sea creature, mesmerized, all awareness was focused only on this experience of spiraling into an endless expanse of space, falling into the deep center of something she could not name or understand. She settled into complete stillness, once again feeling as though she'd dropped out of the world around her, into a place where time and space dissipated.

Match the rhythm of the waves.

Return to the deep quiet of the turtle's eyes.

She opened her eyes. Who had spoken those words? The ocean lay in a wide expanse before her. She blinked a few times to adjust to the light.

Grandmere Grace, was that you I saw? Was that you as a child?

Alice stared out over the ocean. "Send a message," she said, not knowing if she was asking the waves or her great-grandmother or simply the air around her. "Something to help me understand what you want of me, what I'm to do."

She looked down at the jewelry box and the oval mirror inside the lid reflected a flash of sunlight. The face in the mirror was her own but—for a moment—she saw her mother's face, then her grandmother's, then Grandmere Grace's. All with hazel eyes. Staring at her silently.

Slipping the scarf from her neck and spreading it on the blanket, she picked up each item and set it onto the scarf: first the stone, then the doll, eyes permanently open, mouth permanently closed, unable to tell her anything. The hair pins and small squares of quilting material. The notecard with the date on it: June 21, 1923. The note from her great-grandmother.

Use your gifts to protect what you love and create what you desire.

She stood up and walked the few steps to the place where the waves washed up onto the shore. White foam caressed her bare feet and she thought of Ronan, his strong feet that had drawn her attention, the way they seemed almost a part of the sand. She looked at her pink toenails. The cold waves washed over them and they settled deeper into the sand, water pooling around them. A sand dollar appeared as the water pulled away, settling just next to her foot. She picked it up, rubbed her fingers over its smooth shell, and smiled.

A gift from the ocean.

The song Ronan shared earlier came back, the melody of it rising from her chest and filling her ears, and she tried to let it come out, quietly and hesitantly at first. No words, only sounds that came in rhythm with the ocean, rocking her body into a vibrating state of calm as she settled more deeply into the sand, water making larger pools around her feet.

The notes that came through were quiet but resonant, rising and falling like the ocean waves before her, then settling into a sustained hum. Alice closed her eyes, her body dissolving into the seascape. She let the hum fall away until all she could hear was the ocean—waves beating against the shoreline, covering her ankles as she felt herself rooted in place, sucked into the sticky pool of water and crystal sand.

Voices suddenly carried over the music of the waves—a couple walking nearby, interrupting her thoughts. She walked back to her blanket, settled onto it, and placed the sand dollar next to the river rock, then picked up her journal and sketched the tableau she'd created, the sound of the sea washing her mind into silence.

CHAPTER 8—GRACE

July 1934, Richarme, Louisiana

I remember the day your gift for healing washed through you, right in front of us in a way that changed how we saw you. You were five years old. We were on a picnic with Martha and Pierre, the four of us lounging beneath the branches of a big mother oak tree, small creatures living their lives all around us, birds flitting from branch to branch. I'd made a pot of red beans and rice the night before and we were eating the leftovers with cornbread we'd made that morning.

The light streamed through the trees around us, catching little streaks of red in your beautiful hair. You probably got that from your Scottish great-grandparents on your daddy's side, or maybe from Mamou's mother's Irish family. Something about that little hint of red caught my eye that morning, and I thought about the small ways you differed from your siblings. That hint of red hair seemed to go with the magic inside of you, baby girl. It only showed when the light was just right, revealing something that was there all along but that no one could see unless it wanted to show itself.

The branches of the protective oak shielded us from the blazing heat sizzling in the air. You suddenly looked up at the tree, turning your eyes from the roly-polys you'd been playing with, and smiled. We all turned our heads to look, and in that moment a breeze came and washed over us, cooling our sweltering bodies. The smallest branches of the oak tree moved as though they were arms, raising themselves to the heavens. Heralding something. Announcing a moment in time—when your healing powers would be called out of you, showing themselves that day.

As the breeze died down, the sound of a dog barking penetrated the air around us, turning into the cry of an animal in pain. That cry turned into a howl, then lowered itself into a long whine. We all got up and went to the road to see what was happening. A dog, its yellow fur all matted and dirty, lay injured on the ground, and you ran toward it, as though it had a string and was pulling you straight ahead. You slowed down just before you reached it and I yelled out for you to stay back, but your attention wasn't on me anymore, just on the dog and its eyes filled with pain.

It looked like it had been in a fight with another animal. It cowered low to the ground, nursing a hurt front leg covered with blood streaks. The blood was fresh, so its attacker must have just left. You walked right up to it and put your hand on its head.

When I caught up to you, she was looking at you with liquid eyes like she was in love, begging for help. I asked you to back away because I was afraid she might hurt you or that she had rabies, but you didn't listen. You wrapped yourself around her and put your hand on her front leg and started singing to her, a song I hadn't ever heard before. It came out of you as though it had been there all along, a song with no words but a melody that quieted everything around us and seeped into that hurt dog's pain, washing it away.

I was so surprised by what you were doing that I stopped and stood there for a minute. It was like the two of you became one being. When you pulled away, she had stopped whimpering and rested her head in your lap. She closed her eyes like she was going to sleep there, resting in whatever circle of healing you had created around the two of you. You looked up at me and smiled and said, “Maman, it’s gonna be all right now. The warm feeling came over both of us and now it’s gonna be all right.”

I asked what you meant and you told me that the warm feeling that came to you sometimes when you saw something hurting had just come over you, and that it wrapped up the dog too. You asked me if I ever got the warm feeling and I had to say no, I didn’t get that feeling. I wasn’t sure what you meant, but I suspected then what I know now. The warm feeling was the healing gift that came over you when it wanted to go to someone or something that was sick or in pain. We took the dog home and nursed her back to health, and she stayed with us for two more years before she passed away, just a week after you left us. I think her spirit couldn’t stand to stay here while you had gone away, flying with the angels.

You named her Honey Pot and said it was because she was the color of honey, and she followed you around wherever you went. They say some healers have animals that talk to them, and Honey Pot was one of many animals in your life like that, the one who showed us all something of how big your gifts were.

I know you already know this story, Lily Mae. I just need to tell it to myself right now as I unravel so many pieces of your story and mine, the stories of your grandparents, their grandparents. They live inside us. When you healed Honey Pot, I thought of Mamou. I remembered the days when I was a little girl, being in her kitchen in summer afternoons, watching as she stirred a pot of something good and worked with the plants and herbs from her garden. She’d tell me stories about the plants, which ones healed scars of the body and which ones healed scars on the inside of a person.

That day we met Honey Pot, I remembered one afternoon when I was sitting on her back porch peeling potatoes. A young woman came trotting up to the house, her feet trailing dust from the road, her arms filled with a little ball of black fur. It was a kitten with the cutest face I'd ever seen, but it was hurt. The woman walked up to the kitchen door and asked if Mamou could come out. Mamou scooped up the kitten and walked into the kitchen, humming a song. I wanted to go inside but Mamou told me I should keep peeling potatoes. When they came back outside the kitten was perched on the lady's shoulders, purring. After they left, I asked Mamou what she did to the kitten and she said that she just gave it the right kind of love. She smiled when she said that, then went back inside.

I wish now that I had asked her more questions about the kind of love she knew how to give. She seemed to know how to get different kinds of love from each plant in her yard, from leaves and the bark of trees. She said healing came from every part of nature, that everything God created had something to share with us.

I'm telling you this, Lily Mae, because I can see how she lived in you. If I had known how to help you with the things you sensed and knew, I would have. I just didn't know how.

* * *

I want to tell you about some things that happened with Father Comeaux. He's been connected to our family for so long, and you know he was the one who baptized you.

I remember the day of your baptism, your face pink from the sun, eyes wide open taking everything in. You were silent, looking at all of us as Father Comeaux poured the water on your head and blessed you with oil. You didn't cry and I wondered what kind of thoughts you were having. Babies aren't supposed to have thoughts, I guess, just take in images and sounds, but you weren't like others even then. Even then I thought maybe the angels had sent someone special to be with us, maybe one of their own. How could I have thought that when you were so little, so new to us from heaven?

But let me tell you about the day I knew something was coming, even though I didn't want to let myself believe what I knew in my heart.

Do you remember when Father Comeaux came to our house that Easter Sunday when you were six? I remember what you were wearing, because I'd spent so much time sewing it up for you. You loved the color deep green, and I sewed up a dress for you to wear on Easter. I always liked you girls to wear white or pale yellow for Easter Mass, but you begged me to make you a green dress, and I broke down. It was a simple dress, short sleeves and a flared skirt, with a bow made of silky ribbon that tied in the back. You were so happy in that dress that you put it on two hours before we had to leave. You told me you felt like the queen of the forest. That's what you called yourself that morning. I didn't realize then that you meant what you said, that the forest was truly becoming a home to you.

After Mass Father Comeaux came over. What happened that day seemed like a small thing, but it's stuck in my mind. It was one of those moments when I realize that if I had been paying more attention maybe I could have stopped things. Looking back, I understand that we only see and believe the things that feed the stories we want to tell ourselves. Until hard truths bang down our doors and crash things in, I guess it's human nature to ignore what's right in front of our eyes.

You children were in the front yard when he came. We'd just had our big Sunday meal and Pierre was chasing you and Martha around the yard. I always liked for you to get outside after we ate, and you three were running around laughing, still all dressed in your Sunday clothes.

Father Comeaux came in and I gave him a cup of coffee and a piece of carrot cake. At first, I thought he'd come by just because he'd heard how good my Easter Sunday cake was, but as we made small talk, I noticed he was fidgeting and not really eating. His leg bounced up and down and I wondered if maybe he wasn't feeling well. But then he got quiet and I realized that maybe he'd come to talk about something.

Right when I started wondering that, you and Martha walked into the kitchen, sweating from all that running around. Father Comeaux looked over at you and his lips tightened up a bit as he asked how you two were doing. I raised you right—you know that—so you both said you were doing well, thank you for asking. Then you walked into the back of the house and Father Comeaux asked me whether you'd been visiting the woods at night—late, when the moon was up—all by yourself.

I didn't know what to say, and his question frightened me. I asked him what he meant, and he said he didn't really want to ask questions, but a few people at church had come to him telling stories about you. Ricky and Robby Benoit told him they'd seen you walking in the woods one night when they were hunting and wondered what you were doing. It was close to a full moon and they heard something they thought was perhaps a cougar, but then they saw you walking through the woods. It was around midnight and they knew it was you because the moon was shining so much light down into the forest that they could see you clearly.

They watched you stop at a big oak and start singing to the tree. At midnight. In the middle of the woods. They said you danced around the tree like you were possessed. That was the word he used—possessed. They left because they got spooked by what you were doing. They told him all this because they thought maybe the devil had taken a hold of you and that he ought to know.

He stopped talking then. I didn't know what to say. So many thoughts raced through my head, mostly about how this was none of his business, and that you probably weren't out that late *(were you?)*, and that those boys were just making up stories. I did think about the river otter family you visited when you could. Could you have been out there, visiting it? Checking in on the babies? You told me that one of the babies seemed smaller than the others, saying, "If we don't help care for it, Maman, who will? The mamma otter may need our help. I think that's what she's trying to tell me when I visit her—they need our help."

All of these thoughts ran through my head in a flash. What did you mean about the mother otter talking to you? You believed she was telling you something, that much was true. But would you go out at night to see them, to visit the trees you loved so much? I stopped myself, deciding that no matter what was true, Father Comeaux was going to start thinking something about you and our family that wasn't going to come to anything good for any of us.

It took me a minute, but I told him that the boys must have been mistaken, that you always went to bed at nine o'clock and that you slept in the room right next to ours and of course we would hear if you went out of the house because the front door was so close to our bedroom. And, besides, what kind of crazy story was this anyway? There was no reason that you'd be going outside in the middle of the night singing to a tree. I smiled and asked him if he wanted more cake or coffee and he said no, then he stood up to leave.

Right before he left he told me, looking me straight in the eye, that he was sure the boys must have just made up that story to get a laugh out of him because of course it couldn't be true, that they were little pranksters, after all. He thanked me for the cake and looked me in the eye one more time without saying anything, in the way that people do when they're thinking something they want you to understand without having to say it, then he left. Left me standing there with my head spinning.

Of course I wondered about it, Lily. I wondered if it was possible that you'd been in those woods in the middle of the night. I knew how much you loved the woods and the river and all the creatures that lived there, how often you liked to wander through the trees. But I never thought you'd get up in the middle of the night and go to the woods, and I sure didn't think you'd be out there singing under the moon and stars. I just didn't think it was possible. But still I wondered.

When you came back through the kitchen a few minutes later in that forest green dress, I had a feeling in the pit of my stomach, but I didn't let myself pay attention to it. I had a feeling that somehow that forest might take you from us. Right away I thought how silly that was and let it go. And I let you go outside again without asking about what Father Comeaux said. I think I was afraid to. I never brought it up again, to you or anyone else. But I never stopped thinking about it. I never stopped worrying about whether or not something terrible was coming toward us.

That evening I sat in the rocking chair on our porch, my mind spinning with thoughts that wouldn't let me go. I'd always seen the woods as a place of safety and refuge, but that night, a hazy fear moved up my body until it gripped my heart. My mind couldn't make sense of it and I waited until the moonlight calmed me back down.

When I finally went inside, I was more relaxed and I thought about Mamou. It was easy to see how her connection to the water and trees and nature got into you. She may not have been the one who put it there, but it came from her just the same. And maybe that's all that matters. It gives me some comfort to think that, because if it came from her, then maybe you're with her, and I can find some peace in that.

Mamou

My dear Grace, I remember the day of Lily Mae's baptism. What the priest didn't know was that I had baptized her too. From where I sat in the church, I saw my own Maman there above her head, blessing her in the way of those of us who can hear the Earth and the spirits speak.

After we went back to your house, I held Lily Mae in my arms and felt my Maman and all the healers who came before pour down through my arms the love of generations. They poured down the deep gifts of healing and sight. I already knew this child had the gift of sight. It came to me in a dream before she was born. When you told me how she came out with her head and face covered in a way you'd never seen a baby come out before, I knew for sure. That caul over her head was a sign from the spirits that she was one of them, come down to Earth still able to see into the other worlds.

The first time I held her she looked at me, eyes wide open, silent and staring. I knew she could see the spirits who work with me, the guiding spirits and the healer spirits and the dreamtime spirits. They were all blessing and loving her, ma chérie. She was always one of their own, and it was only a matter of time before they'd call her home.

CHAPTER 9—ALICE

June 2019, Berkeley, California

The light from the sun dipping into the sea turned Alice's left arm golden as she drove north on Highway 1. The sandwich she had eaten hours earlier long gone, the thought of oysters, bread, and a buttery glass of chardonnay filled her mind. She hoped her favorite coastal restaurant was open and not too crowded.

Madeline's oyster dish popped into her thoughts. Missing her sister, Alice thought briefly about calling her again, but knew she wouldn't. The day's events were not something she could describe to Maddie. They could talk about cooking and seafood and the travails of her dating life, non-existent as that usually was, but she couldn't explain to her sister what she was experiencing. Feeling isolated with these experiences was all too familiar.

The restaurant came into sight as she navigated a bend, the setting sun warming her arm. *Will Ronan be here?* The thought popped into her mind as she pulled into the gravel lot, carefully sliding into a narrow spot. *Do I want him to be here?* Even with a town this small, the likelihood of that was minuscule. Still, she peered around the dining room when she opened the door, surprised by how comforted she felt by the salty aroma of fresh seafood.

She ordered oysters and French bread to go, then chose a Napa Valley chardonnay she loved and headed back to her hotel. She didn't feel like being around people tonight. *Besides, my great-grandmother is with me, so what do I need with living people*? Grandmere Grace's bright eyes flashed before her. *Yes*, she thought. *Just us girls tonight.*

* * *

She awakened in the dark center of the night, the smell of perfume lingering in the air. The tail of her dream stayed with her: a young girl feeding chickens in a small backyard behind a house, scattering seed around the scuttling birds. A corn-colored dog followed behind, tail wagging. Tall pine trees flanked the back of the house, entry to a small forest.

Once more, the turtle, appearing as a foreign visitor in this rural scene. Swimming slowly through a sudden wave of deep-blue water, moving gracefully through the depths of an endless ocean. Again, Alice felt both unnerved and strangely calmed by it. Her last fleeting image was of its body turning away, swimming into the dark sea as though beckoning her to follow.

She lay nestled under the covers, afraid to wake up completely, wanting to hold the images still swimming through her consciousness. She sunk deeper into the bed, enjoying the quiet. Living in Berkeley, she rarely awoke to silence and wanted to rest within its depths as long as possible.

Slowly, events of the previous day came to mind. Did Ronan live nearby? Was he waking up right at that moment, not far away? Or was he already up, possibly sipping good coffee?

The jewelry box caught her eye, the silk scarf lying next to it. She'd left the box open and the small oval mirror again reflected light. Questions rose like a candle flame, twinkling in her mind. What did Grandmere Grace want from her? And what did she mean about gifts in the family being shut down? If seeing spirits was a gift, she didn't want it.

Or did she? She wasn't sure of anything anymore. Maybe learning more about her great-grandmother would help.

I should call Grandmere Martha.

Alice's grandmother had cared for Grandmere Grace in her last years of life. Alice hadn't spoken to her since her cousin's wedding at the big cathedral in Metairie, a suburb outside of New Orleans where some of their family still lived. Grandmere Martha would know something about the jewelry box and gifts inside. *She can tell me about the gifts in the box. Then I'll know what Grandmere Grace meant. What she wanted. And I can close this up.*

The sand dollar she'd found the evening before rested on the nightstand. The faintly-etched star in the center caught her eye and she rubbed her finger over it gently. The light from the lamp beside the bed flickered. She popped out of bed, shaking off the mist of dreams and cloudy thoughts. Time to go home and get back to real life.

* * *

Alice's new neighborhood was filled with people out enjoying the sunshine, walking their dogs or working in their yards. Anxious to get some things growing in her own yard, she wondered if the growers' market would have starts she could buy. She'd go later that afternoon, after talking with her mom.

Isabella's face peeked out of the front window from her spot on the couch. As the door opened, she bounded off the couch and purred, then gave a clear demand for food, trotting over to her food dish and looking up, waiting for Alice to feed her.

"Isabella, I had quite a trip. I wish you could talk. I could use someone to talk with right now."

Scooping a small amount of puree from the tin, she thought about the call to her mother. What should she say? A flash of memory from her teenage years, along with a tightened feeling in her stomach, slowed her movements. Was it time to try again? Attempt a deeper conversation with her mom about the types of experiences that had haunted her since childhood?

Meow! Isabella rubbed against her, looked up, then butted her head against her leg. Alice dropped the scoop of food into the dish then moved to the couch and sat down, closing her eyes and letting herself return to a conversation with her mother years earlier. She was seventeen and had just broken up with another boyfriend—a guy she'd dated only two months, really, barely long enough to call him a boyfriend. After coming home she'd tossed around in her bed for hours, then drifted into a troubled sleep.

Alice had awoken in the middle of the night from a dream about swimming in a river, reaching for a low-hanging branch from an oak tree at the shore. Beside her bed she saw a hazy image, the little girl—visiting her again. The white nightgown, bare feet, sweet face like an angel. No words, no message, just her presence so close that Alice wanted to reach out to touch her, to see if she was real, but didn't, too afraid to move. She closed her eyes willing herself to stay calm. When she opened them a few minutes later, the child was gone, only an empty space beside her bed.

In the kitchen the next morning as her mother brewed café au lait, Alice started the conversation casually.

"How did you sleep, Mom?"

"Fine. I finished my book and fell right to sleep. You?"

"I slept OK. I woke up in the middle of the night, though. It was strange, almost like something in the room woke me." Alice pulled a green coffee cup from the cupboard, her mind going back to the deep color of the river in the dream.

"What do you mean?" Alice's mom turned to her, eyebrows furrowed slightly, coffee cup held tightly in her hand.

Body tensing, Alice paused before answering. "It's something that happens sometimes. I wake up and . . . feel like someone is in the room. I know no one is there—but . . . sometimes it seems like it. Probably just my mind still closing up a dream." She poured a cup of coffee.

"Yes, just dreaming, Alice." Her mother turned back to the stove, scraping the bottom of the iron skillet a little more forcefully than usual. "You've always had an active imagination."

Alice halted. Say more? Risk having her mother pull back even more? No. Take a sip of coffee. Close it up. Close everything up.

"I know, Mom. Just a dream."

The quiet lie, the one she had told herself many times as a child, now cemented in her mind as one she would use to protect herself in the world: I just have an active imagination—nothing I think I'm seeing is real. What I think I see isn't really there.

The lie had become her anchor when images arose or she felt a rush of cold air around her, suggesting the presence of a spirit trying to get her attention. She repeated it to herself as a mantra until it became a part of her. *What I think I see isn't really there.*

After the events of the last week, the lie didn't seem to be sticking so well.

Her mother picked up on the fourth ring, just before Alice was about to hang up. "Hi, Alice," her mother said in her soft Louisiana drawl. "What are you up to today? My weekend has been busy."

Alice knew what that meant. Her mother often spent weekends with her best friend, Elinor. Both widows, Elinor and Kate had been inseparable for years.

"I'm glad you're keeping busy, Mom," Alice said. "I just got back from a quick trip to the coast. I stayed at a little hotel near Stinson Beach. It was great to be at the ocean."

"I know how much you love it there," her mother said. "What else do you have planned this weekend? Are you going to Mass in the morning? Or are you no longer Catholic?"

Alice sighed, knowing her mother meant the comment mostly in jest, but also knowing that her lapsed Catholicism was a source of sadness and concern. Her family's Catholicism was more than a religion. It was a cultural way of life, going all the way back to their ancestors in France. "Well, I did say a little prayer at the ocean, but I know it doesn't count as Mass," she said. "But, you know, I really think God is OK with it. She told me so right after I said that prayer."

Alice laughed, knowing her mother would lighten at their joke. On her mother's last visit to Berkeley, they'd had many conversations about Alice's changing thoughts about religion, her final decision to leave Catholicism after failing to be able to reconcile her many questions about doctrine with things she had come to believe, and her scandalous idea—at least to her mother—that God was neither male nor female. One of her friends had given her a small statue of the goddess of Willendorf, and when her mother saw the naked deity with heavy child-bearing hips and belly, she'd shaken her head, wondering what was happening to her daughter in California. From that moment, light-hearted comments about God as a "she" became an easy way to avoid any real conversations about religion.

"I'm glad she told you that," her mother laughed. "If she talks to you again, ask her if the Saints are going to win the Superbowl."

"I don't think she knows the answer to that," Alice said, "but if she does ever tell me ahead of time who's going to win, I'll be sure to tell you in time for you to place a few bets."

"You know I'm not a betting woman," her mom said, then added quietly, "But I do wish you'd start going back to Mass."

Alice paused. *Ignore this. Stay focused.*

"I did go for Marie's wedding, Mom, remember? It was great seeing all the cousins that day," Alice said, quickly sidestepping the issue. "I called because I was thinking about Grandma Martha and wondered if you've talked with her recently. Do you know how she's doing? I haven't talked with her in a long time."

"The last time I saw her was a few days ago. She surprised us all and came to the dinner I had for your sister's birthday party. We wished you were with us."

"Can I get her new number, Mom? I'd love to call her."

"I don't know it by heart, but I can text it to you after we get off the phone. Tell her I'll stop by and visit soon. Maybe I'll ask her to cook some of her shrimp etouffee for me. I've never been able to make it like she does."

"Mom . . ." Alice started, uncertain what she would reveal, only knowing she wanted to see if her mother knew anything that would help her with her quest to understand what her great-grandmother wanted. "Do you remember the green jewelry box Grandmere Grace gave me when she died? The one with the scarf in it?"

"I do, but I haven't thought about that for years."

"I was wondering if you know anything about it. Do you know where she got the jewelry box or the things inside? There was a scarf and a river rock with a spiral painted on it."

"I don't remember what was in the box, Alice," her mother said slowly, as though peeling back layers of years in her mind. "Actually, I don't remember seeing the jewelry box much at all before she gave it to you. I do remember the doll. She had it on her dresser when I was a little girl, then one day it disappeared. She must have put it away in that box."

Remembering the images from her dream that morning, Alice wondered if the little girl who kept appearing had been the doll's owner.

"The doll's still in the box, Mom," Alice said. "Thanks for sharing what you remember."

"Enjoy the rest of your afternoon, Alice. I'll have more time to talk next weekend. Hope you have a good week."

"Thanks, Mom. You too. I love you."

"Love you too."

Alice hung up the phone. She started the water in the tub, pulled the jewelry box out of her backpack, then placed the river rock and sand dollar on the side of the tub. *It won't hurt to bring the river and ocean here. I just wish I knew what Grandmere Grace wants.*

As she lit the candle on the counter top, she was surprised by a sudden fear that even if Grandmere Grace could talk with her, she might not want to hear what she had to say.

* * *

When Alice finally made the call, she was disappointed to get voicemail. She hung up before leaving a message. When she went to work Monday morning, her mind was still rambling through all that had happened over the weekend.

Soon after she sat down at her desk, her supervisor walked over with a smile on her face.

"Are you up for a surprise? One I think you'll like?" Amanda asked, leaning onto Alice's desktop.

"I'm not sure," Alice said, laughing. "I've had a weekend of surprises. But, sure, what is it?"

"We're starting a new series on the Pacific coast. Are you up for a little travel?"

"I'm always up for travel. Where are we going?"

"San Diego. Just you. We want to do a story on high-end tourist expeditions. There's a company that leads four-day luxury getaways and we'd like to send you to write about it. How does a few days on the ocean sound?"

The picture of Ronan standing on the beach flashed across Alice's mind, the soft melody of his song. Everything stood still.

"Great assignment. When do I go?"

"We're booking a flight for you this Saturday. Can you be ready that soon?"

"Of course."

"Great. Start packing!"

Alice smiled at Amanda then watched her walked away. She took another sip of coffee and sat quietly for several minutes before finally turning on her computer, her mind jumbled with questions she could not answer.

CHAPTER 10—GRACE

July 1934, Richarme, Louisiana

We are all made of stories, Lily. All of us. The longer I live the more I understand that everything I see is filtered through all the stories I've lived in my life. And without understanding how it happened, I think I've passed them on to the three of you. Somehow, they took hold of you in a different way than they did for your sister and brother. They seemed to line the cells of your body, moving your mind to see and hear things the rest of us couldn't. There were times when the things you said and did frightened me in a way that held me frozen, unable to act, even when you needed me most.

Now that you're gone, I'm starting to understand that the stories that came to me and the ones that came to your daddy, through our parents and their parents and as far back as time, went into you too. Your little body just couldn't hold it all. You were like a little vessel of clay that got filled up with too much, until it seeped out of every crack and opened you wide until you burst into flames, into light, into the air and space and heavens all around us.

I don't know all the stories, but I know some of them. Thinking about Mamou has me thinking about her husband, my Grandpere Antoine. Antoine Beaulieu. His last

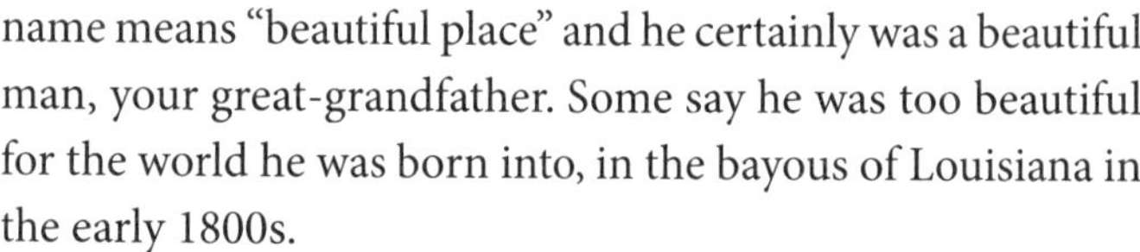

name means "beautiful place" and he certainly was a beautiful man, your great-grandfather. Some say he was too beautiful for the world he was born into, in the bayous of Louisiana in the early 1800s.

Mamou told me he was working in the fields when they met. He was a young man, a tenant farmer, and she was the youngest child of a big family that didn't have enough money to feed everyone. She said when she first laid eyes on Grandpere Antoine, a vision flashed before her of a bird taking flight, a big, brown-feathered bird with wings that spread so wide they cast a shadow across the field where he was standing. She said it was a shadow of light, a wave in the shape of angel wings, passing over the field and your great grandpa as the bird passed over.

This may sound funny to some, but I know you of all people understand, Lily, that things like this do happen. Mamou had visions most of her life, but that one was a sign to her and she took it with both hands. As soon as the sun started setting that day, she went back to the field where she'd seen the bird and the man she would marry, carrying a basket with a blackberry pie fresh out of the oven. When your great-grandfather walked off that field, he was greeted by Mamou, standing there sweet as sugar, offering him not only pie but a chance to woo her into a life together. Of course, like everything else in their marriage, she was the one who took the lead. The wooing started with her wide-eyed smile, and before long, Grandpere Antoine asked her to marry him and join him in the little shack he lived in, next to the fields where he spent his days.

She was seventeen and Grandpere Antoine was twenty when they married back in 1858. They lived east of Bunkie on the banks of the Atchafalaya River, close enough to the water that she could visit every day. Water has a way of shaping things, carving its way around towns, defining the land and the souls of the people who live there. Mamou's connection to the river gave her strength to move through everything life gave her, and she gave her love back to that river, back to every living thing that made its home there.

She had two children right away. Both died before they lived to be a year old, then she had my mother, Rose. I can tell you that by the time my mamma was born, Mamou and Grandpere Antoine were working from the time the sun peered its first rays of light into the sky until after the stars came out at night. My grandpa loved working the land, and he talked to it and understood it the way Mamou could talk to plants and animals.

They were a team, those two. They had something between them that's rare, something that only comes along for some people, the ones who are lucky enough to be born under the right stars. I haven't known any other marriage like theirs. They seemed to be able to understand what the other was thinking, even without talking. More than once, I remember the two of them just looking at each other, not saying a word, then one of them would walk over and pick something up and hand it to the other, as though it had been asked for. They had their own language and we all knew it. We watched them together and wanted to be sheltered by that great big love they shared.

I don't remember as much as I'd like to about my grandpa, but I do have a few clear memories. He didn't talk much, but when he did, everyone listened. He only spoke when he had something to say. One night he and I were sitting out on the porch after supper, and the moon was just a sliver dancing between the branches of the pine trees in their front yard. He was quiet and I sat there, happy to be next to him without anyone else around. After a little while of sitting in silence, he started talking, and he told me a story that helped me understand more about him. The whole time he talked he was staring out into the trees, almost like he didn't remember

I was there, and I barely made a sound because I wanted him to just keep talking.

He started by telling me that the night of the month of the first slice of the moon—that's what he called it—always reminded him of someone he once knew. It was one of those nights when he told me this story. The moon had gone dark and was just starting to come back in the sky, building up toward being full again in a couple of weeks. As we sat under the sliver of moonlight, he talked about a man he'd known when he was a boy. As I said, he'd grown up dirt poor and he'd had to work alongside his daddy in the fields from the time he was young. He said one of the other workers in the field had been a tall man, lanky and too thin, with hands weathered and coarse from years of hard work. He remembered those hands because he watched the man work and was afraid his own hands would get that worn down when he was old. Grandpere Antoine loved the land, but he knew the land could tear a man down if life didn't give him time to rest and take care of himself. That's what he saw in Emile, a man whittled down to the bones by hard labor.

Emile was a tenant farmer like his daddy, working his whole life trying to buy a small piece of land but never getting very far. Grandpere Antoine remembered Emile as a kind man, with eyes that bore through you and a soft voice that lulled whoever was listening into being quiet themselves. My grandpere and his daddy worked side by side with Emile for years, and Emile was always there no matter what, until one day he didn't show up in the fields. They didn't worry too much at first, thinking maybe he'd had something come up with his family. Emile didn't show up the next day or the next, though, and by the fourth day, Grandpere's daddy decided to go and check on him.

Emile lived in a tiny shack with his wife and their three children a few miles outside of town. Grandpere Antoine walked with his daddy to visit them and what he saw shook him for the rest of his life. When they knocked on the rickety front door, a pale, emaciated woman opened the door, her face heavy from crying. She was holding a young boy with two other children standing behind her, staring out at them with wide, empty eyes.

Grandpere's daddy said he'd come to check on Emile because he hadn't been in the fields for a few days. The woman said Emile was gone, that he wasn't coming back, and that he definitely wouldn't be going to the fields to work anymore. She stepped aside so they could look into the house and they saw a body laid out on the kitchen table covered with a ragged sheet. Grandpere knew it was Emile but he didn't want to believe it. His daddy took off his hat and asked if there was anything he could do. Emile's wife said there wasn't anything anyone could do now.

The sheriff and his boys had ended Emile's life after he was caught taking a bag full of carrots and potatoes from a neighbor's field to feed them, and even though he planned to pay them back with some of the food from their own small patch of garden when he could, the sheriff wasn't interested in hearing anything from a man who couldn't take care of his own family. They shot him right in front of his wife and children, almost casually, as though it was as easy for them as hunting a rabbit for dinner. This was a time when a sheriff could do anything he wanted, with no one he really had to answer to, and now Emile's wife and children were left on their own. Grandpere's family helped Emile's family as well as they could after that, but he never went back there again. He was haunted for the rest of his life by the memory of seeing Emile stretched out like that, all the life gone out of him.

My grandpere's eyes got shiny when he finished talking. He was crying, I could see, but he didn't want me to know it. He told me that when they got home later that evening, he walked outside on his own after dinner and looked up and saw "the first slice of moon" coming up in the sky. He prayed then that Emile was rising up in the night sky like the sliver of moon and that his soul would keep rising up to heaven where he belonged. When he stopped talking, we both looked up at the night sky together and didn't say a word. I've always remembered his story, and more than anything it's the weight of his sadness that stays with me, as though he was carrying something as heavy as the moon itself. I think he carried that weight with him until he died, always trying to find a way to relieve everyone he came into contact with from the pain of human suffering that seems to be as old as the dirt we walk on.

* * *

This is what I know about Grandpere Antoine and the way he and Mamou started something they never liked to talk about, but that defined who they were, at least for me. Grandpere used to tell me he didn't know what he would have done without Mamou—*my Claire*, he used to say. He told me she saved him that day in the fields with her fresh-baked pie and eyes that lit up like the stars. He said she made him stronger and braver than he would have been, even heroic by some people's accounts, and he said everything he did was because of her.

According to him, Mamou was the one who took the boy in, the one who showed up in their barn in the middle of the night while all of their children were sleeping. She heard something outside and found a thin teenage boy hiding behind a stack of hay. Grandpere said he was so skinny you could see the lines of his ribs, and his body was covered in cuts and bruises, burn scars sketched across his skeleton back. They fed him that night and Mamou put a poultice on his wounds. They gave him a warm blanket so he could sleep in the barn. They didn't want their daughter—my mamma, your

Grandma Rose—to know, because they weren't sure whether or not they would take him in.

For a week Mamou went to the barn before my mother woke up and then again after she went to bed to feed and take care of him. She was trying to nurse him back to health while they could figure out what to do with him. They knew he was the child of a family that was too poor to feed all of their children, and they figured out he was also the one who took the worst of the beatings from his father's frustration that came out after drinking his shame away at night.

Grandpere needed help if he was going to figure out how to do anything for this boy. He knew he was taking a big risk by going to Father Richarme. He didn't know what the pastor thought about getting into the private business of other families, but he thought he was truly a holy man because he'd always helped the hungry poor who came to the church steps. He was careful in how he brought it up, saying he'd heard about a family nearby whose children were taking the brunt of the family's poverty, just to see how Father Richarme would respond. They eyed each other for a minute, trying to figure each other out, then Father Richarme quietly said that he'd heard about a family like that. He said one of the women at church took him aside one Sunday and told him about a family living in a small house far out in the woods, that they didn't seem to have much to eat and that the children didn't look too healthy in other ways either.

Grandpere said they eased into the conversation slowly, like two people wading into a bayou looking out for the bright eyes of an alligator. They both knew it was part of the code of honor for country people to not get into other people's business, but after a few minutes of talking, they finally trusted each other enough that Grandpere told him about the boy in the barn. Father Richarme said he might be able to offer a little help if my grandparents would consider keeping the boy for a while. He would have to stay hidden, of course, but Father Richarme said that between the two of them, they might be able to find a way to help him and maybe his siblings too. They struck a deal that day. That's how it all started, as far as I understand.

I can't help but think that Grandpere must have been thinking about Emile, knowing he could also end up at the end of someone's shotgun if that boy's father found out where he was. I'm so glad he did it anyway, Lily Mae. I wish I had half of the bravery inside me that he and Mamou had. You had it too, that stubborn streak of love for the world that could override the fear that keeps most of us frozen into doing nothing. For you, for your bravery, and for my grandparents, I'm trying to learn to be brave. I'm trying, Lily.

* * *

I want to tell you a lot more about that story, but first I want to tell you that the reason I keep thinking about him is because I saw how your great-grandfather seemed to live in you. What I remember about him is how he connected with every living creature he met. He seemed to have a way of reaching out feelers in the world and knowing what a person or animal was feeling, and when the feeling was sadness or fear, he did what he could to heal the broken places that caused it. He loved little animals too, Lily. I remember stray animals he used to take in, sometimes a dog or cat, and once a hurt rabbit that found its way to their back yard. He had a way of taming animals, even wild ones, and getting them to trust him, the fear inside of them draining away with his soft words and quiet way of holding a creature with his eyes, looking directly into its soul and calming it down.

You were like that. We all saw it with Honey Pot but it came out in other ways too. Sometimes it came out in ways that frightened us both, and I always watched over you so I could keep an eye on that way you had of feeling the emotions of the people around you. I was always afraid it might overtake you, that you might land in a dark place and not know how to come back from it.

One way it came out for you was nightmares. Sometimes you'd wake us up with sounds you'd make in your bedroom, sobbing or yelling in fear. I'd go to your room and Martha would usually be awake, looking at me, not knowing what to do. You frightened her too at those times. I'd go over and you'd be in such a deep sleep and so much distress that I never knew if I should wake you to try to comfort you or just let you keep going in your dream until you came out on the other side.

Usually, I'd sit on your bed and slowly rub your back, hoping I could bring you back to our world. Sometimes it worked and sometimes you stayed asleep until your body would slowly relax, the dream losing its grip on your tender spirit. When the back rubs woke you up, I'd try to comfort you and sometimes you'd tell me a little about what you were dreaming. Mostly they were stories about small creatures being chased and eaten up by big animals.

Every now and then your body would curl up in a ring around mine, your head nestled on my leg, your thin arms cradling my back like moss curling around an oak branch. Sometimes tears would fall from your eyes even as you drifted back to sleep, leaving wet marks on my nightgown. I'd feel those tears on my legs when I'd crawl back into my own bed and I always hoped that somehow I was helping to lift whatever burden you felt from the world's suffering by carrying a little mark of your sadness with me.

I have other memories of this way you had of feeling other's suffering. One happened just a few months before you left us. You'd been playing by yourself in the back yard, and I looked out and saw you sobbing. Your body was shaking so much I could see it from the kitchen window, and I went out to see what was happening. By the time I got to you, I was afraid you were about to get yourself killed. A little frog had found its way into a snake's mouth, and you were trying to use a stick to get the frog out.

At first I couldn't tell what kind of snake it was. I was afraid it was a rattlesnake. I ran over as fast as I could and yanked you away, but you were in one of those trance-like states and I knew you would fight me. You did, with more strength than I knew you had. You tore yourself out of my arms, staring straight ahead at the frog that was slowly slipping into the throat of the snake, and reached at it to pull it out. We both shrieked as the snake shook its head at your hand and the frog disappeared completely into its mouth. We couldn't save it, and the snake slipped back into the woods as we stood there, me shaking from fear for you and you still sobbing for that poor frog. I was able to see that it was a garden snake that couldn't have hurt you, but it could just as easily have been a cottonmouth from the river. I could see then that this thing that pulled you was stronger than any common sense you had, and I was afraid that one day I wouldn't be able to protect you. You turned into my arms and cried so hard for the frog, questioning me about why the snake had to eat it. You kept saying how unfair it was, how no creature should have to give up its life so another one could live.

I didn't say anything, Lily, because I didn't have the heart to tell you then that the story of that frog and snake is the story of the world, at least as much as I've seen of it.

CHAPTER 11—ALICE

June 2019, In Flight

Alice looked out of the small rectangle window as the plane lifted off from Oakland International Airport. As the hills of the East Bay began to fade into the distance, she settled back into her seat and closed her eyes.

Exhaustion weighted her body from the last few nights with little sleep. The plane ride to San Diego would give her time to let events settle in her mind. More importantly, she needed to let a few unfamiliar feelings settle. Counting backwards, she realized it had been less than fifteen hours since she'd said goodbye to Ronan. Still reeling from the unexpected surge of emotions when he said goodnight to her at her doorstep, she marveled that they'd seen each other again at all. And she wasn't sure how she felt about it.

His call had surprised her. She hadn't been able to stop thinking about him, but was focusing her mind on her trip. She'd gone to a small bookstore and poked through guidebooks on San Diego, hoping to find something that would give her ideas for the article. She was just about to move to the travel memoir section when her phone rang. By the time her hand got past her wallet, lipsticks, pens, and checkbook and finally landed on her slim phone case, it had stopped ringing. She looked at the number—not one she recognized, but it had a 415 area code. San Francisco.

The phone pinged with a message, bringing a sudden tightness in her stomach. She walked outside and heard Ronan's quiet voice. She called him back immediately, before she lost her nerve, and he suggested they meet in the city for an early dinner the night before she left.

"Just curious. How'd you get my number?"

"You told me where you work. I took a chance that the number listed might be your cell. Lucky for me—it is."

"See you soon, then," she said, catching a glimpse of her reflection in the glass window. *A date. How long has it been since I've been on a date?*

* * *

After struggling for thirty minutes trying to decide what to wear, she chose a simple black dress with black flats. At the last minute, she pulled her great-grandmother's scarf from the jewelry box and tied it loosely around her neck. Adding a small set of gold earrings from her mother, she felt ready.

BART was the easiest way into the city. She still felt a rush of excitement when she stepped onto the underground trains, watching the wide array of people moving in an unspoken choreographed dance of boarding, finding a space to sit or stand, bags and backpacks jostling as everyone found a place before the train whizzed from the station. A few stops from where she boarded, they would travel below the San Francisco Bay into the city.

As the train slid into the last station in the East Bay, Alice looked out the window and saw a woman waiting for the doors to open. The deep green scarf wrapped around her neck, large silver drop earrings, and wide-set eyes caught Alice's attention. Her skin was the color of café au lait. The woman sat next to her on the crowded train car, sliding in quietly without looking anyone in the eye. Her gaze held steady on the seat in front of them, as though she was lost in her own quiet world, unaware of the people around her.

Alice noticed her perfume, a blend of coconut and tropical flowers. Instinctively bringing her hand up to her great-grandmother's scarf, she wondered if anyone could smell the faint floral scent it still held. Images from her dreams began to rise in her mind, starting with the turtle-women coming out of the ocean. As the train picked up speed Alice's vision blurred, her body suddenly heavy. The image of the shotgun flashed before her, then the turtle women from her dream rose around it, a quiet song humming in her ears. Alice closed her eyes as the melody rang through her. She gripped the rail in front of her, willing herself to focus on the cold metal of the bar and her present surroundings.

Relief washed over her when the train pulled into the Embarcadero station. As she left the train, she turned and looked back, wondering if the woman was getting off at the same stop, but the flow of people carried her out the door and onto the train platform. Within seconds, the door closed and the train zipped away.

Surfacing on the street, Alice paused, the sights around her a sharp contrast to her visions. Women in slim-fit business suits carrying Gucci purses, tourist families eyeing street maps on their phones, college students sporting backpacks—this part of the city always bustled with energy. Alice took her time walking the few blocks to the restaurant in Chinatown where they'd agreed to meet. Her breath caught in her throat when she saw Ronan. Leaning against the brick building, his face turned in the other direction, he looked as though he was part of a photo shoot. She had not imagined him as part of the sleek city scene in San Francisco, but dressed in a crisp cerulean button shirt and black pants, he looked like a model.

He turned and looked at her then, his face breaking into the wide, easy smile she remembered.

Dinner passed quickly, with easy conversation flowing between them. She opened up more than she expected to, feeling surprisingly relaxed with this man she'd known less than a week.

They strolled for miles after dinner, not ready to end the evening. As they turned the corner onto Columbus Avenue, City Lights bookstore loomed before them.

"I'd love to stop in," Alice said.

"Good idea." Ronan took her hand in his as they turned toward the iconic bookstore entry.

Books lined the walls from floor to ceiling, signs celebrating banned books and posters for poetry festivals perched strategically. Alice looked for something of interest about San Diego but found nothing useful. A book about marine life caught her eye just as she was about to give up. She leafed through it and images of ocean mammals came to life—harbor seals, sea otters, spinner dolphins. Mesmerized by the colors and images of the beautiful creatures, she decided to buy it. Maybe her story could include tidbits about sea life in Southern California.

Ronan took her hand again as they walked out of the store. Warmth rushed through her body. He led her to the Vesuvio Bar next door and as they ducked in, she squeezed his hand without thinking, then second-guessed herself. Maybe it was too early to give him signals that she was attracted to him? Would he think she wanted more than just a night out? Did she?

"If you've never been here, this place is almost as famous as the bookstore," he said. "Jack Kerouac and Allen Ginsberg are a few of the famous people who've visited. I can share with you some of what I know about the animals in your book over a drink. Ocean cartography was my favorite subject in college."

They ordered drinks—gin and tonic for him and a Tom Collins for her—then nestled into their seats in the tightly packed bar. She leaned in slightly as she asked him about his work.

"So you work at a company that maps waterways around the Bay. Does it include the Pacific Ocean?"

"Not at this point. We're looking at areas that feed into the Bay. So much of the water around here leads to it. What I do is considered science, but I think of it as art. You write stories, which is definitely an art, and I create detailed maps that track the ways water moves around us, nourishing everything we do."

"That's beautiful. I never thought of it that way, but you're right. Maps are really pieces of art that show us nature's designs."

"I volunteer at the Marine Mammal Center in Marin on weekends. I love having the chance to be up close with seals and other mammals we share this part of the world with."

"What do you do as a volunteer?"

"Feed and care for the animals. They take in a variety of seals, along with other mammals that have been injured or are unable to live in their natural habitat safely. I've been doing it for years now. When I was really young, we lived in a small town right on the ocean in Ireland. Some of my best childhood memories are there. In the early mornings we had the beach near our house to ourselves. I'd walk right up to the water line, playing games with the waves, trying to not get more than my ankles wet. It felt to me like the water was alive and I was dancing with it."

"I love the ocean too. We used to drive to the Florida panhandle for summer vacations. The beaches there are so incredibly soft. I loved walking in the mornings too. I always hoped something special would wash up. Once I found a tiny seahorse. It must have died not much before I found it—it was perfectly shaped. It felt like a gift just for me."

"I've never seen a real seahorse. What I loved in Ireland were the seals. They seemed like my friends, coming to the shore in small families. At the center, we work a lot with Pacific seals, occasionally monk seals from Hawaii. Have you heard of them?"

"No. Are monk seals different? Great name, by the way."

"They're the oldest seal species on Earth. As far as we know, they only live in the waters around the Northern Hawaiian Islands and in the Mediterranean. They once lived in the Caribbean, but they're extinct there now."

"The name makes me think of a little old guy, wise and silent, with big eyes."

"That's about right—they're beautiful animals. When they swim up to shore in Hawaii, ropes are put around them to create a barrier so people stay away and let them rest. They give birth each year in the bays of Kauai. The mother and pup stay for weeks, until the baby seal can start hunting on its own."

"I should definitely do research on marine life in Southern California for my article."

"If you want, I'll hook you up with my aunt. She lives down there and volunteers at the Pacific Marine Mammal Center. She's the one who got me interested in volunteering."

"That would be great. Where is it?"

"Laguna Beach. A bit of a drive from San Diego, but if you have time, it might be interesting."

"I'd love that."

"I'll text you her number."

"Thanks. Do you see her often?"

"Not as often as I'd like. She's my mom's oldest sister. She came to America with us when we moved, then went down to Southern California with a guy. He isn't in the picture anymore, but she stayed. I visit her occasionally. I like being there—the water's warmer. I love getting away from the city lights to see the stars over the ocean. Makes me think of my ancestors who mapped the sea following the stars."

Your eyes look like stars, Alice thought.

Ronan pulled a small turtle, carved from dark wood, from his pocket. Alice stared at it, her mind pulling up images of the turtles from her dreams.

"It's beautiful," she said. "It's carved so delicately. I can see a slight expression on its face, as though it knows something it isn't sharing."

"It was carved in Ireland by a craft person. I picked it up there on my last visit. I brought it because I thought you might like it, and now that I know you're headed to Southern California, I'm glad I did. Maybe you'll see one on the beach there." He smiled with his lips closed, the smile she was quickly coming to know as the one that came across his face when he finished speaking, as though to punctuate his words with a silent, warm gaze that enveloped her.

"Thank you."

Picking it up, she moved her finger across its shell, which was made of a deep green gemstone—malachite, the same stone on her great-grandmother's hair pin. She let out a small gasp when she noticed the spiral carved across the turtle's back, just like the one on the river rock. She looked into the turtle's face, turned upward to her, then turned her eyes back to Ronan, unsure of what she felt. Fear? Excitement? Or something deeper than that?

Before she could decide, he squeezed her hand, a gesture that settled the swirl of emotions. She leaned in closer and he kissed her, his hand folded over hers, the turtle gently nestled within her palm.

The memory of his cologne still lingered in her mind as she leaned her head back on the airplane seat. A heady mix of ocean breeze and . . . sage? Light and clear with a hint of something woodsy. Earthy. Something she couldn't quite define. *Like Ronan himself*, she thought as she closed her eyes, thoughts of his soothing presence bringing a smile to her face.

* * *

The Pacific Ocean glistened sapphire blue below the plane as it began its descent to the San Diego airport. The flight had gone quickly. The plane skidded on the runway, bouncing slightly before coming to a complete stop. The passengers around Alice began to gather their bags, but she stayed completely still, gazing at the mountains outside the tiny window. She wanted to take in the beauty of the day before moving through the bustle of the airport.

"Welcome to San Diego," the captain's voice rose above the sounds of shuffling bags and snapping seatbelts. Alice finally moved, gathering her backpack and books, joining the others in line to deboard the plane.

CHAPTER 12–GRACE

July 1934, Richarme, Louisiana

I remember when Mamou first told me about the family they took in and how haunted she looked as she talked about it. The boy who showed up in their barn that day was one of seven children, all of them hungry, all of them with a hollow look in their eyes that made you want to look away when you saw them. Mamou had seen them in town a few times, but until that day, she didn't know their names. The boy's name was Samuel. He was fourteen, and the youngest child, a girl, was four. Mamou said she was such a little wisp of a thing that it always seemed like she was about to fly away back to wherever she came from before she was born.

The whole family lived in an old house deep in the woods. Mamou told me later that when they took Samuel in, what they were most concerned about was how to get the other children away, because without Samuel, they would be the ones taking the brunt of their daddy's rage. Mamou and Grandpere couldn't take them all in, though. Back then, people really minded their own business and families like that were left alone. They didn't know what to do about that, so they started by caring for Samuel. Father Richarme helped by sending over food and supplies to put together a makeshift bed in their barn. I still think about how brave my grandparents were to step in the way they did.

Mamou was the one who told me how it all happened, once she thought I was old enough to hear some of the harsher things that happen in this world. My mamma didn't want her to tell me, but Mamou thought I should know, and as hard as it was to hear, I was glad to hear it straight from her rather than learn only pieces of the story.

She told me that after about a week of staying in their barn, Samuel started telling them how worried he was about his siblings, how guilty he felt for leaving them behind. He wanted to go back, but his body was so weak from being on the brink of starvation and so tattered from his father's abuse that even as he talked about it, Mamou could see he didn't have the strength to do it. She also saw the fear in his eyes, fear that never seemed to leave him.

Eventually Grandpere decided that the most honorable way to support his family would be to go over to the house and offer to help. He knew the father might not want to accept help from strangers, but he wanted to give him the chance first. Mamou was worried, of course, but she put together a basket filled with good things—special cakes for the children, fresh baked bread, vegetables picked that morning. They didn't tell Samuel what they were doing, because they didn't want him to try to go with Grandpere or worry about what might happen if his father discovered where he was.

Grandpere wasn't going to tell them Samuel was with them, of course. No father with any amount of pride would handle that well, especially one broken down by poverty and shame.

Grandpere got to their house mid-morning, hoping to be able to offer a good lunch. He walked up to the front porch and knocked. The door was open and he could see Samuel's little brothers and sisters running around inside. One of them saw him and yelled for their mother, who came to the door wearing a thin nightgown, her face pale and gaunt, her eyes wide in a way that gave her the look of a ghost, lost between worlds. Grandpere smiled at her, hoping to get her to smile back, but she just stared at him with a vacant look, not sure, it seemed, how to talk to this stranger on her porch. Grandpere said he was just stopping by because they had so much growing in their garden that he wanted to share what he had with them, and he wondered if they might like to take the basket of extra vegetables and things off his hands.

Three of the children came up to him, peering into the basket with eyes filled with hunger, and one of them started to reach in to grab one of the cakes Mamou had made. The mother stepped up then and thanked Grandpere and said that she appreciated the neighborly kindness, and she looked like she was just about to reach out and take the handle of the basket when they heard loud bootsteps coming from the back of the house.

The mother and kids all turned around quickly, as though the sound of those bootsteps held a chain that pulled at them, keeping them in line. They all backed up and two of the younger children ran behind the house. The children's mother stood frozen—like a deer caught by a hunter—and Grandpere said he saw her eyes glaze over in that moment and her face went slack, as though the sound of those bootsteps turned all the lights off inside of her.

When Samuel's daddy came out to the front porch, he smelled of liquor and was carrying a shotgun. Grandpere saw the nose of the shotgun before he laid eyes on the face of the man holding it. The boots came next, then the tall body and a mouth and eyes contorted by alcohol and anger.

"What are you doin' here?" was the first thing Grandpere heard. "This is my house. Get yourself outta here now, before I shoot you."

Grandpere knew he only had a few minutes to try to make things go in a different direction, so he tried to pretend that he didn't smell the whiskey coming out of the man in front of him or understand what the shotgun pointed at him meant. Grandpere told the man his name was Antoine Beaulieu, his neighbor from a little distance away, and that they had too much growing in their garden and wondered if the family might take some food off their hands to keep the critters out of their garden at night.

The man said his name was Billy and that this was his house and that they weren't interested in talking to any neighbors or taking any food off anyone's hands. He said that if Grandpere didn't leave right away, he'd show him what his shotgun could do to a basket of food and any man stupid enough to come into his yard. Billy walked up to his wife and grabbed her by the hair, yanking her back into the house.

Grandpere was shaken by what he was seeing, but he wanted to give it one more try before leaving. He tried to keep his voice calm as he said he understood they probably didn't need anything but that his wife, Mamou, had also baked a few sweet cakes for the children. Billy walked up to him, pulled one of out of the basket, and said he might just need to try one himself. Then he backed up two steps and pointed the shotgun before Grandpere knew what was happening. The sound of the shot made everyone jump, Grandpere and Billy's wife and the one boy who was still standing nearby, frozen in place until the gun went off.

The shell went right through the basket, sending vegetables spilling onto the dirt, and my Grandpere's hand felt a blaze of heat either from the shell itself or the fear that finally rang through his body. He looked up and later told Mamou that for the first time in his life, he saw what he thought was the sign of pure evil. Billy's eyes had a look in them that seemed to come from some dark place where light never entered, and the smirk on his face let Grandpere know that he was taking pleasure in watching everyone around him jump in fear.

Whether or not he thought he was really in danger then, I don't know, but he told Mamou that he drew a breath and pulled in all the gentlemanly strength he could find, for Billy's wife and children if nothing else, tipped his hat to Billy, and backed off the porch and out of the yard, not once turning around with his back to Billy until he got to the edge of the trees. Mamou said that when he got home, Grandpere was shaking and couldn't tell her what happened for a couple of hours. He took the pieces of the basket home with him, and it was still gripped in his hands when he came into the house. He put it on the kitchen table and walked out to the back woods without saying a word.

Mamou decided that day that she would have to use other kinds of healing to fix what was happening with the boy in the barn and his brothers and sisters. She and Grandpere made decisions that day that set off a chain of events that stayed with them for the rest of their lives. And now I know that maybe it carried itself through the family chain to you, in a way I still can't understand.

The family they helped has descendants living right here in town with us now.

Billy's last name was Benoit. He was the great-grandfather of Robbie and Ricky, the boys who were sitting in the pew at church at your funeral.

The boys I know had something to do with your passing from this world.

Lily Mae

Maman. Maman. I love you. I wish you could see me now, where I am. I'm with all of our relatives, even some you don't know about, some who lived way back when our family was still in France. We talk about everything, what happened when we were in bodies with all of you and how all our stories weave together like a tapestry or get patched together like a quilt. Sometimes we braid two stories together to see what happens, like mine and Mamou's. Or sometimes we weave together lots of them and then we watch to see how they are all still playing out there with you and everyone else who is still alive.

Maman, Haydee is with me too. She's the one I came here to find. You know that, don't you? She and Mamou called me here. They didn't mean for me to cross over and be with them, but that's what happened. Sometimes after those dreams, I'd go out to the woods because I could feel the pull of those trees, and Mamou and Haydee were pulling me too. And the river pulled me, like it had a water spirit calling to me, almost singing to me to visit it. I wanted to be connected to it, Maman, the water and everything there at the river.

I watch you and hear you and know you are talking to me. Maybe you wonder if I can hear you? I can, Maman. Where I am, we can hear everything. We have to choose where we listen, just like you do there, but here, we can listen to lots more things at the same time, and we can see lots more. I can see the stories you are telling me and now I also know some parts of those stories that you don't know yet. You will one day, Maman.

Je'taime.

CHAPTER 13—ALICE

June 2019, San Diego, California

A thin sliver of moon rose above the ocean. The view from Alice's hotel room balcony was almost enticing enough to draw her outside for a walk on the beach after dinner at the hotel restaurant, but fatigue from a long travel day and the late night with Ronan hit just as the sun began to set.

She sat down on the bed, sinking into the mattress, grateful that her room had a view of the beach. The jewelry box lying in her partially unpacked suitcase caught her eye. Pulling it onto her lap, she opened the lid and pulled out the scarf, stone, and doll. The hairpins—turtle, seal, whale, bright yellow fish—fit in perfectly with the view of the sand and sea before her. She put them on the dresser next to the bed, the stone beside them, and placed the doll on the pillow, wrapped in the silk scarf. She put the sand dollar next to the hair pins and picked up the acorn, holding it in her palm.

Martha, do you really talk?

Maybe she didn't want to know. She placed the acorn on the dresser next to the stone, traced the painted spiral with her finger, then put on her pajamas. She drifted off almost immediately once she slid into the cool sheets, the tiny doll beside her. Sleep came quickly, pulling her deeply into another world.

* * *

Warm water washed in waves over her body. She stretched her limbs out in the shape of a starfish then pulled them inward, bringing her body into a tight curl, floating beneath the sun. Waves rolled over her, until one pulled her under and immersed her completely. All sounds ceased, swallowed by the totality of the water's depths, holding her in a still-point float, submerged close to the shallow bottom.

Feeling part of the water itself, she drew her torso upward, rising toward the waves above, then crashed through like a sleek dolphin, head and arms pointed toward the sky. As she broke through the water, her body twirled up until she was midair, high above the waves. Just as she was eye level with the mountains hugging the cove, she took a nose-dive then swooped up again.

She flew toward the mountains. Cliffs rose into thick, white clouds, waterfalls cascading down into deep green canopies. Her eye caught sight of an opening in the mountain wall and her body moved toward it, pulled by an invisible force. The opening widened as she neared, then soared toward it on a wave of air, headfirst. Just before she reached the opening, she saw a mound of sand and swooped down, landing gracefully. The contours of a cave opened before her, water pooling just inside.

Would it be safe to enter? Only the first few feet into the cave were visible. To the right of the opening was a solid wall of earth. To the left, more water curved into a dark hollow.

A breath of wind pulled her into the opening, lifted her, then dropped her gently into a boat.

Silence, then soft sounds of water dripping. High walls folded into a ceiling of rock. Crystals gleamed from crevices. Rivulets of water dripped down the walls, passing over moss and fern leaves. She picked up an oar and paddled forward, craning her neck to see around the bend. An endless body of water extended before her.

"Welcome," a woman's voice said. "You are here now. The cave goes deep and has many turns and dark hollows, all with hidden secrets. It will take you your whole life to explore it, and you will never fully understand what you find. You can never leave once you have entered."

An old woman stood in a boat ahead of her, coming out from one of the passages within the rocks. Alice turned to look behind her and watched as the opening of the cave began to close until it was only solid rock, no sign of a doorway or path to the world on the other side. Her breath became shallow, her chest tight. She turned back to ask the woman what to do. The water before her shimmered, rippling in tiny waves, the boat and the woman gone. She was alone in the cave.

The only sound was the steady flow of water dripping down the walls, dropping into the ocean pool, in rhythm with the thrum of her heartbeat.

Alice awoke, startled by birdsong outside the open window. Frightened by the dream, disoriented, she turned to the clock: 6:42. Grateful for time to let the dream fade away before she had to get ready for the day, she slipped lower under the covers, closed her eyes, and felt herself slowly being rocked back to sleep, as if in a boat, moving gently on the water.

* * *

She arose at eight, had a quick breakfast, then put her bathing suit on with a t-shirt and shorts and walked out to the ocean. Just looking at it filled her with a sense of peacefulness that surprised her. She'd always loved being near the sea, but each time she visited it she was amazed at how instantly it affected her, as though it had an invisible power that reached out and held her as soon as she came near.

She walked toward a group of people gathered down the beach. They stood around a rope-enclosed area, snapping photos. A large animal lay sprawled on the sand in the middle of the circle, oblivious to the attention. Alice read the sign hanging from the rope. *Male, age 7, harbor seal. Please keep at least 10 feet away.*

A seal, right on the beach! She was struck by his face, which looked almost human. His eyes were closed and his mouth was curled in a way that gave him the look of a smiling old person, napping quietly. Either that, she thought, or of a baby, peacefully sleeping on a blanket of sand.

She was instantly in love.

After taking several photos of the spotted seal from different angles, Alice decided to get into the water. She had time before she was scheduled to meet the travel agents who would be her guides on her stay. The seal moved a few inches toward the ocean, its wide tail creating a trail in the sand. The dreams of turtles came back to her, calling her to follow them.

Alice slipped off her t-shirt and shorts, stepped out of her flip flops, and walked toward the water.

When she reached the edge where the waves lapped onto the sand, she stopped for a moment, looking out to the horizon. Blue sky, seemingly endless above her, met the line where the ocean curved away from sight, far into the distance. Marveling at the expanse of water before her, wondering what life was swimming just out of sight, she stepped in slowly, expecting the water to be cold. She went in until the waves hit her torso, then looked down. Any fish or sea life floating close by?

An approaching wave came quickly, crashing into her and tossing her in a swirl before she pulled herself back up, breaking through the surface, into gleaming sunlight.

She settled her feet on the sand below, standing in gentle waves that rose to her hips. The sight of a large sea turtle, moving slowly through the open water, stopped her. Seeing the turtle here seemed unreal: dream world or physical world? *Where am I? What's happening?* Alice's eyes squinted in the bright sunlight as she slowly approached the beautiful creature, not wanting to disturb it but drawn to see the details of its face and body. She'd never seen ocean animals like this so close before. The turtle seemed ancient, moving steadily.

It pulled itself onto shore a short distance from the seal. She swam in that direction and walked up to the gathering crowd. A lifeguard stood there.

"Hi. I'm Alice," she said. "I'm here to write a travel story about San Diego and I'm curious about the seals and turtles. Do they come up on the shore like this often?"

"It depends. In some areas they do, and we have to work to keep people away from them. This guy will nap for a while then push off into the water again."

"He's beautiful. I'd love to learn more. Do you have recommendations on where I can do some research on the sea life around here?"

"The Pacific Marine Mammal Center, in Laguna Beach."

The same place Ronan's aunt volunteered. Coincidence? Maybe these sea creatures were going to be a bigger part of her visit than she expected.

"Thanks."

Alice wandered away, moving toward the turtle, pushing back out into the water. She watched it glide through the shallows then head into the open sea.

Her meeting with the tour guides started soon—she had just enough time to go to her room to change then get to their office. She took one last look at the blue water topped with the white foam of waves and turned toward her hotel.

* * *

The large *San Diego Sun Tours* sign stood out in the shopping center. Decorated with a sailboat in the harbor at sunset, it mirrored the website Alice had viewed in preparation for her trip. She opened it on her phone before stepping out of her car. Two smiling faces greeted her, followed by their welcome message.

Kaitlin and Jeff invite you to join us in sunny San Diego for a vacation of a lifetime!

Alice scanned the list of sights on their four-day adventure. One of their best sellers, it included a harbor cruise with lunch, a shopping day in the Gaslamp District, a beach day in La Jolla, and a four-hour whale-watching cruise. The cost was much higher than she could imagine paying for a vacation, but they seemed to have plenty of satisfied clients.

The silk scarf from her grandmother was wrapped around her neck. *Let's go meet the tour guides, Grandmere.*

A young woman about her age stood in the door of the office, waving, her arm moving so quickly and with a smile so wide Alice stopped, self-consciously smiling back, and took a deep breath. Highly extroverted and overly happy people always made her a little nervous.

Kaitlin greeted her at the door and a rush of air conditioning greeted her. Jeff was waiting just inside, hands in the pockets of his khaki shorts, smile as wide as Kaitlin's.

"Welcome!" Kaitlin said. "We're so excited you're here! We have such a great trip planned for you. How was the flight? How's your hotel?"

"Great, both the flight and hotel—great. Thanks."

A tall plastic palm tree stood in a wicker basket in the corner. The walls were lined with framed photos of smiling tourists. Alice's eyes were drawn to one of a family on a beach, waving to the camera. In front of them, a large sea turtle rested in the sand. They stood so close the youngest child was touching its back.

"Great photo, huh?" Jeff said. "People love when we see turtles and seals on our adventures. This photo was taken several years ago. The girl wanted a ride, but we pulled her away before she could climb on it!"

Alice thought of the turtle she'd seen in the water. How could they let tourists get so close to these ancient creatures?

Before she could complete her thought, Jeff offered her a seat. "Let's talk about the next few days."

Alice pulled out her notebook, ready to take notes.

"We were so excited when your magazine called us to say you were coming," Kaitlin said

"You did a good job of convincing our editors that they should send me." *You probably don't take the word "no" for an answer,* she thought. Then *Don't make quick judgments*, a voice in her head said. Alice looked at her notebook, steadying herself, thinking of her grandmother's voice.

"OK. Let's jump into the itinerary for tomorrow," Kaitlin said. "Jeff, can you give Alice her tour folder? We have so much to talk about!"

CHAPTER 14–ALICE

July 2019, San Diego, California

Her cell phone rang as Alice was slipping the card key into her hotel room door. The jangling sound and the phone's vibration in her purse made her pull it from the door too quickly. The light on the lock flashed red and the door handle wouldn't turn. She tried again as the phone rang two more times. *Could it be Ronan?* She pulled the card out too quickly a second time, watched the light flash red again, and slipped the card into the front pocket of her purse while unzipping it and reaching in to grab the phone.

"Hello?"

"Hi, Alice, it's me." Ronan. *Answered just in time.* "Are you back at your hotel?"

"Yes, trying to unlock the door as we speak. Can I call you right back?"

"Sure. I'm happy to wait for you."

Happy to wait for you. Good. Does he mean wait until I figure out whether or not I'm up for trying to make this last for more than one or two dinners out?

Alice finally got inside. Dropping everything on the bed, she looked at herself in the mirror. *What will I say if he asks me out again? Yes, of course. But . . . what happens next?*

He answered on the first ring.

"How's it going? I hope you're enjoying the bright sunshine."

"I just met the tour guides and have the rest of the day to myself, but I have a lot of work to do. This article is going to be a big spread. They want me to include local history and details on other tourist sites here, so I'll need to be doing research when I'm not actually out on tours."

"Excellent. I have just the thing for your research. My Aunt Annie wants to take you to dinner tonight if you're free. I told her about your work and her voice lit up. I hope you don't mind."

"Not at all." *Do I?*

"She'll talk your ear off. And she's bringing her best friend, Tutu Amelia, from Hawaii. They met about ten years ago and have been hooked at the hips ever since. Both sea lovers, both missing their homes. They volunteer together. They'll show you a fine time."

"Thank you. Should I call her?"

"She said to just meet them at the O'Toole Irish Pub in the Gaslamp Quarter. Easy to find. I doubt you'll have any trouble finding them—they tend to stand out in the crowd. They'll be there at 6:15."

"Great. It'll be nice to have dinner with someone tonight. I was going to eat in the hotel restaurant."

"What are your dinner plans tomorrow night? Fancy an online dinner with me?"

"Oh—yes—I'm free. Tomorrow we're taking a harbor cruise and lunch is included, but I don't have plans for dinner. I think I could be back at my hotel room and at the computer by six."

"Perfect then. Text me your hotel name and room. I'll have dinner delivered to you at six-thirty and will send you a link for our date."

Alice looked in the mirror again. *Smiling. I'm smiling. Can he hear it in my voice?*

"Wow. No one has ever had dinner delivered to me before."

"Enjoy the aunts tonight. They're really something. And enjoy the boat cruise tomorrow. See you tomorrow evening."

"Yes, see you then. And thank your Aunt Annie for me—I'm looking forward to meeting her."

Dinner with the aunts. And tomorrow with Ronan. The trip was turning out to be more than what she'd expected. But everything was turning out to be more than she expected these days.

* * *

Alice dressed in a pair of white cotton pants, sandals, and a new top. The soft green color was a perfect backdrop for her great-grandmother's scarf, so she put it on, breathing into it first to see if the floral smell remained. It was there, faint, like the whisper of her great-grandmother's voice in her ear. "Let's go, Grandmere," she said quietly.

O'Toole's Irish Pub stood on the corner of two busy streets, bookmarked by an Italian restaurant on one side and a sushi bar on the other. Patrons were fenced in by a black wrought iron gate. Mostly men sat on the patio, giving her a sense of entering a sports den. Alice kept her eyes on the door as she walked past, ignoring one man who whistled at her. The smell of stale beer wafted past her nose.

Adjusting her eyes to the dim light, Alice stopped and scanned the scene. A hand waved toward her from a back table. The aunts. Aunt Annie with bright red hair—similar to Ronan's—framing her fair-skinned face. Tutu Amelia wearing a loose-fitting cotton top in ocean tones, her black hair flecked with gray pulled into a loose bun.

Alice walked toward them.

"You are Alice," Aunt Annie greeted her, holding out both hands. "Ronan said I'd know who you were by how beautiful you are and your smiling eyes. You must have some Irish in you."

"Actually, I do, on my mother's side."

"Sit. We took the liberty of ordering a pint for you. Best ale in town. At our age we can only drink one, but we enjoy every sip. Not as good as the kelp gin my uncle used to make, but we do enjoy it."

Alice adjusted her purse and settled in, focusing her attention on the two women before her. Aunt Annie—fair skinned, a few freckles scattered across her face and arms, light green eyes. Sea glass. Eyes the color of sea glass.

Tutu Amelia. Dark eyes that seemed to be taking in more of Alice than just her own brown hair and eyes. Almost looking past her. Or into her.

Both with big smiles.

"Thanks for inviting me." Alice spoke quickly, wanting to break past her sudden nervousness. "I don't know any restaurants here and would have eaten alone at the hotel tonight."

"Ronan says you're here to write a travel story about San Diego. We'd love to share with you a little of our San Diego. Tell us about what you're planning." Aunt Annie's voice was loud, boisterous, able to rise above the cacophony of voices around them.

"I write for *Pacific Travel* magazine and I'm doing the San Diego Sun Tours four-day package, then will write about it. Tomorrow we start with a bay cruise. We'll do a day shopping and eating here in the Gaslamp District, a day at La Jolla, and end with an ocean cruise."

"Sounds like a good itinerary," Aunt Annie said, picking up the menu. "Let's order some food and talk about what else you may want to see while you're here."

The laminated menu featured the house special fish and chips, fried oysters, fried clams, and chicken strips. Burgers and grilled cheese sandwiches were listed at the bottom. The back was covered with every kind of beer and ale Alice could imagine.

"Fish and chips sounds good to me," she said, taking a sip of her ale. Slightly fruity and bitter at the same time, it slid down her throat easily.

"That's what we both usually get," Tutu Amelia said. The waitress walked up with a note pad in her hand. Her green t-shirt and black baseball cap both bore the pub's logo—an Irish man whistling, playing a harp.

"What would you like today? Looks like you two brought a friend," she said with a slight Irish lilt, winking at Aunt Annie.

"Yes," Aunt Annie said, nodding back. "We'll have our usual fish and chips, and an order of the same for our friend Alice."

They handed over their menus. Alice leaned in to thank them again for inviting her but was stopped by a voice booming from the small stage in the corner.

"Welcome to O'Toole's! We're glad you're here and hope you like what we're playing for you tonight. We'll introduce the band in a few minutes, but for now we'll start with a song we love about the sea."

A group of four musicians with different instruments—a harp, fiddle, mandolin, and hand-held flat drum painted with a Celtic cross—stood on the stage. The man who had been speaking held the microphone in his hand and turned, then nodded toward the band. They were silent for a few seconds, then he began singing a cappella. His voice silenced the restaurant—clear, lilting, haunting, then the instruments joined, one at a time. The harp first, then the mandolin. Alice watched, mesmerized by the sound. The words were in a language unfamiliar to her. Gaelic? Celtic? The song was similar to the one Ronan sang to her at the beach the day they met.

She settled into an almost hypnotic state as the melody deepened. The musicians closed their eyes and swayed slightly, voice and instruments in perfect sync. The crowd in the restaurant was silenced by the song, most patrons now looking at the band, as though responding to an invisible wave of energy being woven with their ancient-sounding music and movements.

Time stood still for a moment. Alice couldn't take her eyes off the singer and the men behind him. Dressed in shades of green and brown, one in a tan shirt the color of tree bark, they seemed like tall trees—stately and commanding sentinels in a forest. A flicker of light floated in front of her, and a familiar wave of dizziness passed over.

Scenes came rapidly: a small girl running near a stream, wearing only a thin, white nightgown, moonlight coming down through the trees on the path before her. Trees all around, moss hanging low to the ground from the large oaks. Then the sound of a shot ringing in the air, freezing the images and jolting Alice from her reverie.

The musicians sang their last note just as the gunshot rang through her ears, a sound she knew only she could hear. The audience broke into thunderous applause, sound exploding around Alice in waves.

She pulled herself out of the dream images and blinked twice, forcing herself to focus on her immediate surroundings. Tutu Amelia was looking at her directly, eyes boring quietly into her own. Alice smiled, wondering what she must look like and whether or not Tutu Amelia could see what had just happened to her—whether either of the aunts could.

"You must come and see us tomorrow, or as soon as your schedule allows," Tutu Amelia said.

Alice turned and focused on her, still trying to pull herself out of the vision of the girl and the shotgun.

"We should take you to Sunset Cliffs cave. It's a magical place. We can meet you there at four tomorrow, if that works for you, Alice. I'll bring my granddaughter. She loves going there." Tutu Amelia smiled again and raised her glass as if to finalize the plan. Aunt Annie raised her glass and clinked it with Tutu's.

"Perfect place!" Aunt Annie said, winking at Alice, mirroring what the band leader had done just before starting his song.

"I think that time would work for me," Alice said, unsure what she was being invited for. The bay cruise the next day with Kaitlin and Jeff would end at three, so the time would work. She raised her glass. The clink of the glasses mingled with the chatter of the people around them.

"The song was beautiful," she said. "I heard Ronan sing a song like it. Do you know what it's called?"

Aunt Annie leaned forward. "I don't know the name of it, but it's a traditional type of song from Ireland called sean nós. They're old songs, often about the sea, sometimes about love. Haunting, isn't it?"

"Yes," Alice said, still lingering in the space between the world in front of her and the one she'd been pulled into by the song. Ronan's singing hung in her mind, the silhouette of his body standing by the shoreline flashing in front of her.

"Maybe you can write about this pub and the music in your story about San Diego. Ronan said you love writing," Aunt Annie's voice was quieter now, eyes focused on Alice.

"Yes, I guess I've been a writer most of my life. It's something I've always loved. I like my work at the magazine. It lets me travel a bit."

"What do you like about writing? I think it's a great gift." Tutu Amelia's voice was quiet too. Alice put her hands in her lap, clasping and unclasping them before answering.

"I just love stories. I love stories about all of the people who've lived on the Earth. I love reading about other cultures and time periods, imagining myself in other worlds. When I write, I guess it's my small way of trying to capture some of the magic of stories." She paused. "I'm not sure if I'm very good at it, but I do love writing travel pieces and I'm glad I got put on this assignment."

"What stories do you want to capture here, in San Diego?" Tutu Amelia's hands were wrapped around her pint of ale. Alice brought hers back up to the table and took a sip before answering.

"My assignment is to write about the great travel experiences people can have. I'm not sure yet what stories I'll find within that, but I'm open to anything you two can share to help me get started."

Tutu Amelia leaned back in her chair. "We can start by sharing with you a little bit about ourselves and see if that sparks anything for you. Do you know how we became friends?"

"No. Ronan didn't tell me that story—he just said you wanted to take me to dinner tonight. Thank you, by the way."

"Ronan's aunt and I met at the Pacific Marine Mammal Center in Laguna Beach. We're both two older women from islands a world apart, but we connected here over our shared love of the ocean and the animals that live in it. I'd been volunteering there for a few months when I met Annie. Her Irish accent immediately drew my attention because I knew she was a kindred spirit, living far away from her homeland."

"Tutu introduced me to the monk seals. They're the oldest seals on Earth and live in the Northern Hawaiian Islands."

"Ronan told me about them. He said they're in danger of becoming extinct."

"Yes," Tutu Amelia said. "They're beautiful animals, so graceful. One was being treated at the center when Annie came to volunteer on her first day and we bonded over mutual love of that seal. He's back in the islands now. He was brought back after he recovered."

"What had happened to him? Why was he there?" Alice leaned forward, curious about the seal being treated in California rather than Hawaii. "Did they bring him here from the islands?"

"Yes," Tutu said. "He had been causing trouble on Molokai, eating too many of the fish that the fishermen wanted. He got caught in the net of a boat and was wounded. They sent him here for treatment because the treatment center there was full and we have some specialists who've worked with these animals before."

"So he was stranded here, far away from his home—like you two are far from your homes—right?"

"Yes," Aunt Annie said. "He brought us together and we've been friends now for years. We both feel more connected to our homelands when we're together, and it makes us both feel a little less lonely for the places where we grew up, where our families are from."

New Orleans rose to Alice's mind, a city that lay below sea level, surrounded by the Mississippi curling around it. A city shaped by water, similar to Ireland and Hawaii. An island of its own, with its own culture and stories made up of so many types of people who've lived there over the centuries. The faces of her grandmothers flashed before her.

"Right now one of our patients is a sea turtle," Aunt Annie said, breaking into Alice's thoughts. "Her name is Emerald, like the color of the sea at certain times and places."

"I'd love to see her. Can I visit the center, or do you have to be a volunteer?"

"We'd be happy to introduce you to our sea friends, if you can make the time to drive to Laguna Beach. It's about a ninety-minute drive. What day could you go?" Aunt Annie took another sip of her ale, leaning in toward Alice.

"I think I could make it the day after tomorrow." Alice calculated the time it would take to finish her day with the tour company and meet them. "I could meet you there late afternoon."

"We'll give you directions," Tutu Amelia said. "Although, you probably just need to put it into your phone, right? My grandchildren try to get me to use mine more for things like that, but I still like the old-fashioned way. I still like maps. On paper!"

"Paper maps are good, but I'm better with my phone map, I think. Can we meet at 3 p.m., day after tomorrow?"

"Yes," Aunt Annie said. "So, we'll see you tomorrow at the caves and the next day to meet the seals and turtles. And we never know what beautiful sea creatures may be there when we go. Who knows—maybe we'll have a selkie come ashore to greet you."

"A selkie?"

"Selkies are seals that transform into people. Most of the stories are about them being women, but there are male selkies too." Aunt Annie winked again. "And you never know when you might meet one."

"In Hawaii," Tutu Amelia said, "we also have stories about sea animals turning into people. There is a legend of a sea turtle that would come ashore and become a woman, watching over the children, then return to the sea."

Alice's dream washed through her mind. Turtles and seals coming ashore, becoming women. Circling around her. She sat back in her chair, wondering whether or not to tell the aunts about it.

Aunt Annie broke into her thoughts. "Every sea culture has these stories. Some of us think they aren't just stories. Maybe that's one thing that brought the two of us together. We're both believers in things the eyes may not always see. Or that the eyes may see, but the mind doesn't believe."

Alice's mind spun. Didn't Ronan say something about what the eye could see when they met on the beach? Or what some could see and others couldn't?

"Have you heard of the green flash on the ocean?" Tutu spoke quietly.

"I haven't."

"It happens only occasionally when the water and sky and light come together in just the right way. When all conditions are right, a green flash appears over the ocean, right where the water meets the sky. You have to be looking at just the right place—at just the right time—to see it. It happens in Hawaii and occasionally people have seen it here."

"I'll watch for it."

The waitress approached the table with a large tray, momentarily halting the conversation. She placed three plates of fish and chips on the table. Light from the window reflected from her hair. Alice noticed ginger-colored tones highlighting the barely visible freckles on her cheeks.

"Mahalo," Tutu Amelia said. "Thank you for bringing us such a beautiful meal to enjoy together."

The waitress winked at Tutu with a smile.

"Sláinte!" Aunt Annie said, raising her glass in a toast. "Alice, we speak lots of languages here, so you have to keep up. "

Alice was suddenly famished. She picked up her fork and waited for the aunts to do the same before diving in.

"Enough talk for a while," Aunt Annie said. "Let's enjoy our dinner."

An Irish dance song started up from the corner where the band had been playing. A few people began pushing their chairs back, gravitating to the small area by the band cleared of tables, moving their bodies in cadence to the music. Alice took a bite of fish, sweet and crispy from the batter, then a sip of ale. She sat back in her chair, taking everything in. A lot to write about. A lot to think about.

Grandmere Grace, what do you think of all of this? Alice took another sip of her ale, catching a faint whiff of perfume in the air.

PART 3

Healing

CHAPTER 15–GRACE

July 1934, Richarme, Louisiana

Lily, do you remember our visits down to the Gulf of Mexico? There was something about that place that pulled us, more than just for the fishing and shrimping your daddy did there. The water whispered to us in our sleep, I think, because some mornings we'd all wake up saying we should go over together and put our feet into the sand. When we were there, it seemed to me like we all became different people. Or at least different versions of ourselves.

We visited just a few months before you left us and stayed a few days with your daddy's shrimping partner's family. The wind and rain came and went while we were there, every day bringing waters down from the heavens and blowing anything that wasn't firmly attached to something swirling into the air. It felt magical, or like a sign that something was coming.

One afternoon after the rains stopped, I walked down the jetty and found you sitting at the end, looking over the water. I could tell before I even got near that you were in another world, in that trance-like state that would take you away from us. You didn't seem to hear me walk up behind you. You were sitting there with your legs crossed, staring out over the horizon. I wondered what you saw there, who you were talking with. You were at peace. I sat beside you and didn't say a word, just tried to quietly enter that place you were in.

You started humming, a melody I hadn't heard before. The song melted all around us, swirling us into another world. As you hummed the wind picked up and your voice got louder, singing that melody coming from someplace inside of you. You closed your eyes and the song kept coming, music with no words, made only of sounds that rose out of your spirit, mixing with everything around us.

The wind died and you slowed your singing, then let out one last note that hung in the air between us before it floated out over the water. It was a gift to every living creature in the sea. I took your hand, Lily Mae, and you looked back at me and smiled.

"The clouds look like sky paintings, don't they?" you said.

Yes, ma chérie. Sky paintings. That's how I see them now.

You left this world so soon after that day, and I will always be grateful for the memory of that moment. Your voice lives inside of me, helping me to heal. I'm grateful for that.

Your song goes on, even if I'm the only one to hear it.

* * *

Mamou had songs too, Lily. They were prayers, all of them. The night after you sang on the jetty, I remembered where I'd heard that before. Mamou sang it to you before she passed away. She hadn't been feeling well so we went to visit her. I was cutting vegetables for soup when I heard it, a melody that pulled me out to the back porch to hear where it came from. You two were sitting on a bench, looking out at the big oak in her yard. It seemed to me that she was giving you a gift, so I didn't intrude—I listened for a few minutes then slipped back into the kitchen. You were only six years old.

She died in her bed one night several weeks later, peaceful as could be. She just went to sleep and didn't wake up. My mother found her with a smile on her face, rosary in her hands. We couldn't even feel too sad because she left us all with love and a feeling that she was happy in whatever place she had gone to. She died as she had lived—as a healer.

* * *

She always told me her healing powers came from God, and as a child, I accepted what she said and thought everyone had people in their family with these gifts. No one ever called her a *traiteur*, but I know now—that is what she was. A faith healer. She used her hands and her prayers, ones that had been given to her from her grandmother, to heal people's bodies and hearts. She had strong faith in what she could do for people with her song-like prayers and gentle touch. She used what she knew about the healing powers of plants to make the magic that came through her stronger, and when she put all three together—her song-prayers and the energy that came through her hands and the properties of the plants she worked with—it seemed like there was nothing in this world she couldn't fix.

When Mamou was a little girl, her mother, my Great-Grandmere Mae, taught her the healing ways of the French people. I think her mother saw in her what I saw in you, the gift that lands where it will in each generation.

Mamou told me that Grandmere Mae started teaching her the prayers when she was seven. She would take her out for long walks in the trees and show her which plants to use for headaches, which ones helped with women's pains, which ones might help heal the anger of a man torn down by life. Grandmere Mae taught her about the dangerous use of anger, that it was always caused by life beating a person down until the only way they could find any power was to boil up inside then spurt it all out on anyone around.

Mamou also knew about hoodoo, the dark side of these gifts, but she never went that way. She told me that when my grandfather came home from Samuel's daddy's house after he shot the gun at the basket, she wasn't sure how she was going to help that family with such an angry, dangerous man ruling over them all, but she knew that trying to fix darkness with darkness never works, even when it seems to be the only way. She chose the right way, Lily. She chose to go the way of love.

She went to the water to think that day. She walked through the trees down to the river, listening to the sound of the wind, feeling the energy of the spirits of the Earth around her. She asked those spirits for help and listened quietly, waiting for an answer. She harvested manglier she found among the trees and brought it home to make tea. As the woodsy aroma of that tea started rising in her kitchen, it came to her what she had to do.

Mamou believed that Billy's anger was from his feeling he wasn't really a man if he couldn't feed his wife and children, so the only way to feel good about himself and have his family respect him was to lash out at them. Mamou thought she could help him by using her gifts to help him feel power in a different way, the power that comes from knowing you are loved, that you belong in the place where you are.

She was wrong, Lily Mae. She learned that lesson too late, but when she smelled that manglier tea brewing in her kitchen that day, she really thought she could turn Billy around with prayers filled with the healing love of the grandmothers who came before her.

She started by going back out to the woods and gathering up as many healing plants as she could. She harvested more manglier and found some mamou, the plant that seemed to speak directly to her. She gathered mint and rosemary and brought all of these plants home in a big bundle and set them out to dry. Grandpere Antoine asked her what she was doing. She stayed silent as she worked, her fingers weaving the herbs together, eyes cast down on what she was creating. She knew Grandpere was so shaken up by what he'd witnessed that he wouldn't believe she could do anything to help. He saw and understood her gifts and knew she was a powerful healer, but she knew his pride was knotted up in all of what happened, and she didn't want to have to untangle that along with what she was doing with Billy. She knew it would take everything she had. She didn't want to waste any drop of power coming through her.

Mamou couldn't read or write, so she had all of the prayers in her head. She thought about which ones to use and decided that the best way would be to use one prayer and say it over and over, keeping it all focused in one place. She never told me the prayer—she never told anyone the words to her prayers—but she said she started saying this one over and over in her head as she prepared the plants to make a little altar. When they were all dried out, she created a space on an old stump out in the back yard where she laid them out. She asked the spirits of those plants to come together and help her. She was used to having the person she was trying to heal right in front of her, but she couldn't do that this time, so she decided she would find a way to put something of Billy's there in the middle of the altar of herbs. She went out to the barn and asked Samuel if he had anything of his daddy's on him. He told her that the only thing he had from his daddy was the scars on his body.

Mamou decided that using something that came straight from Billy's anger might be the best way to do her work, so she asked Samuel if she could put a new poultice on his back. She put it on the freshest scar she could find, one where the tear in his skin was still open. She knew some of the blood from his body would come out on that poultice and it did, just enough to make the herbs closest to his skin turn a little pink, like the bottom of a gulf crab when it's still a baby. She knew she would also need something of his to make the prayers work the way she wanted them to, so she gave him one of Grandpere's shirts to wear and took his, saying she would sew a new one for him.

She wrapped the poultice in the shirt, brought it back to the stump, put it in the middle of the herbs, and set her river rock next to it. Then she started praying. She prayed day and night, whispering that prayer while she cooked and cleaned, during supper, and when she laid down to sleep at night. She kept focusing it on Billy, on whatever had happened in his life to fill him with the kind of rage that ends with a person being shot at and children running away in fear. She pictured Billy as a little boy and tried to send him healing love, all the love that had come to her through the generations. She guessed that he hadn't felt that before, or he wouldn't be able to hurt his wife and children the way he did.

Even as she slept, some part of her was still praying, still whispering into the heavens.

A dream came to her on the first night. A huge wave from the ocean rose above her, bigger than anything she'd seen before. At first it scared her. She thought it was going to swallow her up completely, but just before it came over her head, she was picked up by a seagull that came swooping down from the sky. The seagull carried her above the wave and she was able to look down into the waters and see all sorts of creatures of the sea there—some beautiful and some frightful, all of them swimming around together, spiraling around each other, some eating from the bottom of the ocean and some eating smaller creatures in one bite. She saw it all and knew when she woke up that her healing prayers could only do so much to change the order of things, to change Billy's rage or what became of it.

She saw in one flash how big the world is and how much we don't know about what's happening around us. She realized we are all a part of that swirling ocean, moving through our piece of it, trying to stay alive the best way we know how. She saw that we aren't all made the same way. Some of us are going to attack and eat smaller creatures no matter what. But she knew it was her nature to try to heal things, so she decided she would just keep saying her prayers for Billy and his wife and Samuel and all the other children in that family, because that was her place in the order of things. She realized that morning after the dream that she had to stop thinking about how things turned out and focus instead on how well she did her part, the thing that was hers to do when she came face to face with hatred and pain.

After three days of saying her prayers and waiting for a sign that a shift was happening with Billy and his family, Mamou woke up early and walked out to the stump with her herbs and prayer altar and found Samuel there. He had come out of the barn for the first time since he'd arrived, and she came upon him staring at that altar with his eyes wide with fear. He looked at her and didn't have to say what he was thinking. She could see he was wondering why his shirt was there wrapped around herbs and a candle.

She decided it would be best to turn his stare away from what he saw and coax him into eating some breakfast. She offered to cook him a slab of ham with fried eggs and suggested he wash up so she could bring it out to him. He didn't say a word. He walked back to the barn then stopped at the door, turning to look back at the altar one more time. She knew something was starting to happen in that moment. She just didn't know what—or which direction things would turn.

CHAPTER 16–ALICE

July 2019, San Diego, California

The morning started with the ping of a text on her cell phone. Alice sat up in bed, shaking off the remnants of an early morning dream. Smoke rising. A bird circling the sky. A downpour of rain over a darkened forest. Just before waking, Ronan had appeared in the dream, reaching his hand to hers, his eyes piercing through the darkness of the thick grove of trees.

Pulling herself out of bed, she focused her attention on the pale light of early morning. A seagull circled the ocean just beyond her balcony, looking for breakfast near the shoreline, replacing the dark shadow of the bird in her dream.

She picked up her phone. The text was from Jeff, giving directions on where to meet. Still unsettled, she stood still for a moment, willing herself into the present. Maybe calling her oldest sister would ease her thoughts.

She sent a quick text. *Hey, Sophia. Thinking about you. Do you have time for a call?*

The answer came back immediately. *In a meeting that ends in five minutes. Call me then.*

Alice settled in a seat on her hotel balcony before calling. Sophia picked up on the second ring.

"Hi, sis. San Diego? Sounds like a nice assignment." Sophia's soft voice—still with a slight Southern accent even after living in New York for ten years—made Alice smile.

"Yes, it's fabulous. I've been here a couple of nights and am enjoying the warm weather and scenery. Thanks for picking up. Do you have a little time to talk?"

"Just a couple of minutes. I have another meeting soon and it's across town. What's up?"

"I just wanted to say hi," Alice said, pausing, pushing the dream from her thoughts. She and Sophia talked often, mostly checking in about small things happening in their lives. *Take a risk and talk about Ronan?* "And maybe ask you for a little dating advice. You're the only one in the family with a solid marriage, so maybe you can help me out here."

"Advice? From me? I've been in my relationship so long I don't know how much I could help you now. Things have changed a lot in the dating world in the last ten years. Did you meet someone online?"

"No, actually. I met him on the beach. He's a cartographer from Ireland."

"An Irish guy, huh? When did you meet?"

"About a week ago. We had a dinner date before I flew here. I have an online date with him tonight—he's having dinner delivered to my hotel room."

"Sounds like a romantic. Thinking you should probably give this guy a chance. Maybe open up a bit this time?" Sophia's voice was soft, kind.

"Maybe. He gave me a beautiful carving of a turtle. The shell is made of malachite. It has a carving of a Celtic spiral on it. It's beautiful."

Bring up the river rock in the jewelry box from Grandmere Grace and the spiral painted there? Ask Sophia what she thought about that, about all that was happening? No. Keep it safe. Stick to dating, which was risky enough to talk about.

"I love malachite," Sophia broke into her thoughts. "Most of the jewelry we work with is made with precious stones, but occasionally semi-precious stones show up in estate jewelry sales. Malachite has been used in lots of cultures. It's said to be a stone that brings protection and healing. I think it's one of the gemstones that was used to create the ink for The Book of Kells, an ancient Celtic book of the New Testament."

"The turtle carving is so intricate. The spiral on the back, carved into the malachite, gives it an ancient look."

"This guy must really like you."

Alice paused. "Maybe," she said, looking far out over the expanse of the ocean. "I'll let you know how things go. Say hi to Camille for me. Didn't you two just celebrate your anniversary?"

"Yep. Five years married on the summer solstice. Ten years together. We think of 2014 as the year all of our friends got married—the gay ones, at least. Lots of five-year anniversaries this year."

"Have fun celebrating."

"Have fun on your trip. Send pictures. And let's talk again soon when I'm not rushing to a meeting."

"I'd love that." Alice pictured Sophia's smile on the other end of the line—wide, expansive, her eyes always sparkling. "I'll call again before too long."

They hung up at the same time and Alice sat staring at the water, thoughts about their conversation and her past reluctance with men swimming through her mind. Growing heat from the sun rising higher in the sky finally nudged her back inside to start her day.

* * *

The drive to the marina took longer than she expected with morning traffic. Kaitlin was waiting for her at the dock, waving her arm in the air to welcome Alice, her high-pitched voice ringing out. "Hop on, Alice. I've got a spot for you at the front of the boat."

Alice watched as a line of tourists poured out of a van with the company's logo then boarded the large cruise boat. People gathered around Jeff, who was handing out drinks with slices of pineapple poking out of pink-tinted glasses.

"Welcome to our first excursion," Kaitlin said as Alice took a seat next to her. "We'll leave in a few minutes."

"Welcome!" Jeff's booming voice carried across the boat from speakers. A few tourists still boarding hurried to empty seats.

"We're a group of thirty this week and we have a great set of adventures lined up for you. Today we'll enjoy a beautiful cruise of the bay. Take lots of pictures and enjoy the ride. We'll have lunch for you to enjoy and music during our cruise. Let us know if we can do anything to make your day more enjoyable."

The boat pulled away from the landing, moving into the slow-flowing water. Alice looked down into its depths, thinking about the rivers of Louisiana. She loved rivers as much as she loved the ocean—the mystery, the way the light danced on the water at different times of day, and always the pull to jump in, to swim deep into the distance and be connected to the world beneath the surface.

After snapping a few photos and sipping on a pineapple drink—which tasted too sweet for her to finish—Alice decided to use the time to learn more about her guides.

"How did you and Jeff meet?" she asked Kaitlin.

"In college at Sonoma State. He grew up here. I'm an Army brat, so I've lived all over."

"What made you decide to settle here?"

"We decided this was a good place to start a business. The scenery can't be beat, and he's lived here long enough to know the area well."

"How do you like living here?"

"I love it. Growing up, our lives were centered around my father's career and wherever it took us, so I never felt like I could really settle in anywhere. With Jeff's family connections here, it feels like home."

Before Alice could respond, Jeff joined them.

"I heard my name," he said, kissing Kaitlin on the cheek. "How's it going?"

"Good. Talking about the business." Kaitlin turned to Alice. "We're going on six years now and the business is growing."

"We're grateful for the article you're writing," Jeff said. "Kaitlin, I can use your help with the drinks. Alice, do you mind?"

"Not at all."

Kaitlin joined Jeff at the bar. Alice noticed a family sitting near her, a teenage girl with long brown hair in between her mother and father, staring out at the water. *Reminds me of myself.* The thought came quickly, as though a mirror had been held up and she was seeing herself back in time. Images of Louisiana rivers in her childhood mingled with a memory that began to surface from a trip she had taken with her family when she seventeen, ten years after Grandmere Grace died. They had gone to Hawaii, a place Grandmere had always wanted to visit.

She remembered a river cruise on the Wailua River, going deep inside the island to a grotto filled with ancient ferns. Alice had loved the name of the river—the word *Wailua* ringing in her ears like a song.

They had stopped halfway through the boat ride, at a landing near the grotto. The scenery—multiple shades of green, hanging ferns, ancient trees—and the scent of water hanging in the air all mingled to create a sensory experience that took her from one world to another. The tour guides led people through the small park area, sharing history and pointing out plants with Hawaiian names.

We're going back in time, she remembered one of them saying, followed by: *You may even want to watch for spirits of old as you walk!*

Alice had walked slightly behind her family members, who were snapping photos of flowers. She stopped and sat on a small, flat rock on the path. A fine mist splayed in the air, creating a halo of light around everything. *Going back in time.* The words played over in her mind. *Is that possible? To really go back in time?*

A Hawaiian chant began in the background, slow, low-toned, voices far away. The musicians on the dock? The sounds of the voices increased, loud and clear enough for her to hear words she could not understand. The graceful melody held her body, her mind drifting, visions of deep blue water filling her mind. *Am I going back in time? What would that feel like?* She remembered keeping her eyes closed, slightly afraid but mostly curious. Her thoughts had been interrupted by her mother telling her it was time to get back on the boat.

On the ride back, a light rain began to fall, first barely noticeable—heavy mist almost—then heavier water coming down, large plops of water soaking everyone and everything not under the cover of the middle part of the boat. Tourists began crowding into the covered area, complaining about getting wet. Alice had stayed put. She loved the rain, feeling like she was back home in Louisiana. Raindrops—heavy, laden with a clean, slightly salty smell—poured down her face, drenching her clothing. The water refreshed her, waking her body and washing thoughts away. The river became muddied, a soft brown color as the rain pelted it.

As suddenly as it started, the rain halted. Alice looked up at the bank passing by just then. As the mist rose from the water, a silhouette rose from the bank. A figure in white, a willowy shape of a child. A hand waving—at Alice? A girl? *The* girl?

Alice had blinked, wiping the rainwater from her eyes. Looked again. No one was there, just the passing shore lined with trees, the sound of tourists returning to their seats as Hawaiian music piped in around them, more clearly audible now as the song of the rain ended. The lie surfaced in her mind before she could stop it: *what you think you saw wasn't really there.*

"Alice, would you like another drink?" Kaitlin's voice broke into Alice's memory, cutting through space and time. She was not a teenager, but a writer working on a story—on a boat in San Diego, not Hawaii.

"No thanks, not now," Alice said, trying to hide her momentary disorientation. She sat up straight, pulling her thoughts back to the present. "But I'd love to hear about the sites we're seeing."

"I can tell you all about them," Kaitlin said, sitting down on the bench. Alice pulled out her notebook and took a breath, ready to take notes.

* * *

The tour ended in time for Alice to jump into her car and meet the aunts at four. The cave at Sunset Cliffs was tucked deep into the rocks on a beach not far from the marina. The tides were out, which was the only time the cave was accessible.

Tutu Amelia was holding her granddaughter's hand at the spot they agreed to meet, Aunt Annie walking beside them.

Memories of Grandmere Martha came to Alice, how she had loved taking her grandchildren to the school playground near her house on summer days. Heat rose off the sidewalks in that old New Orleans neighborhood during the summer, and the smell of gardenias filled the air. *I loved to hold her hand on those walks*, Alice thought.

Still feeling the warmth of her grandmother's hand holding hers, an imprint of memory anchoring her in the distant past, she walked toward the trio, all wearing bright-colored summer dresses.

"Aloha. You made it," Tutu Amelia said. "Mele is excited to meet you."

"We brought you lilikoi pie!" Mele said quickly, as though she had been waiting to share this news all day and could hardly keep the words in. "Tutu grows lilikoi in her yard and we made the pie just for you."

"Thank you," Alice said, scanning her memory for what she knew about lilikoi. A Hawaiian fruit? "I've never tried it, but it sounds wonderful."

"We made the pie together to share with you," Tutu Amelia said, looking down at Mele. "It's a favorite of ours, and we don't give away our secret recipe to anyone!"

Giggling, Mele put her hands to her face and shook her head up and down in quiet agreement. Her eyes twinkled with their shared secret. A warmth rose in Alice's chest as she realized, with a small amount of wonder, that the aunts were welcoming her in a way she didn't expect. Like the type of hospitality she was used to in Louisiana, where strangers could quickly become part of the family.

"It's become my favorite pie," Aunt Annie said as she adjusted her large sunhat on her head. "We'll have some at the cave, along with the Irish tea I brought." She held up a green thermos decorated with a Celtic spiral sticker and a small sticker of a seal.

Alice noted the spiral appearing again, this time next to an image of a seal. Unsure if it felt comforting or unsettling, she turned to look at Mele.

"Come, Mele. Time for us to show Alice some things," Tutu Amelia said. "She's here to learn about our beautiful part of the world."

Mele giggled again and twirled around, her feet making a circle in the sand.

"You know about this cave, yes?" Tutu Amelia grinned, as though she was revealing another secret.

The dream of the cave crashed through Alice's consciousness. Did Tutu know about her dream? Once again, Alice was at a loss for words. She turned to Aunt Annie, whose grin mirrored that of the woman in her dream, the one who had led her by boat deeper into the cave.

"I . . . I'm not sure. I read about it this morning. The tour guide said it's a great tourist attraction."

"Tourists do visit it, but we love to go when it's not too crowded. We can walk to the mouth of the cave from here and you can tell us what was happening for you last night as the sean nós song ended, yes?" Aunt Annie smiled again.

Alice didn't know whether she felt relieved that the aunts had seen what happened or frightened. "You saw?"

"Yes. It's not hard to see when the spirits of other worlds and times visit us if we open ourselves and are not afraid to look," Tutu Amelia said. "You do not seem to be afraid. That's good. The spirits welcome those who are brave in their hearts and minds. Bravery in the face of challenge is what helps us through everything in life, especially when people around us don't know what to do. The world needs as many of us as possible to be brave now." Pausing, she put one hand on Alice's arm and looked at her, softening her gaze. "You are stronger than you think. Maybe braver than you think?"

Alice paused. What was she referring to? Aunt Annie was still smiling, eyes softened around the edges. Should she tell them what she'd been experiencing? Simple things rattled her these days, her mind seeming to be slipping off a cliff she couldn't see. Images of Ronan's smile, memories of his touch on her arm at dinner, visions of the little girl appearing everywhere—was she losing her ability to function in the real world?

"I'm not feeling very brave," Alice said, chest tightening as she gave words to her jumbled thoughts. "I've been having some strange experiences lately. I don't know what they are really, something like visits from my great-grandmother, perhaps. I can't really tell what's happening to me, but images come to me from out of the blue and I'm not sure what they mean."

Mele gazed at her with a quizzical look. *Am I revealing too much?* Alice put her hands into her pockets. Her cheeks burned and she suddenly felt self-conscious. Being around Mele reminded her of being a child with her own grandmother, of times when she didn't need to restrain her feelings or guard her thoughts.

"You must be very connected to your great-grandmother. Perhaps she has a message for you," Aunt Annie said. "Come. Let's walk to the cave. It's a good place to talk. The mouth is a place between the water and the land, the wide open sky and the dark places in the Earth. A perfect place to talk about the thin lines between the worlds. That's what you're experiencing, Alice. Let's walk."

She moved toward the cave. Tutu Amelia walked behind her in a steady pace, her earth-worn feet making a slight shuffling sound in her slip-on sandals. Mele turned and reached for Alice's hand. Alice reached back and, connected, they walked together toward the cave, which she now saw was only a short distance down the beach. The opening rose up before them into the low-hanging clouds. The sight mingled with her memories of the cliff in her dream. As she stood before the cave in front of them, a familiar sensation ran through her, as though she had been here before. She marveled again at the ocean's ability to evoke such strong emotion. A simple shift in the wind or scent on the breeze had the effect of tapping into her subconscious, drawing her into the world of dreams and distant memories. The cave pulled her forward now, her focus on the water pooling just inside its rocky opening. The cliff line above shrouded in hazy white clouds looked like a scene from a fantasy movie, another world rising just above them.

Mele ran straight toward the side of the cave's mouth and began climbing the rocks that reached toward a small tree, jutting from the cliffside. Alice's face softened into a smile as she remembered herself as a child, always wanting to be closer to nature, longing for the feeling of merging with trees or grassy meadows or rivers during afternoons playing in the sun. The breeze shifted, bringing with it the briny smell of the ocean, filling her nostrils, inviting in more memories of her childhood. Visiting the Gulf of Mexico with her family. Picking up seashells on early morning walks, searching for treasures left behind at low tide. Tracing the shape with her fingers of small crab shells fading from red to pink on the hot summer sand.

Mele picked something up and ran back to Alice. "Here," she said, her smile so wide it seemed to seep into her eyes, her whole face lighting up. "It's a seashell I just found. I think they have stories and sometimes I hold them to my ear and see what they say. Do you ever do that?"

Mele, in her light-colored sundress, her feet bare in the sand, suddenly seemed to be a mirror image of the child from the park. *Her name is Martha. She talks if you ask her questions.* Alice's stomach lurched, her breath shallow.

"Not often, but . . . maybe I'll try," Alice responded as Mele put the perfectly-shaped clam shell in her hand. "Are you sure you want to give it to me?"

"Yes! I'll go find more." Mele giggled then turned and ran back toward the cave. Alice looked at the shell, then up at the aunts.

Tutu Amelia sat on one of the small rocks facing the cave's opening, Aunt Annie on her other side. She motioned for Alice to sit beside her. The rocks formed a low wall surrounding the cave, creating a barrier from the world of the ocean behind them. Alice sat slowly, easing into a smooth, curved space on the rock that seemed carved to her shape.

The lilikoi pie and tea came out, placed on a flat rock.

"Isn't it wonderful the way children talk to beautiful things in nature? Sometimes we forget when we become adults that it is possible to communicate with everything around us." Aunt Annie smiled as she poured tea. "The world is so much more interesting when we remember that nature is just as alive as we are—and maybe more intelligent!" She laughed, a playful sound, swirling in the air around them.

"Pie?" Tutu Amelia offered Alice a slice.

"Yes, thanks."

"Now, tell me what happened last night," Tutu Amelia said. "What took you away for those few minutes during the song? I too felt a presence, one that was unfamiliar. Who was visiting you?" Tutu's face was more serious now, dark eyes soft and warm. Alice felt an urge to reach for her hand but stopped herself and folded her hands into her lap, looked up, taking in Tutu's appearance: weathered skin, soft eyes, close-mouthed smile. Strong arms and legs emerging from her muumuu, a multi-colored print splashed with tropical flowers—red, purple, green, gold—draping her like royalty. The three colors of Mardi Gras in Louisiana came to mind, the same purple, gold, and green. *Yes, royalty. Tutu Amelia is indeed royalty, descended, perhaps, from kings and queens of Hawaii.*

"I think it was my great-grandmother, Grandmere Grace," Alice said. "I think she's been visiting me lately. That may sound odd, or maybe you don't think so? I'm just not sure what it means or if I'm supposed to do something with it."

Alice's voice caught in her throat. This was the first time she'd spoken with anyonc who might understand what was happening to her. Years of holding silent about her experiences had taken a toll, years filled with confusion, fear, vulnerability she always had to keep hidden. She turned to look at Aunt Annie then looked down again.

"I don't think it's odd," Aunt Annie said. "Spirits visit us everywhere. Most people don't listen or know how to hear what is being shared. You have a gift, to be able to hear and see beyond this world that surrounds us. It can be a burden when we don't know how to use it, or when we feel alone with it. But you're not alone. Your great-grandmother is with you. She's probably always been with you, even before she died. What do you know of her? Was she alive when you were born?"

"Yes," Alice said. Something in the way the women listened so steadily gave her strength. "She died when I was seven. I remember her as a petite woman, but with a strong presence. I was always mesmerized by her. I felt she and I were connected in some way, even though there wasn't really anything different about my relationship with her in comparison to her other great-grandchildren. When she died, she left me a jewelry box. No one knew why she left it for me."

"Do you still have it?" Tutu Amelia's voice was gentle.

"I do. I even brought it here. There was a note inside telling me to remember who I am, to know that others came before me and more will come after. There was a river rock in the box too, painted with a spiral and stars. The note said to use the spiral to help me find my gifts, then to use my gifts to protect what I love and create what I desire. I'm still not sure what she meant."

"Ahhh. She's left you a present and a blessing, along with an assignment, yes?" Aunt Annie leaned toward Alice as she spoke. "That means she believes in you, and probably knew that you have this gift of being able to see into other worlds. Perhaps she had it too. That is why she would know she could trust you with the box."

"I never thought about that. I don't talk much about these things," Alice said. "I've had these experiences ever since I was a little girl but I've never had anyone I could talk with about them. I talk with my sisters sometimes, and every now and then I'll say something to my mom, but none of them are comfortable or know what to say. I don't remember anything that happened that made me think my great-grandmother had these experiences, but I guess she wouldn't have necessarily said anything to me about it." Alice paused. "There's one other thing. The box contained a scarf, the one I was wearing the day we met. I had never worn it before, but when I opened the box for the first time in years a couple of weeks ago, I decided to put it on. And, as strange as it seems, I think that when I wear it, it brings on some of the experiences I've been having." She looked down at her hands. "It frightens me, if I'm being honest."

"If you have this gift, it probably comes from others in your family who have it too," Tutu Amelia said, taking Alice's hand. "It's sad that no one could talk about it, but that is the way of many cultures now. In Hawaii, it is not such a strange thing. These experiences are a way we are linked to our ancestors and the worlds beyond this one. You are with us, so you can speak of these things. We do not see them as unnatural. And the scarf may be a way your great-grandmother can speak with you, can share things with you that she thinks you need to understand."

"You may even find yourself having more of these experiences, now that you've shared your story with us," Aunt Annie said. "Being by the sea helps. The creatures of the water draw them out of us, those of us born with the ability to see between the worlds. Especially the sea beings who move between the land and water, like the turtles and seals."

There they were again, the turtles. The seals. The hairpins from the jewelry box—sea creatures in brilliant gem-tone colors. Her eyes locked with Aunt Annie's. Asking a question. But what? What was she asking? Alice turned back to Tutu Amelia.

"Thank you," she said. "I don't know why you decided to invite me here today, but I'm grateful."

"We have a responsibility to the past, Alice, and—more importantly—to the future," Tutu Amelia said. "It is in your hands, in mine. We come from our ancestors and must carry forth the work they began, whatever it is, wherever we find ourselves in the stories they leave for us. You will find what you are looking for by turning to the stories of your family, to the culture which birthed you." Tutu stopped speaking, squeezed Alice's hand, and turned her face to the opening of the cave. "As to why we invited you here, well, we've grown fond of you rather quickly. And it seems we're not the only ones." She smiled at Annie and in that moment, Alice could see the likeness to her nephew, the curve of the chin, the color of her hair so like his.

Alice's face flushed with the thought of Ronan. She turned her face to the mountains just as Mele ran back over to where they were sitting. The sun beamed down and the child was wreathed in light.

"Come! Look into the cave with me. Let's go inside it!" Mele's small hand reached out in a gesture of invitation. Alice thought of the family of river otters the girl in the park in Berkeley had spoken of, playful creatures of the water, sometimes holding hands as they floated together.

Tutu Amelia stood up, taking Alice's hand in her own, and walked toward the cave. Alice reached out and took Mele's hand and they walked together toward the opening in the cliff, Aunt Annie keeping pace beside them. The warm sand caressed her bare feet. As they entered the cave she felt as though she was walking through an invisible barrier into a space completely removed from the world behind them. The low ceiling and the water pooling at their ankles created a sense of an ancient world. Alice marveled at the thought that maybe the ocean and the caves did create a way to move between the worlds she experienced, the worlds others seemed to experience—at least the aunts did—with hidden doorways allowing one a sense of moving through time simply by stepping into a different space of sand and rock.

They stopped where the water covered their ankles. Alice saw that the water deepened inside the cave, creating a river as it disappeared around a bend just inside a cavern to the left of where they stood. She was awestruck. What she saw before her was the exact image from her dream. A primordial womb. She half-expected to see a boat waiting. Turning toward the aunts standing silent beside her, she felt herself drawn into her dream again, realizing that she had been led to these women who seemed to see through her. She felt as though the dream layered itself over them and she turned to look at Mele to keep herself in the present. Mele looked up at her and smiled.

"Can we chant, Tutu?"

"Yes." Tutu turned back toward the river of water before them. She began to chant in a low-pitched, powerful voice that first startled Alice, then held her, silent and still. Mele began to chant quietly with her grandmother, her higher pitch creating a balance to the depth of Tutu's voice. Still holding hands with both Tutu and Mele, Alice closed her eyes and allowed herself to be carried by the sounds.

Within a few seconds, a woman materialized—her great-grandmother standing before her in a white cotton dress, old, as she had looked at the end of her life. In her hands she held a letter, and though she did not open her mouth to speak, Alice heard words come through.

Protect what you love, Alice. Create what you desire.

The image before her slowly vanished. She opened her eyes and looked to her right. Mele was there, chanting with her grandmother, no longer smiling, eyes opened wide. Tutu Amelia stood with her eyes closed, chin raised slightly as the sounds coming from deep within her reverberated through the cave. Aunt Annie stood to Alice's left, eyes closed, her chin held high, her face lifted toward the top of the cave.

Tutu chanted a final note, ending with the sound of *Ha!* She and Mele were silent. The chant rang in Alice's ears for a few seconds, then she felt herself washed over with the silence. She closed her eyes and called to her great-grandmother, but no image appeared before her. Tutu and Mele let go of her hands and walked back out into the sunlight. Aunt Annie followed. Alice stood alone in the cave until their voices disappeared, listening to the occasional *plink* of water dripping from the walls of the cave.

CHAPTER 17–GRACE

July 1934, Richarme, Louisiana

Mamou spent the rest of the morning cooking, stirring a big pot of gumbo to keep her mind focused. Cooking always soothed her soul when she felt troubled, and she turned that morning to the smells of chicken cooking in a pot, melting off the bones into a soup of onions, celery, bell pepper, and garden herbs.

She was stirring the gumbo when Samuel left the barn and headed down the trail through the woods, back to the one place she didn't want him to go. If she hadn't had her head in that pot she may have seen him leave and been able to stop him. As it turned out, Antoine was the one who saw him leave, heading through the woods back to his family's house. I doubt my grandfather even thought about it before he started following Samuel. Mamou told me that when she walked out on the porch she saw Antoine headed down the trail, his body moving faster than it usually did, with a sureness that seemed rooted in something beyond what he could control. It was as if something had begun that none of them could stop and he was destined to do his part.

Mamou went out to the stump where she'd made her altar and sat down. Words came through her in a steady rhythm, creating a melody that rocked her into a quiet place inside.

She closed her eyes, hoping to see what was happening, but nothing came. Sometimes she could see things beyond what most of us can see, but that day all she saw was the smoke swirling up from the chimney of their house, carrying her prayers that Antoine and Samuel would come back safely.

* * *

Mamou must have spent an hour at the stump, singing, drinking manglier tea, and waiting for Antoine to come home. The tea tasted more bitter as time passed and the sky darkened itself while she waited. Rain clouds gathered above her and she wanted the water to come down, hoping it would wash clean what was happening at Samuel's house. The sky became darker as she waited, bringing with it a sense of dread she couldn't shake, even as she prayed harder, rocking herself with her song-prayers.

When Antoine finally came home, his body slowly dragging itself out from the woods, he wouldn't raise his face to look at her, and she didn't need to hear him speak to know what had happened. She didn't know the particulars, but she could feel in her chest that the dark birds of death had come swirling around them. She looked down, startled to see that the herbs had turned black. Her hands were warm and prickly, like they got when she knew someone near her needed healing. As Antoine walked past her, he turned for just a moment and she saw a look in his face that told her something had changed between them, changed in the world around them. His eyes were cold and glossy and his mouth grimaced into a shape that frightened her. He didn't stop to talk to her. He walked into the house, and as the screen door banged shut behind him, a streak of lightning came out of the sky. The world closed in on her, with a darkness descending that she thought would never lift.

Mamou felt a fast swirl of a spirit circling her, then as it rose up into the sky her cotton dress flew up as though a big wind had arisen. She looked up and knew it was Samuel. His face flashed before her as the rain came down and she said that even though he wasn't her son by birth, she felt in that moment as if one of her own children had been ripped away from her.

I know what that feeling is, Lily. I live with it every day. Mamou told me this story before I even knew your daddy, but it stuck with me, maybe to prepare me for what I've lived with twice now, losing you and Haydee both in just a few short years. And like Mamou who blamed herself for Samuel's death, I blame myself for yours. I guess when we can't make sense of something, the only way to get any sort of peacefulness is to take it upon ourselves to own the guilt of the thing. It doesn't change what happened, but somehow it seems as if we had some control over it, even if that power we think we had brought about suffering that can never be fixed.

Antoine finally told her what had happened, but only after a few days of not speaking to her at all. He told her that when he got to the shack he walked right into a fight between the boy and his daddy. He tried to jump in and help Samuel, throwing his body between them. Samuel's daddy walked onto the porch, picked up his shotgun, and aimed it straight at my grandfather. Antoine felt ready to die right there if he had to, because somehow Samuel and his siblings had woven themselves into his mind so he couldn't think about anything else. He told Mamou he thought it had become his responsibility to save them, but he ended up killing Samuel instead.

My grandfather didn't kill Samuel, of course. Just as the shot rang out, Samuel threw himself in front of Antoine. He fell to the ground with his eyes open wide, and Mamou said that as long as Antoine lived, he'd wake up from nightmares of those eyes staring at him. My grandfather was never the same after that. And because he blamed Mamou for what happened, for scaring Samuel into running back home, their family was never the same, either.

I know that in some way I can't understand, your life was taken over by the ghosts of what happened there. Your life seemed to be haunted by so many others who came before us too. And here I am, like Mamou that day, feeling helpless to change any of it.

The story of what happened that day has lived on like a curse for us. Mamou shut her gifts away and she never touched the river rock again. She put it away in a box beneath her bed and left it there until she died. Grief is not rational—it spirals and moves on its own timeline, and I don't think Mamou ever fully recovered from the way it overtook her that day.

You were the one who found the stone, the day after her funeral. You drew it from the box and took it to your room. I only learned that after you died, after I found you that morning at the river, lifeless, holding it in your hand. Martha told me later that you'd been keeping it, seeing it as a way to stay connected to Mamou. And by then, it was too late for me to do anything for you, to tell you anything of what that river rock had come to mean for our family.

I wonder if I could have saved you, Lily, if I, too, had not been shut down to what those gifts that run in our family mean. You bore the brunt of that day, and I think I will never forgive myself for it.

Lily Mae

Maman, I'm right here.
I never really left you.
I left my body, that's true, but it was only the faintest part of me,
the container that let me love everything in the beautiful world around us.
I wish I could tell you what really happened
but I know you can't hear me,
not in the way I wish you could.
And I'm still here.
I'm still with you, Maman.

CHAPTER 18–ALICE

July 2019, San Diego, California

The water from the shower washed across Alice's skin in a warm drizzle at first, becoming a waterfall as she turned the handle on the shower head. An online date with Ronan in an hour. Only a few days had passed since seeing him—how could that be? Worlds had moved through since then. Magical, mysterious, even frightening. Haunting dreams, Mele dancing at the caves, Tutu Amelia chanting an ancient melody. And the song at the pub, so similar to the one Ronan sang on the beach the day they met.

Years of pushing men away came back. College dates that rarely ended with a second one and close to a decade of studying or working long hours, avoiding opportunities for anyone to push past the walls inside her. Walls built to keep away the very types of experiences that were happening at every turn now. The land and water around her seemed to call them out, leaving her as out of control as she had felt in the warm, humid world of Louisiana as a child, when she felt porous, unable to keep out the spirits of other worlds.

It all connected now, the rivers and bayous surrounding New Orleans, ocean water around her, the cave and rocks and fauna of Southern California mingling with the images of moss hanging from oak trees and winding paths along rivers and streams in Louisiana. The scent of pikake and jasmine filled the shower as she poured body wash into her hands. Pikake brought memories of the sweet scent of flowers in her mother's garden. And the jasmine—similar to the flowering jasmine at home. Camellias and roses in Grandmere Martha's garden in New Orleans rose before her. Eyes closed, water soothing away any thoughts, more flowers appeared: African violets in small pots, lined neatly under the window of Great-Grandmere Grace's home. Remembering being tall enough to see just over their royal purple flowers, small and fragile, she had always marveled at their tiny perfection.

The magnolia tree in Madeline's yard in New Orleans came to mind. Maddie had the grandmothers' touch with plants. What would she say now about this date with Ronan so soon after their first one? How did it all feel so natural and scary at the same time? Similar to the experiences of being visited by the little girl, by ghosts and memories of the past. Like walking into another dimension of reality with no door to walk back through, no way to return to the world she had lived in before.

Alice turned the water off and stepped out of the shower, wrapping herself in a towel. The reflection of herself in the bathroom mirror—light brown eyes, oval-shaped face framed with shoulder-length brown hair—made her pause. Did she look like Grandmere Grace as a young woman? Or other women from her family's lineage? Were they all here with her now? A tingle of anxiety about where everything was going in her life moved through her body, but knowing that Ronan's bright smile would greet her on her computer screen soon brought some comfort.

* * *

The knock at her door came fifteen minutes before their date. A gangly teen greeted her. "Here you go," he said, handing her a white paper bag, a tattoo of a surfer on a longboard spreading up his arm, wrist to elbow. "The tip was paid too."

Alice smiled. The sweet, spicy aromas of fish and lemongrass curled up from her dinner.

Her laptop was already set up on the table, ready to join Ronan. She pulled out the boxes—one with grilled fish covered in a light-colored sauce, a slice of lemon on the side, and a scoop of creamy polenta, the second with a small salad. Taking a last look at herself in the mirror, she sat down and opened the browser. Ronan was waiting, his face lighting up her screen. She noticed a slight stubble on his face, as though he'd missed a day or two of shaving, giving him a slightly boyish, unkempt look.

"Hi. I hope your dinner arrived on time."

"Yes—it looks amazing. How did you know I love fish?"

"Just a guess. I love almost anything from the sea and hoped you might too."

"How did you know which restaurant to choose?"

"I picked one my aunt took me to last time I visited her. I had the grilled fish of the day and it was delicious. That's what I ordered for you."

"What are you eating?"

"I ordered something similar for myself—baked fish with creamed spinach sauce over rice."

Creamed spinach. Just like her mother cooked, an old New Orleans recipe that had been handed down from her grandmother.

"That almost sounds like a Louisiana dish. My mom cooks a great version of that. My sister Madeline is a professional chef in New Orleans and does some great things with spinach. Oysters Florentine is one of her specialties." She took a bite of fish, letting the tangy flavors of lemon and dill linger in her mouth. Ronan leaned forward, his face coming into closer focus on her computer screen. His eyes, flecked with green and gray, lit up as he watched her enjoy her meal.

"Oysters. That's an aphrodisiac, isn't it?" He smiled, then leaned back slightly and took a bite of rice. Warmth flooded Alice's body. She froze, hoping her face wouldn't become flush, giving away the unexpected sensation his words brought.

"So they say. I have to admit, though, that I've never had an experience of that. Oysters are a part of lots of menus in New Orleans. Do you like them?"

"I like almost anything from the sea."

Alice leaned back into her chair. Seeing herself on screen next to him, she wondered if he could see the way her eye liner was off a bit. Too much on the right eye. She pulled her attention back to him. *Gorgeous. His eyes are gorgeous.* The dappled color of the ocean when the clouds were low, filtering out the bright rays of the sun.

"I enjoyed meeting your aunt and her friend," Alice said, changing the subject. "They took me to a cave on the beach."

"There are some great caves there," he said.

She noticed a framed map of an island on the wall behind him. "What's the map behind you?"

"My beloved Ireland. I love islands, the way they seem to be isolated but are really all connected. If you think about it, the water connects all of us. Aunt Annie and Tutu Amelia talk about how their islands are connected by the same big pool of water, just stretched across the planet." Ronan turned and pointed to the bottom left corner of the island on the map. "This is where my family is from. Lived here for generations. In the summers we'd go to Cape Clear Island," he said, pointing to a small dot just south of the edge of Ireland on the map. "Best gin in the world is distilled here, and the whole island is gorgeous. I miss being able to visit it every year."

Alice sank back into her chair, thinking about her family's trips to Grand Isle off the coast of Louisiana and to the small town of Buras, close to the mouth of the Mississippi River below New Orleans. Her mother's grandfather's family came from Buras. The memory of crabbing off the docks there in the early evening came crashing through her memory. The water—everywhere—mixing in her mind.

"Do you think living on an island is part of what made you decide to become a cartographer?" she asked. "I sometimes wonder if growing up so close to the Gulf of Mexico and the Mississippi River ruined me for life for any possibility of living in the middle of the country. I can't imagine living more than a few hours away from the ocean."

"Yes, me too," he said, looking at her with a wry smile. "I'm not sure if living on an island is what made me decide to become a cartographer, but I think it did feed my curiosity for what else is out there in the world. I love discovering new things and I'm constantly interested in understanding the natural patterns behind what we see around us. I like the illusion it gives me of creating some sense of order and control in this world that is constantly changing."

"Do you have other maps? Do you collect them?"

"All cartographers collect maps," he said, his bright laugh opening something in Alice's chest. A warm flush rushed through her again. She sat back and took a sip of water.

"What do you love most about maps?" she asked, trying to take her focus off of how unsteady she felt being with him. Trying to chart a course through a territory she usually managed to avoid by cutting men off after the second or third date.

"I love old maps for what they show us about the way the world looked to people who lived before us. And I love to see how maps change over time. We think we know everything there is to know about something, then new knowledge comes along, a new discovery is made, and we realize we have to open our minds a bit more."

"That's a great way to think about it," Alice said, relaxing back in her chair. "Great metaphor for life, really."

"Yes. Maps teach us how much we know, and the evolution of maps shows us how much we're still learning. One of the next big areas to map is the ocean floor. We know so little, really, about the deepest parts of it. There are sea creatures we don't even know exist down there, living their whole lives without human interference. That gives me comfort, really, knowing that there is at least one area we humans haven't managed to fully intrude upon yet."

"Except for the waste that we throw into the ocean," Alice said.

"Yes, except for that. I'm sure even the sea beings way below us are having to learn to adapt to whatever is falling down from our inability to deal with what we produce."

"Are you interested in oceanography?"

"I am," Ronan said. "I'd actually love to move into that field at some point. Help to map the ocean depths—but do it in a way that teaches us to be more respectful of the life living on this planet with us."

Silence for a moment. Alice wished they were together in person, that she could reach over and touch his arm, hold his hand.

"Hey," Ronan said, breaking into her thoughts. "There's a great map museum in San Diego. Maybe you can find time to fit it into your schedule while you're there."

"I'll look it up. I'm not sure if I can squeeze anything else into my time here, but I'll check it out."

"Looking at old maps always reminds me that people have been trying to find a way to control the chaos in the world around them for as long as we've been on this Earth."

"Do you think the world is out of control now? Chaos beyond what we can fix?"

As soon as she asked it, she realized they could be moving to shaky ground. They hadn't discussed anything political or related to the growing shift in perceptions in the country about what was right, what was wrong, and what the government should be doing about all of it.

"I'm not sure I think it's out of control. I do think, though, that we have some big problems to deal with." Their eyes held for a moment, each silently deciding whether or not to move the conversation toward current social topics that could reveal rifts in their beliefs or, if not that, at least bring a heavy weight to the evening.

"We do. I can't stop thinking about the horrifying stories of children at the Southern border being separated from their families. I can't imagine that—fleeing violence and terror in their own countries, traveling thousands of miles to the US, then literally being ripped from their parents' arms."

"It's hard to comprehend what's happening there. One of the things that keeps me up at night is what's happening at the EPA. A billionaire oil guy in charge of protecting the environment? Unbelievable. The planet is for sale to the highest bidder. The Earth will survive one way or another, shaking us off if needed, but it puts humanity in a pretty vulnerable place."

Vulnerable. Alice felt a tingle run up her spine.

"I've had my focus on what's happening right in front of me, the project I'm here to work on, and personal things in my own life," she said. "It's hard to miss things in the news, though."

"All the things we see happening in the news are just new versions of things that have been happening since the beginning of time. People can be unbearably cruel to each other, and we seem to have lost the understanding that we share this Earth with other species—and they depend on us to do our part to take care of it," he said. He spoke with an intensity, a conviction, that Alice found both appealing and reassuring, even if the words themselves brought up a feeling of despair.

"I know. It amazes me that some people don't seem to think past the next few years, past the money they can make off a deal. As though what we do doesn't impact the future of the next generations."

"It feels personal to me, having spent the first years of my life on an island. I look at what's happening with sea creatures and ocean reefs around the world. Sea animals are dying, and their bodies are filled with plastic bits that have been dumped into the ocean. You're absolutely right about that—the pollution traveling around the planet through the oceans. And the people who dropped those bits of plastic into the trash someplace will never see where it ends up, in the body of a turtle, perhaps, so they don't feel a connection to it. But we're all connected to all of it."

Ronan looked at her, his eyes softened, head tilted slightly. The room spun for a split second, as though they had just walked through an invisible doorway.

"I wonder sometimes if we'll ever get it right," Alice replied. "It can feel so hopeless when I read the news. But then I look out at the ocean. It's so beautiful and everything seems like it will go on this way forever."

She turned to look through the glass door on her balcony. The sea glittered, stretching endlessly before her.

"I want to let myself think that the things we love will be here forever," Ronan said.

"The stars have been in the sky forever, right? I can't see them from here with the lights from the city, but I know they're up there. It gives me comfort."

"I wonder if the Seven Sisters are visible tonight. Do you know what they are?"

"I've heard of them, but I can't remember much about them. Are they the stars in the Big Dipper?"

"No, although some people think they're the same. The Big Dipper is also made up of seven stars, and it's part of a larger constellation called Ursa Major. That name means *great bear*—as though a big momma bear is watching over us from the sky. The Seven Sisters are the star group called the Pleiades. Myths and stories have been told about them all over the world and they're thought of as star sisters watching over us. I love that idea, that stars watch over us at night. It makes me think that, in the end, we'll all be alright."

Alice thought of her great-grandmother watching over her, of the love she felt from the jewelry box she'd been given. *The world needs as many of us to be brave as possible now.* Tutu Amelia's words rang through her mind. For a moment she and Ronan looked at each other, something quietly passing between them.

No words were needed as they sat in an easy silence, their eyes holding each other as closely as if they were in person. The gentle lapping of the waves coming through the open door on her balcony washed away thoughts of anything other than Ronan before her. Something was shifting in a way she couldn't predict. And, to her surprise, she felt herself smile, Ronan mirroring her in response, his face lighting up the screen on her laptop like the stars she knew were above them, shining over whatever was beginning.

CHAPTER 19—ALICE

July 2019, San Diego, California

The lilt of a bird singing an unfamiliar song was the first thing Alice heard, pulling her into the waking world of her hotel room. The melody coming from the tree branch just outside the window woke her gently, and as her thoughts slowly focused on the birdsong, tangled with hazy images from her dreams, she stretched beneath the soft sheets. *I could get used to having birds wake me up every morning,* she thought. *Much better than an alarm clock.*

Slowly opening her eyes, the light breeze from the open window and the sounds of the tropical bird pulled her from the dream images. She looked out of the window and saw the red and white bird that had been singing to her, sitting on a branch alive with hibiscus—blood-red flowers with black pistils reaching out, highlighted with yellow dots at the end. The bird continued to sing. *I'm in San Diego*, she thought, slipping into the silkiness of the sheets. *And I had a date with Ronan last night. Magical. Beautiful.*

Time had seemed to be slippery since she'd met him. Compressed and expansive at once, moving her between worlds, between the spaces of past and present.

The green jewelry box sitting on the dresser near her bed drew her attention. Without thinking, she reached over to open it and pulled out the scarf, silky between her fingers. Grandmere Grace's letter was starting to make sense. Maybe.

Time to talk with Grandmere Martha. It was 8 a.m. in California but already 10 a.m. in New Orleans. She picked up the phone and called, not sure what she would say. After the first ring, her grandmother picked up and Alice was immediately carried back to Louisiana by the Southern voice on the other end of the receiver.

"Hello?"

"Grandmere Martha, it's Alice. I'm calling from San Diego. Mom gave me your number. How are you?"

"I'm so happy to hear from you, Alice. What are you doing there? Your mom told me you were going for work, but she didn't have many more details."

"It happened quickly and I'm not sure I had the time to tell her everything she wanted to know. I'm here on a work assignment. It's beautiful—everything seems so alive here. I feel pretty lucky that they sent me here."

"How are you doing? I haven't talked with you in a long time. What's happening in your life, besides taking trips to beautiful places?"

"I'm doing well. Life is good. Lots of . . . interesting . . . things happening."

"I talked with your mom the other day and she did tell me you were asking about the jewelry box your Great Grandmere Grace gave you when she died. I can't really remember what was in it."

"It had a doll and some of her hairpins in it, and it also had a scarf wrapped around a stone with a spiral and stars painted on it. I don't know if you remember, but she also left a note for me, and there was a card inside with a date on it—June 21, 1934. Do you have any idea why she had that date on a card in the box?"

Silence hung between them for a few seconds. Grandmere Martha let out a small sigh, a puff of air followed by a few more seconds of silence before she spoke.

"Oh, Alice, honey. That's the date my sister Lily died."

"I'm so sorry. I didn't know. I'm sorry to bring this up now."

"Alice, there's no need to apologize. When I gave you that box, I followed what my mother asked me to do, which was to give it to you and leave you alone with it. I never asked what was in it. I don't know why she had the date of Lily's death on a card that she gave you. I do remember now that she had a note in the box for you. I wondered what she said to you in that, but I didn't want to ask. You were so young, and you took that box so quietly. I remember you went to a chair and pulled out the note, and I just left you to read it. It was such a sad day for all of us. After that we were all caught up in the funeral and family coming into town, and I kept thinking about the deaths of my two sisters, so long before that. I don't think I ever asked you about the jewelry box again. What's bringing it back up now after all these years?"

"I decided to put the jewelry box on a new bookshelf I bought and I opened the box and read the letter again. It said I should take the box to the ocean one day and I finally did it. I went to the ocean near where I live, and then when I went back to work the next Monday, I was told I was being sent here to San Diego for an assignment. So now the box and I are here, right on the ocean. I've been feeling Grandmere Grace with me through all of this."

"I feel her with me often too. The jewelry box was special to her, so I'm not surprised you're feeling her. I always wanted to know what she kept in it, but she usually had it put away in a drawer. She was quiet, like you. Powerful in her own way."

Alice hesitated before speaking.

"This may sound funny, but did she ever talk about her dreams? Or did she ever talk about having . . . strange experiences? Like seeing things . . . spirits . . ." Alice's voice trailed off, leaving the word *spirits* hanging in the air between them just as the silence had before.

"I don't think she ever talked about seeing spirits, honey, and she never spoke to me about her dreams, not that I remember, anyway. But I can say that she often seemed haunted to me, particularly after we lost Lily, and little Haydee had died not long before that." Grandmere Martha paused. "I know I shouldn't, but sometimes I still feel a little pang of guilt about Lily's death. We don't need to go into that, but I know my mother felt the same way. I can't quite explain it, but she often seemed like she was suddenly far away for no reason that I could see. I used to wonder where her mind went in those times. She'd just seem like she was drifting away from us every now and then. I could see when it would happen. She would get quiet, like she was thinking about something, then she would seem pulled away by something none of us could see, and she'd usually go into her room or the yard. She loved to garden and that always seemed to bring her back to us. After Lily died, I knew she'd never be the same and I came to stop expecting much attention from her. It's just the way it was. Something closed up inside of her after both of my sisters passed away."

"I'm sorry if I'm bringing up something painful, Grandmere Martha."

Silence again, an unusual thing for conversations between women in their family.

"Don't worry about it, honey," Grandmere Martha said. "We all have memories and burdens we carry."

"I'm not sure if I should ask, but—you said you feel guilty about your sister's death?" Alice took a breath. "You were just a little girl, weren't you?"

"I was, honey. But that doesn't mean I didn't feel like I should have done something to prevent it. To protect her. I'm sure your sisters feel protective of you too, being the youngest. By the way, how are they?"

"They're both good, I think. Madeline is going a mile a minute, as always, being a mom and a chef. And Sophia seems happy. She's busy too, of course. Not much to report on either of them, I don't think."

"Well, you tell them I said hello and to remember to call me sometime. I love all of you, you know.

"We all know it, Grandmere. Maybe we can all plan a time to get together in New Orleans before too long. I have some vacation time coming up."

"That would be wonderful, honey. I'll cook whatever you'd all like, although I know Madeline will want to share some of her dishes with us. Or she might enjoy having a break from being the one to have to cook."

"I'm sure she would. I'll talk with them about it. It would be great to see you." Alice stood up, looking out at the ocean. "I miss you, Grandmere Martha."

"You're always welcome here, Alice."

"Thanks. I know that. I'm so glad I caught you at home today. It's good to hear your voice."

"You too. Enjoy San Diego. How long will you be there?"

"A few days. I need to go to work now. I'm looking forward to being outside today—the weather is perfect."

"Well, you have a good day. Call again soon."

"I will. I love you."

"You too. Bye, honey."

As Alice hung up the receiver, a chill slid down her spine and she pulled the blanket from her bed up and around her shoulders. She looked up to see if a wind had come through the open window, but everything around her was perfectly still. The bird that had woken her up was still sitting on the branch, now peering inside her window, its head cocked to the side. She held its gaze for a moment before it flew from the branch into the bright blue sky, leaving behind only the lingering trill of its song.

* * *

The day was blindingly bright. Alice had decided to visit the beach and explore an area she'd seen with a cliff overlooking the ocean. She had an hour before she needed to meet Jeff and Kaitlin and the others on the tour for the visit to the Gaslamp District that day, so she'd grabbed a cup of coffee and a muffin to eat in the car.

As she drove along the shoreline looking for the turnoff, the conversation with Grandmere Martha replayed in her mind. Maybe she and her great-grandmother had more in common than she knew. She could relate to feeling haunted. Her own experiences of feeling haunted by images beyond the world around her seemed to be growing. The conversation the day before about her great-grandmother possibly having the same types of experiences that Alice had—of seeing things from the past, or of a hazy possible future—lingered in her mind. What did it all mean? Were these experiences a type of gift, to be used in the world in some way, or were they more of a curse, just making life more difficult?

"Grandmere Grace, let's go see the water," she whispered under her breath as she pulled into the parking lot and walked out to the beach.

The air smelled of salt and sand. Waves lapped the shore in a rhythmic cadence, sending splashes of water into the air in a flurry of white foam. She stood at a distance from a group of tourists laden with blankets and picnic baskets, allowing the breeze to wrap around her. Wanting a solitary experience away from people, she closed her eyes, settling into the sound of the waves.

She waited, hoping for a message from Grandmere Grace, a sign from the other side that would break through the veil of time separating them.

Turning her face to the sun, she closed her eyes, grateful for its warmth. A sudden crashing sound startled her, and she opened her eyes in time to catch a brilliant whirl of water splashing onto rocks. Within seconds, waves of water and white foam dropped back into the ocean and Alice was struck by how quickly the view before them changed again, returning to a calm sea. White clouds scattered lightly across the sky. She felt a sense of endlessness, as though anything could happen.

She spotted something swimming through the water, a sleek head creating a line breaking through the waves. As the seal came up onto the shore, Alice let out a breath. Sliding forward, the large sea animal dragged its tail to create a wake in the sand until it found a resting spot near a cluster of flat rocks. Alice was mesmerized by the way it moved so gracefully, then nested itself against the rocks, almost becoming one with the shoreline.

The sound of music whispered across the sand to her, mingling with the whir of the wind and the splash of the waves. Turning, she saw a man standing on a crest above the seal looking out over the water, playing a flute. Barefoot and wearing only board shorts, his weathered skin and long brown hair gave him the appearance of someone who spent a lot of time outside. A black bird with a white underbody swooped above him. Alice took a step forward without thinking or looking down, the bird, the seal, and the song from the flute pulling her toward the shoreline.

She slipped so quickly that she barely felt her body hit the ground, her hands cut by sharp rocks as she reached out to catch herself. Her ankle shot a signal of piercing pain up her leg, and she looked down to see her foot caught between two rocks, twisted unnaturally.

Grandmere Grace—help me. Later she'd remember only the sound of the flute continuing its haunting song as she let herself collapse fully onto the sand and jagged rocks.

PART 4

Returning

CHAPTER 20–GRACE

July 1934, Richarme, Louisiana

You had a recurring dream, Lily, that haunted me, and I don't know why I didn't put it all together in my head until now. You had this dream every few months in that last year before you left us, and I always sat by your bed trying to comfort you, but you couldn't be comforted, no matter what I did.

The first time you had it, I heard you calling out in your sleep. I went into your room and Martha was awake, looking over at you, not knowing what to do. Your little arms were waving around, and you were so clearly afraid and upset that I wasn't sure if I should try to wake you. I sat on the bed and gently rubbed your head, hoping that might bring you back to our world. You kept calling out, "No! Don't!" I finally got you to start waking up and you curled your little body around mine, wrapping me so tightly I could only respond by curling my body back down around you, holding you in my arms. You asked me if the shotgun was gone, and I wasn't sure what you meant. Your daddy's shotguns were locked away. I told you there weren't any shotguns around, that we were all safe. You started crying, the pillow beneath your head wet with the fear you shed. You were in that place between worlds, and you started telling me about the dream, saying you were walking through the woods when you tripped. You saw a shotgun pointed at you. You kept hearing the sound of someone stomping around but you couldn't see who it was, and no matter what you did, you couldn't get away from that gun pointed at your face, threatening you into terror.

Later when you had the dream, more things came out. Someone was laughing, eerie-like, and you could hear it as though the person was laughing right into your ear, and still you couldn't see who was pointing that shotgun at you. Sometimes you said you heard the click of a trigger being pulled, then you'd hear that mean laugh, and you'd realize the gun didn't have a shell in it, that the person was just trying to scare you. When you'd wake up after that part of the dream, your little heart would be beating so hard I thought it would lift you right out of the bed. I'd cradle you in my arms until you were settled, rubbing your back until I could soothe you into sleep again. I'd always stay in your room after you fell asleep, hoping I could be a guardian for you to keep those dreams from coming back.

The last time you had the dream you woke up and opened your eyes. You were wrapped around me again and I had my hand on your back, asking Mamou to help me comfort you. You said, "I saw him, Mamma. I saw the man with the shotgun." I asked you who he was, and you said, "I don't know him, but his eyes were like little beads of hate, Mamma. There wasn't any light in them. His eyes were what scared me the most, like he wasn't even a person but more like a devil. Mamma, who is he?"

I couldn't answer you. I didn't have any answers, Lily. How could I know what I now think was happening to you? It didn't seem possible and it's only now that you're gone that I'm able to think past what my mind set up to keep me from being too afraid for you. I think you were dreaming about Billy, about that family that your great-grandparents took in. But how could you? How could you have been dreaming about something that happened so long before you were born? And now I see how Billy's great-grandsons carried on his legacy of cruelty, how they had a hand in what happened to you. That I know with all my soul.

I don't understand these things, Lily. There is so much I didn't understand when you were with me. So much I wish I could do over. Maybe if I'd figured it out and told you about what your dream was about, let you know that it was something that happened a long, long time ago and that it was over, maybe you could have stopped trying to follow what kept pulling at you from the other side. Maybe we could have put the pieces together and you'd still be here with me, on this side. But you had to work out these puzzle pieces on your own, and I'm so sorry for that.

I have to stop thinking about all this now. My own face is wet with sadness just thinking about how I failed you. And now you are gone forever from my arms. Gone to the other side and I'm still here, still trying to clean up what's left behind.

I miss you, Lily Mae. I miss you.

Mamou

We are here, Grace. Watching over all of you.

I called Lily home to me. I didn't mean for her to come all the way, to be here with me in spirit, but Haydee and I did call her. Lily would visit us at the oak tree at night, hearing us singing, I guess. And she would visit the otter family. They spoke to her and she could hear them, even if she couldn't always understand what they were saying. She only knew they wanted to connect with her, and she knew she would do anything she could to protect them if they needed it. She was a protector of the animals that lived in and near the water, as I was.

She had such a thin veil shielding her from this world where we are now, that she could hear things others couldn't. She lived between the worlds, slipping in and out as light as a feather drifting on the wind. And she was so young that she didn't know how to keep herself in the world she lived in with you once she felt herself in our world.

We would talk to her, sing to her, let her feel the beauty and grace that fills where we are now. She'd dance a bit to our songs, joining us under the moss of that tree. It seemed to soothe her soul, help her be able to go back into the world after those times, knowing that we were always close by, in the trees and the water and air around her.

She is safe with us, Grace. We are holding her, always, as we are always watching over all of you.

CHAPTER 21–ALICE

July 2019, San Diego, California

Blood spooled onto the rock from the cuts on her hand. Alice was grateful that she'd been able to catch herself as she fell, even though the searing pain from her twisted left ankle brought tears to her eyes. She was finally able to wrench her trapped foot from the rocks and look at the damage. Besides the cuts in her hand, she had scrapes on her legs and what she knew would become bruises above her swollen ankle. It throbbed as she tried to put gentle pressure on it. The day was going to be difficult. She wouldn't be able to walk without pain.

She looked over to where the flute player had serenaded her to this accident. He had stopped playing and looked at her from across the sand. Thinking briefly of asking him for help, she decided she didn't want to bring any more attention to herself, so she started hobbling back to her car, leaning heavily on her right leg. The seal that had been resting on the beach pulled back out into the water just as Alice got into the car, its sleek head dipping under the waves and out of sight.

She sat in the car before turning it on, allowing the sunlight to pour through the windshield and soak her body. Tears ran down her face. The dreams and images that had been coming to her for weeks flooded her mind and she found herself shaking with intense feelings she couldn't name. She wondered what was pulling her more, her desire to understand what her great-grandmother had asked of her or something deeper, a pull from some place beyond her awareness.

The seal was far out at sea by the time she pulled herself together enough to drive. As she headed to downtown San Diego for the day's tour, she let herself feel strengthened by having seen its sleek body moving gracefully through the water. Grateful for that gift this morning, at least.

* * *

The Gaslamp District brought to her mind scenes from New Orleans, memories of walking through its historic streets flooding her mind. Black wrought iron fences and balconies, restaurants and buildings made of brick and wood, warm air caressing her body as she walked down the street, careful with her ankle which still throbbed from the fall. Would camellias grow here? Magnolias? Probably. Similar weather, near the ocean, even close to the same latitude. A drive east on I-10 would take her straight to her family's home.

Kaitlin and Jeff stood in the center of the group of tourists in front of the restaurant they'd chosen for lunch. Alice had a chance to look more closely at some of the group as she walked up to the restaurant. A couple both dressed in black pants, the woman wearing close-cut capris and the man in linen, sported expensive silky shirts. Hers was a Dior, his a crisp short-sleeved button-down with a designer icon on the pocket. A woman next to them clutched a large Gucci handbag, big enough to hold a small poodle. Two older teens stood next to their mother, both scrolling on their phones, the girl in shorts cut close to the top of her thighs, the boy in ripped jeans and a Supreme t-shirt. Alice looked down and wondered if everyone there could tell by her simple cotton dress that she was not among those who could afford a trip like this. An interloper, in some ways. Not quite one of this crowd.

"Alice," Kaitlyn called out as the group began moving into the restaurant. "Join me at my table. They have sushi to die for here."

"Thanks," Alice replied, waiting for an elderly woman to scuttle through the heavy door into the air-conditioned bistro. "Will everyone be seated at different tables?"

"We have three large tables, and everyone can sit where they'd like. It's fun to watch people connect and make new friends on these excursions. Today we'll walk through the downtown area after lunch and do some shopping. Great boutiques here. And everyone gets a massage today or this evening. You know, you can still schedule one if you'd like."

"No thanks. I'll just wander around and look at the shops after lunch, then I need to get started on the article."

"Ok. We'll start off now with mimosas to get everyone going!"

"I think I'll probably just have tea, but the day sounds like fun." Alice smiled, wondering who could drink champagne at this hour and keep going all afternoon. She sat down next to Kaitlyn at a table set for ten guests.

"I asked for a Bloody Mary a few minutes ago. Can I please get it before I order my meal?" the woman to Alice's right asked the waitress, who was hurriedly putting glasses of ice water down at each place setting, smiling as she juggled the large platter of glasses. Alice turned, taking in the woman asking for a drink. large gold earrings swung from her ears, dancing between the long, smooth curls of her platinum-dyed hair. Heavy mascara, bright red lipstick, the heady scent of perfume hanging in the air around her. The woman turned to Alice and smiled, her pearl-white straight teeth glistening. "Seriously, don't you think they would know to give everyone their drink as soon as they order it? We got here a few minutes ago and ordered and it still hasn't come."

Alice smiled back, suddenly self-conscious, then turned to the waitress and nodded slightly. "Thank you for the water," she said.

"Where are you from?" the woman to her right asked, putting her napkin in her lap.

"Berkeley. You?"

"Connecticut. We've never been to San Diego—oh, this is my husband Jim," she said, waving toward the man next to her, his head turned down, peering at the menu. "And I'm Aurora. We love California. At least parts of it. We visit San Francisco and LA at least once a year and this time we decided to drop down to San Diego after our annual week in Malibu. Do you come here often?"

"Actually, no. I write for a travel magazine. I'm here to do an article on tours of San Diego—I think this is a beautiful area."

"Yes, it's beautiful, if you stay in the right places. I find that's true everywhere, though. It's sad to me how gorgeous cities let people trash them. I'm so glad I haven't had to see any homeless people so far on this trip. I can't say that for our last trip to San Francisco. We practically had to step over them on our way to the theater."

Uncertain of what to say, Alice turned back to the waitress who was taking Kaitlin's order. "It looks like it's time to order food," she said, hoping to change the subject without appearing rude. Burying her head in the menu, she wondered how she would get through the meal. Still shaky from the fall at the beach, she didn't feel ready to engage in a long stretch of small talk. The waitress circled around the table to her.

"Are you ready to order?"

"I'll have the Cobb salad. And just water is fine for me."

Aurora jumped in with her order before Alice had time to hand the waitress the menu. "I'd like the prosciutto grilled sandwich with gruyere cheese, no mayo or tomatoes, with extra pickles on the side. I'd like grated parmesan added to the salad—can you do that?"

"Of course," the waitress said, scribbling on her notepad. "Can I get you anything else? Your bloody mary is on the way."

"Just get that to me as soon as you can, and I'll want another one before too long. If you can keep an eye out, when my first one is close to finished, can you bring me another? I hate it when I don't have anything to drink, especially when I'm on vacation." Aurora tilted her head slightly as she spoke, punctuating her last words with a slow blink of her eyes and a close-lipped smile.

"Of course," the waitress said before moving on to Jim.

"Seriously," Aurora said quietly, leaning toward Alice. "I've found that if you tell them what you want more than once in the beginning, it lets them know you aren't someone they can slack around with. I expect to get what I pay for."

"I understand," Alice said. *Not really. What do you expect, exactly?* She took a sip of water. Maybe turning the focus to the tour would help her get through this conversation. "What are you looking forward to on the rest of the trip?"

"Well, I love shopping, so that will be fun today. Tomorrow when we go to La Jolla, I'm looking forward to being on the beach. I bought the greatest new bikini for this trip. And on our boat ride the next day, it will be fun to see the whales and maybe some dolphins. They sure better plan ahead to make sure we get to see some. A friend of mine paid for a boat tour like this here last year and they didn't see a single whale. Can you believe it? You'd think the tour guides could figure out how to make sure that happens every time."

"I've loved seeing the seals and turtles so far," Alice said. "I'm not sure they adhere to the schedules of the boat tours, though." She let out a small laugh, hoping it sounded more genuine than it felt.

"They certainly should." Aurora said, "That's one of the main things we're here for."

The waitress walked up behind Alice, placing a large glass in front of Aurora, a pink umbrella and slice of celery poking out of the blood-red cocktail.

"Thank God, it's here," Aurora said then picked up her glass and turned to Jim to make a toast. He leaned in, clicking his beer mug with her drink, then looked over at Alice.

"I hope she hasn't been boring you," he said after taking a sip of beer. "She probably hasn't told you why we're on this trip. It's our anniversary—fifteen years together. We've earned a celebration."

Maybe they have, Alice thought. *Everyone here probably deserves a little celebration. Frame the article that way. Focus on the article.* She picked up her glass and toasted the smiling couple.

* * *

After several hours of lunch then a walk through the Gaslamp District, Alice was happy to finally get in her rental car and head North on the highway up the coast. The aunts were waiting for her when she pulled into the parking lot of the Pacific Marine Mammal Center. She gave them a small smile as she winced getting out of her car. After those few hours downtown, her ankle had swollen up, sending dull pain up her leg with each step. Realizing she couldn't hide it—and didn't really want to, after pretending all afternoon on the tour—she decided to make a small joke of it.

"Something caught my ankle when I visited the beach earlier. Maybe it's meant to slow me down, so I pay close attention to the beauty around me."

"What happened?" Tutu asked.

"I was listening to a guy playing a flute on the beach and also looking out at a seal coming to shore and forgot to look down. I need to pay more attention."

"Speaking of seals, I'm sorry to say we've a bad situation here today," Tutu said. "One got caught in a fisherman's net that was floating in the ocean. We call them *ghost nets* because they swim the waters after being dropped off of boats. Whoever dropped it probably didn't think about the harm it could do."

"There are a lot of expensive fishing expeditions for tourists that happen here and it looks like this fishing net may have been dropped from one of those boats. The seal got wrapped in it. Volunteers are trying to carefully untangle it now."

"That's horrible! Will it be OK?"

"Hopefully it will survive," Aunt Annie said. "We can never tell what happens to the spirit of an animal, though, once it has this kind of interaction with humans, the mess we make of their habitat. We can walk down and look if you'd like."

Hesitant to see the animal suffering but pulled by a growing feeling that she wanted to understand more about their plight, she followed the aunts up the beach, skirting a crowd of tourists trying to get pictures. A rope barrier had been set up to keep people away.

No one spoke as a man and woman in life vests worked to extricate the seal. One fraying chord was stained with blood from a cut in the seal's side. Just as the last strands were released the seal let out a bellow that pierced through the babbling of tourists. The haunting cry shook Alice and she recoiled from it. For a moment she was blinded by flashing lights, dizzying sparks that made her wonder if she would lose her balance. She blinked to get her equilibrium back and took a few steps away to avoid having others see what was happening to her.

Images of a school of fish swirling in a pool of water close to the banks of a muddy river flashed through her mind. She closed her eyes, hoping to steady herself as the scene in her mind grew larger. The fish swam in water that swirled with streams of pink, turning deeper red closer to the bank. One of the fish darted through the streak of blood-red water and bounced off skin, a tiny face, eyes closed, brown hair floating. Blood spooled from a wound in the child's head, trickling out into the river. Alice saw a flash of a small body dressed in a white nightgown, lying completely still, only the hair and gown moving slowly with the gentle lapping of water. One small fish swam close to the figure, grazing the white nightgown before moving back into deeper water.

The girl in the white nightgown . . .

Alice counted to steady herself. She followed the image of the trail of the fish away from the shoreline, the small body lying there. By the time she counted to five she could only see water. She opened her eyes. Aunt Annie was standing there, looking at her intently.

"Are you OK?"

"I'm fine. The bright sun just made me dizzy." Barely able to get the words out, connections began to snap together in her mind. Who was this child in the white nightgown?

"Take some water." Tutu pulled a water bottle from her bag then put a hand on Alice's back.

"Thank you," Alice said.

She turned back to the seal, watching it drag its body slowly back into the ocean. It let out small cries as it moved. The volunteers held back tourists as some moved close to the seal to take photos. Alice closed her eyes again as she tried to integrate the image of the seal with the overlay of the fish in the bloody stream. What was real? Where were these images coming from?

"Are you ready to go meet our favorite turtle?" Aunt Annie smiled.

"Sure," Alice said, grateful for the chance to move inside, away from the ocean and its endless depths—and the images it called up, threatening to overtake her.

* * *

That evening, Alice settled into her hotel room. She'd been struck by the impact of seeing what she'd previously only known through news stories—how human interaction with the natural environment was destroying the conditions that allowed other species to live. She'd seen close up the ways the destruction was happening, how each piece connected with the next, how each creature in the web of life on the planet needed the others, and how humans seem to forget that we too are part of that web.

Allowing herself to sink into sadness rather than push it away, she stopped herself from opening her computer to do research for the article until she moved through some of the deep emotion stirring inside. Using her mind to try to understand things was one of her favorite ways to avoid feeling anything, particularly when she believed she was helpless. An hour passed as she sat on her balcony, watching waves come to shore then roll back out into the sea, a mix of emotions rising and falling with each one. She wondered about whether the vision she'd had earlier connected with her great-grandmother's stories.

She walked over and opened the jewelry box, then picked up the doll, wrapped it in a piece of quilt square, and placed it gently on the dresser. She picked up the stone and traced the painted spiral with her finger. *What do you want of me, Grandmere?*

No answers came. She started searching for articles on the area. Her own article was due in less than a week and she hadn't started it yet. Within minutes, she found several sites that gave history, detailed tourist information, and tips for visitors. Her body relaxed as she found her way into something she understood.

Two hours later, she pulled herself from her computer and dropped onto the bed. She had several pages of notes and an outline. The doll and river rock were still on the dresser next to her computer, temporarily forgotten in her focus on writing the article. She picked them up, placed them gently back in the jewelry box, and closed the lid. Enough for one day. She said a silent prayer that she might be able to sleep peacefully through the night.

* * *

"Alice. Come here. Alice. We need you."

Alice shifted between the sheets, floating up from the world of dreams towards consciousness. The quiet roll of ocean waves outside her open window pulled her toward the present, but the dream pulled her back down, a stronger current from the past that wouldn't let go.

"We're here. Just look up." Alice's legs felt like lead, weighted down by something she couldn't see. She looked up and immediately put her arms over her eyes. The brightness of light coming through tree branches made her squint. She couldn't see anything beyond the light dipping through big, leafy limbs.

"We're here, ma chérie. We are always here. I've never left you, just like my grandmothers never left me. Lily and Haydee are with me now and I'm with my Grandmere. Her name is Mamou. Do you remember?"

Alice tried to open her eyes. She recognized the voice. "Grandmere Grace? Where are you? Where are we?" She tried to move her legs again, but they felt anchored, weighted by something invisible. She saw that she was lying on the bank of a stream. Small fish swam around her feet, coming onto shore where water puddled in small pools, then darted back out into the stream. Turtles moved toward her from the stream, their ancient eyes poking inches above the water. As they got close enough to the shore that she could almost touch them, they started walking, legs suddenly stretching out, lengthening, becoming long and slender. The turtles, changing before her eyes, started walking upright, shells disappearing into their backs as hair began to cascade down their bodies—which were transforming into figures of women, rising from the water.

"Grandmere Grace, where are you? Where are we?" She reached out with her hands, hoping to feel her grandmother's hands reaching back.

"We're here, ma chérie. We're here. We need you. Remember who you are. Remember that you aren't alone, no matter what happens. And the fish and turtles, the seals and sea otters, they all need you. You have something you can use to help them. Your voice, Alice. Your voice. Remember that you have a voice to speak, words to write. You're carrying gifts that have been passed down from one link to the next in our family, and now it is you who must decide what to do. You are the one who matters now because you are the one who is there, still living. Our ancestors knew everything about the Earth and connections with the animals and plants, but many have forgotten. We're always here with you, Alice. But it is you who must choose what to do next, how to act, how to carry these gifts forward. The world needs you. The animals need you. And many others have gifts that are also needed now. We carried the gifts and stories through each generation, holding and protecting them, sometimes using them well and sometimes finding great sorrow from opening to them. But now it is you and others like you who must choose what to do. You are not alone. You are never alone."

"Grandmere! Where are you? I can't see you."

* * *

Birdsong from just outside her slightly-open hotel window pulled Alice back to the room. She opened her eyes and looked around, disoriented, her mind swimming between worlds, waking to questions she could not answer.

CHAPTER 22–ALICE

July 2019, San Diego, California

The ocean breeze washed through the car, ruffling Alice's hair. The drive to La Jolla took twenty minutes. Even midweek, at this time of year the long stretch of sand and palm trees drew visitors.

Alice arrived a few minutes after the tour group. Grabbing a visor and her backpack, she joined them as they walked out toward the ocean, Jeff leading, carrying an ice chest. Kaitlin lagged behind, waving to Alice as she caught up to the last couple getting off the bus.

"Beautiful drive, huh?" Kaitlin wore a bright red bathing suit cover up, large designer sunglasses, and a floppy hat.

"Yes, gorgeous," Alice said, glancing down to watch her step as they started across the stretch of sand. No rocks here. Her ankle still throbbed slightly from her fall the day before.

"Lunch is in the bus, but Jeff has a cooler of drinks if you're thirsty."

"Thanks."

Alice watched as a team of young men walked past, carrying chairs and umbrellas. Her eyes followed the men as they abruptly slowed to a halt. Alice and Kaitlin stopped behind them. A large crowd was gathering near the water.

Alice took in the scene: a huddle of people with cameras pointed toward something she couldn't yet see. A heaviness settled in her stomach, a sense of dread. A loud voice boomed directions to the crowd.

"Step back, please. Everyone stay at least ten feet away."

Alice stumbled forward, following Kaitlin who had jogged to catch up with Jeff, now gathering their tour group to a tight circle, giving his own directions as he seemed to try to turn their attention away from the scene near the shoreline.

Alice felt it before she saw what had gathered the crowd. A large sea lion lay unmoving, just at the edge of the water, gentle waves swishing its body slightly each time one gently rolled to shore, leaving foamy bubbles in its wake. Its body lay at an odd angle, as though the water was now shaping it, rather than the animal itself moving its body with any will or life force.

She understood in a flash. It was dead.

She watched as two men moved toward the large animal, gently squatting low enough to look at its face, then turned away. Jeff and Kaitlin were guiding their group in the other direction and began spreading out the blankets. Many of the tourists followed Jeff and Kaitlin, seeming to want to avoid what was happening with the sea lion. A few couples stood still, watching the scene at the shoreline unfold, their faces draped in sorrow. Alice felt drawn to them, grateful that a few of the members of her group felt as she did. Pulled by a sense of professional responsibility, she reminded herself that she had a job to do, and she'd already been distracted from it more than she wanted by visions that came at every turn. The heaviness in her stomach now turned to a churning sensation. The sun pouring down on her body brought on a light-headedness and she closed her eyes. *No memories now. No visions. Please. I need to do my job. I can't take any more of this.*

But what happened to the sea lion? Why is it there?

The desire to turn back and be part of the group with the sea mammal was almost strong enough to make her turn around. But she couldn't. Taking care of that animal wasn't her job. Writing this article was. *Keep moving forward. Focus on what's right in front of you—this tour group.*

Alice peered ahead, watching Kaitlin and Jeff quickly set up a beach paradise for their clients. The ice chest was already open, guests helping themselves to cold drinks.

She turned and took one more look at the scene behind her. Volunteers were still holding tourists back, but people were snapping photos of the sea lion. A flicker of the girl in the white gown, her body laying still at the shoreline of a river, washed through Alice's mind.

She turned back toward the tour group, tinkling laughter coming from a small group of them.

Just get through this day. Do the job you came here to do.

* * *

The sun was still high enough on the horizon to enjoy sitting on the balcony, the warmth of the sun soaking away some of the sadness pulsing through Alice's body. Almost 6 p.m.—time to eat something, but she wasn't hungry. The rest of the afternoon had gone relatively smoothly. Kaitlin and Jeff had done a good job of distracting everyone from the scene down the beach. Alice had fought the urge to walk over and find out what had happened to the sea lion. Haunted by everything she'd been experiencing, she focused on staying with the tour group, hoping it would shift her unsettled feelings. It hadn't worked very well.

How could there be a seal trapped in a net and a dead sea lion washing up in just a few days' time, right when she was there at the beach? Surely this couldn't be a common occurrence?

Pulling out her laptop, she typed in "dead sea mammals washing up to shore in California" and articles immediately popped up. Toxins in the sea. Boat injuries. Did this really happen so often? If so, why wasn't she seeing more of it on the news?

The word "malnourishment" caught her attention, and she clicked on the first link to a story about a grey whale that had washed ashore a few months earlier. How could a whale be malnourished? The article cited melting ice caps in the far Northern hemisphere as the culprit. This impacted the food chain from tiny organisms up to the largest sea mammal of all, the whale. She clicked on a photo of the one that had washed to shore, its face reminding her of the turtle she'd seen on the first day of her trip.

A wave of sadness came over her, threatening to bring a deluge of tears.

No. Focus. The article. Get something to eat, shake this off, and write a solid draft.

She closed her laptop. Maybe talking with Ronan would help. He seemed to have a way of giving her space to talk about whatever was on her mind. His gentle smile and light-green eyes popped into her mind. She picked up her phone, pausing only a second, then clicked on his icon. He picked up on the second ring, before she had time to second-guess herself.

"Hi, Alice." Ronan's gentle voice soothed her worries.

"Hi, Ronan. I'm glad you were able to pick up."

"How's your day going?"

"It started off alright, but something pretty upsetting happened. We went to La Jolla and a sea lion washed up on the beach. It was dead . . ." Alice's voice trailed off. She stopped herself before it cracked.

"Alice, I'm so sorry. What happened?"

"I'm not sure. I don't know how it died. I was just looking online to see if the story had popped up on any news channels, but I haven't seen any. It must have just washed up as we were arriving. People came and took it away." Alice paused. Ronan's silence on the other end felt comforting. Even with the distance of talking on the phone, she felt he could hold her sadness, not needing to talk or try to make things better. "It was awful," she said quietly. "I stayed with the tour group because that was my job today, but it was hard. I couldn't stop thinking about the sea lion, or about the seal I saw yesterday with Aunt Annie and Tutu Amelia, trapped in a net. So many terrible things happening to the sea life. I never really knew how often it happened."

"Yes," Ronan said quietly. "It happens more often than any of us would like to think."

"I did a little research. A whale washed ashore recently from malnourishment."

"I read about that. I've done a lot of reading about what's happening to the oceans because of warming of the ice caps at both of the Earth's poles. That's changing things in ways we're not prepared for. Most people have no idea what's coming."

"There are so many ways things are coming at us." She tried not to sound as despairing as she felt. "I keep thinking about the trash that goes into the waters everywhere, areas where there are pools of plastic floating in the ocean that go for miles. We just keep going about our business."

"My grandparents used to say that living on an island reminds you of the impact of everything you do. When you live in a small community surrounded by water, you realize we all have to work together."

"The tourists on this trip don't seem to have grown up knowing that—at least they don't act like it. They don't seem to see what's happening, or maybe they do and just want to enjoy their vacations. Money can protect people from suffering, I guess. At some point, though, no amount of money will protect us. We're all caught in the same big net. And I know I'm part of it. I'm writing an article to get people to take expensive vacations in places like this. It seems we all choose to live in denial most of the time because it can feel so overwhelming."

Ronan sighed. "I wish I was there with you. Maybe we can have dinner when you get home? I'd love to take you to the Marine Mammal Center. Working there makes me feel better because I see people doing something about the mess we're making. By the way, have you ever seen a sea otter close up? Their faces remind me of my grandfather's smile!"

"I've only seen otters in big aquariums. I'd love to go with you."

"It's a plan, then."

"That sounds like just what I need right now." Alice looked out at the ocean, realizing her body was relaxing for the first time in hours.

"And Aunt Annie called me. You've charmed them! They'd like to see you one more time, if you want."

"I'm free for brunch just before my plane leaves."

"Great. I'll text Aunt Annie and let her know."

"I'm glad we had a chance to talk."

"Me too."

They were both quiet for a moment, Alice looking up at the sky, wondering what constellations were ready to make themselves visible when darkness washed over the horizon. Comforted by the knowledge that they were there, even though she couldn't see them, she closed her eyes. Ronan broke her thoughts with a few words, spoken so quietly that they sounded like a lullaby.

"Good night, Alice. Sweet dreams."

"You too, Ronan. See you soon."

* * *

The water sparkled with an iridescence that seemed unnatural. Gem-toned blue—the deep color of sapphires—rippling in all directions. The breeze caressed her skin, the warm rays of the mid-morning sun melting away her thoughts. Stunning. The boat ride out to see dolphins and whales gave a breathtaking view of the wide expanse of ocean and sky, the sunlight pouring down creating a luminescent glow around everyone on the boat.

The tour would take four hours, bringing them far out to sea. The story of the malnourished whale washing up to shore had made its way deep into Alice's psyche. Even with the gorgeous view around her, she wondered how many of the whales they may see would be suffering the same fate. She'd continued her research on whales deep into the night.

The article she had to turn into her editor about this trip was still eluding her. She had to force each word, the draft so far written in bright, peppy language, including information about each day's adventures, the extra touches offered. Today the lunch would include smoked tri-tip, grilled salmon, prosciutto-wrapped asparagus, tropical fruit cups, Caesar salad, sparkling cocktails, and several choices of dessert, finished off with champagne toasts. Even if they didn't see dolphins or whales, the group would enjoy good food.

Alice looked out to the horizon. Blue whales migrated past San Diego at this time of year. Her research had brought up articles about their majestic presence in the sea, their skin pale blue, some with bodies as long as three buses. Hearts the size of a small car. And they were endangered, like so many other species in the sea and on the land. One article detailed the whales' unique language, their songs echoing for miles, a sound both haunting and melodic. Scientists tried to decipher it, understand what they were communicating with different tones and pitches. Alice had clicked on a link to hear it. The sounds mesmerized her, bringing her back to the moment she and Ronan had first met, his song on the beach. An Irish love song of the sea, of longing, the melody still lilting in her ears.

She closed her eyes, allowing thoughts of music of all kinds to wash over her. Whale songs. Underwater singing. Songs from the sky, the songs of the stars scientists had been discovering, reverberating across galaxies as large stars were birthed by gases blending and creating new masses, others dying in brilliant explosions larger than the human mind could comprehend. Songs of humans in every culture—chants of Pacific Islanders, drumbeats from Africa, haunting a cappella songs from Eastern European countries. The French melodies of her childhood, sung by uncles on Saturday evenings, accompanied by guitars, accordions, sometimes a fiddle. Insect songs—grasshoppers rubbing their legs together. Cicadas. Bird song. Brooks babbling, waterfalls pouring over cliffs. The hum of a small child playing with sounds. The imperceptible sound of butterfly wings that can start a hurricane on the other side of the planet. The songs of her dreams . . .

"Alice, want a cocktail? We have a special rum punch that's perfect with these appetizers." Kaitlin's voice broke into Alice's thoughts.

Startled, Alice turned and gathered herself.

"Sure." She pulled herself back to the people around her, then followed Kaitlin to a table set with platters of cheese and berries.

"Hopefully we'll see whales once we get farther out." Kaitlin handed Alice a bright pink drink. "For now, just enjoy the view."

Alice sat down. Time to talk with a few guests to get their view of the week. The sharp pang of alcohol hit the back of her throat as she took a sip of the cocktail. She pulled out a notepad and turned to the woman beside her. The article had to be her main focus today.

* * *

At her hotel that evening, Alice wrote the article, keeping her words to what she knew the editors—and their readers—wanted to hear. Bright beauty everywhere, for the right price. Guided tours, gourmet food, breathtaking sights. They'd only seen one whale earlier, so far away that just the distant spout of water it sent up into the air was visible, but enough to bring cheers from everyone on the boat. As they were returning to the bay, a school of bright orange fish swam by. Alice watched as they turned in unison and swam in another direction, as though pulled by an invisible current below the water. She watched in wonder as a pod of dolphins poked their heads from the sea. The tour group, replete with cocktails, seemed happy for this final treat, most standing at the rails taking photos.

After finishing the article, she walked over to the dresser and opened the jewelry box, running her finger over the spiral on the river rock, then touched each star painted around it. *Am I any closer to understanding what I'm supposed to do?*

She picked up Grandmere Grace's hair pins—seal, turtle, whale, brightly-colored fish—and walked out onto the balcony of her room. She looked over the horizon, wondering how many of these beautiful creatures were out there, just beyond view, in their own underwater world. Deep blue water connected with the hues of red and yellow of the sky as the sun dropped on the horizon. Just as the sun dipped into the water, a flash of green lit up the sky in a luminescent glow. The green flash—what the aunts had told her to watch for.

A small gift to end her day.

CHAPTER 23–ALICE

July 2019, San Diego, California

"Alice," Aunt Annie said. "I'm so glad you could join us for breakfast. Sit down and tell us about how you've enjoyed our little area of the world here."

Alice wrapped both hands around a mug of coffee, happy to sit in the bright yellow chair at the breakfast table, nestled into a bay window looking out over a beautifully tended garden. Tutu Amelia sat beside her, scooping fresh papaya, melon, and strawberries onto her plate. A perfect way to end the trip, Alice was grateful for the unexpected hospitality by these two women she'd just met.

"It's a beautiful place, that's for sure. A bit of paradise."

Aunt Annie served scrambled eggs and sausages then held up her mug in a toast.

"Here's to the beauty of the ocean and the warmth of new friendships. We'd love to see you again." Aunt Annie winked as she said this. Alice wondered if the invitation applied whether or not she was dating Ronan. She pushed the thought out of her mind. She wasn't ready yet this morning to take on the growing surge of feelings she was experiencing each time she thought of him.

"Thank you. I'm grateful for the way you two have offered me a different kind of tour than what I would have experienced otherwise." She paused. Should she tell them about how much the experience of seeing the sea life being harmed was hampering her thoughts, coming into her dreams? The strange connections it all seemed to have with her grandmothers, even though she couldn't pinpoint how it all connected?

"What did you think of our visit to the Marine Mammal Center?" Tutu asked.

"It was a bit of a contrast to the tourist attractions, and to the way this area is presented to visitors. I don't think many people pay much attention to the ways our everyday actions affect this paradise, or how endangered sea life is. We take it for granted. Or we don't think about it. I'm actually feeling conflicted about writing this article, enticing people to visit areas like this without also talking about the impact everything we do has on the environment."

Aunt Annie leaned in, her eyes softening. "Alice, what you are feeling is not yours to carry alone. It can feel overwhelming to see all that is happening." She took Alice's hands as she spoke. "Despair has no place here. Let the ocean take away your sadness, wash away the scars of things that have happened in the past, even of things that are happening right now. Everything we need is inside of us. And we must remember we all have ancestors who are here to help us. Some of us have ancestors who loved and cared for the land and people. Some have ancestors who lived their lives in ways that harmed those things. Many of us have both. Either way, it's our work to listen and do what is before us." She leaned back in her chair, pausing. "Return to your grandmothers, Alice. What you are looking for is there, in your own family. You don't need to look for anything outside of that. Sometimes we just need to look a little farther back to find what we need. Go back into the stories of your own family, your people, to understand what is asked of you in your life."

"I'm not sure how to listen to them." Alice was surprised

at how quickly the conversation settled into places where she could open up with these women. "I'm also not sure what they're asking of me. Something seems to be pulling at me, but I don't know how to understand it."

"Everything is singing, Alice. You know this, yes?" Tutu Amelia spoke now, softly. "The moon and stars, whales and dolphins, all of the tiny creatures and flowers around us. Even scientists are learning this now. Everything is singing. We only need to stop and listen. Not everyone can hear the songs, so those of us who do must share what we hear. The songlines of the Aboriginal people in Australia, the drumbeat of the ancient hula, the whispers in the wind blowing by—all of it is showing us the proper way to live, to be in alignment with all of creation. The songs are always leading us into the rhythm of living in sync with everything else. In Hawaii we say *mālama pono,* which means to care for the things we love, to live in alignment with what is right, what is truly important. Listen to the thrum of the ocean waves and follow what you hear, Alice. The cells in your body are singing their own song. Everything has its own melody. When you aren't sure what to do next, stop and listen and remember—everything is always singing, always guiding you home."

A tingling sensation ran through Alice's body. How could they know what she'd been thinking about the day before on the boat? She looked down into her lap.

"The world is changing so quickly," Aunt Annie said. "We're all standing at the water's edge together, facing the unknown. How will we learn to manage it? Perhaps like our friends and teachers, the seals and turtles, the beautiful sea otters. They are amphibious, able to live in the water and on land, move between worlds seamlessly. Always facing a bit of the unknown. Something for us to learn there, no?"

"Wisdom is just below the surface, Alice," Tutu Amelia said. "Even when it's been hidden for generations, it's always there."

"Some people say we all come from the sea." Aunt Annie smiled as she spoke. "Some believe all our stories started there, all of us descended from the magnificent beings of the ocean. And maybe we're all still guided—if we let ourselves be—by memories in our bodies of where we came from. No matter what we believe, there is some wisdom there. No matter what we believe about how we humans came to be on this Earth, the sea animals can certainly show us a lot about how our world is changing and what we need to do about it."

"Some even say," Tutu Amelia leaned in as she spoke, "that we all came from the stars. The pictures they are taking now in space of galaxies far, far away? Those are filled with stardust that nourishes us. The very air we breathe comes from the heavens. We are quite literally fed by the stars, if you think of it that way. And we know we all come from a long line of mothers and grandmothers that go back before memory. Where did we all start? Who really knows? We can all tap into the wisdom that comes from our ancestors, though, if we are brave enough to listen."

"We are part of the Earth, Alice," Aunt Annie said, taking Alice's hand. "When it suffers, we suffer. We are connected to each other and have the same fate. You have a gift and it is opening. You have wonderful things ahead in your life. Know that you have what you need to face whatever comes."

Alice looked at them, unable to respond. What was coming? And what did her grandmothers think of all of this? Grand-mere Grace's face appeared between Tutu Amelia and Aunt Annie for a moment. Only a flicker, like the green flash on the water at sunset the night before. Almost too faint to see . . . or notice it was there.

* * *

Alice pressed "send" on the article the next morning, sitting in her apartment in Berkeley drinking her second cup of coffee. Just the right word count, complimented by photos from Kaitlin and Jeff capturing the light on the water, the smiles of tourists toasting with bubbly champagne in crystal glasses. A few staged photos of elegant meals plated perfectly. Her editor would be happy. The article would come out just in time for people who could afford it to start planning winter getaways to sunnier climates, away from harsher weather.

A walk would help shake the feeling that something was off, the nagging sense that writing the article was contributing to the destruction of the natural world and sea life. But that thought was crazy. Visiting beautiful places brings in needed money for the people who live there and gives people a better understanding of the world. Tourism was not the problem. Or was it? What was the problem? And why couldn't her mind let things go? The seal caught in the net came to mind, tangled and unable to pull itself out.

Alice stood up from her desk and Isabella stretched her lithe body, awaking from her nap on the back of the couch. Eyeing Alice with a silent gaze, she stood up and walked toward her, taking tiny steps then reaching out one paw and placing it on Alice's arm.

"I love you, Isabella." Alice scooped up the cat, cradling her and holding her close to her chest. Isabella's body vibrated gently as she began to purr in a quiet tone, the only sound in the apartment. Alice put her face into Isabella's fur, finally allowing tears she had been holding in all week to be released.

CHAPTER 24—GRACE

July 1934, Richarme, Louisiana

Lily, I had a dream last night. Mamou came to me and told me you were safe. She took my hand and walked me through a house, only it wasn't like any house I've ever been in before. The front door opened off a big balcony made of gold, shiny and bright, and when the sun hit the railings, the light glittered in a way that brought tears to my eyes. In my dream, I owned this house, but not just for myself. It was your house and your siblings' house and the house that your children would have owned, if you had ever had any.

When I walked into the front room, it looked like the home I've lived in all these years with your daddy. But then I started walking back through the kitchen, and when I got to the hallway behind the cupboard, there was a door. I opened it and walked into a room I'd never seen before. It was beautiful, full of fancy furniture and pictures of important people on the wall and expensive-looking china and crystal in a glass cabinet. I walked through it, wanting to touch everything, but my eyes were drawn to another door and I walked through that one too, then I found another door, this one leading into a room that was about to fall through the wooden floor. The slats were broken and it looked like a hurricane had come through, with everything thrown across the room and glass broken on the ragged carpet. I stood there thinking I was going to have to clean it all up and wondering how I would pay for it, when I saw a little window next to an old couch. The window was open, like it was letting in the breeze. I walked over to catch my breath and there was a hallway on the other side of the window leading to lots more rooms, each one leading off the hall. I climbed through the window to see, because I couldn't believe all this existed in my house all this time, and I never knew it was there.

Every time I wanted to stop and rest in one of the rooms, I felt a pull to just keep going, to keep exploring until I could see everything there was to see. I never did see it all. I woke up to the early light of morning coming in through our bedroom window, and in that hazy moment between sleeping and waking, I couldn't tell which world was real, the one I was waking to or the one I was coming from. I slowly opened my eyes, put my hand over and touched your daddy's arm, and knew where I was, that the house with all those rooms had all been a dream.

But it felt so real, Lily. I keep thinking about it. And I started thinking maybe all these stories coming through my mind, all these stories of our family and our ancestors, maybe it's like the house with all those rooms. Maybe all these stories are always in us, part of us, and we just don't know it. Sometimes we have rooms we have to clean up from big storms, and then sometimes, if we're lucky, we find ones that are draped in gold and beauty.

I can't stop thinking about those rooms and how they may be like what happened to you, all these stories mixed up and rambling on like an old house that never seems to end, stories that live inside you and that you live inside of at the same time. Just like in my dream when I had to keep walking through the house, it seems we have to keep walking through all of it until something in our own lives makes sense again. That's what I'm going to keep trying to do, my sweet Lily Mae.

* * *

How do I start to talk about what happened to you at the end? Losing you was the darkest day of my life, and I still can't think about it without crumpling up inside like a burned-up leaf, charred and hopeless.

My mind goes to all the things I should have paid more attention to, times I felt something rise up my spine as a signal. It happened at times when I'd see you do things that made it seem you were getting farther away from us. In those last few weeks, you were more distant than usual, your eyes often with a far-off look in them. You seemed peaceful, though, almost happy. You seemed to be part of a secret story that you couldn't share. I think I decided in the back of my mind—the place where we make most of our decisions, back behind the thoughts that are loudest in our heads—that what you were experiencing was good, a gift. I think I thought you were going to share it with me some day and that we would have our own little secret story, our own world, one that you lived in and that I got to visit because I was your mamma.

Now I pray that wherever you are you can hear me. I pray that somehow you can let me in on whatever private world was pulling at you until it took you all the way out of your body and away from me.

* * *

My mind goes back to those boys, Ricky and Robbie, every time I think about how your life ended. We see the family every Sunday at church and both boys always put on their best clothes and look like little angels, cleaned up, the threat of their daddy's anger coming out at them if they don't behave like gentlemen. But there's something about them I never quite trusted. Something about the way they smile at the adults, then their faces change to something hard and glassy-eyed when they think no one is looking.

Since they are both a little older than Martha, I thought one of them might take an interest in her. That never happened, but it was clear to me that they always had their eyes on you in church. I noticed them snickering when you walked by, their faces changing as soon as an adult looked over. I always felt that prickly feeling in my spine when I'd see that, but there wasn't anything for me to connect it to, so I let it go. I convinced myself I was just an overprotective mother making up stories. Even now, with things settled and the two of them going about their lives as though they had nothing to do with what happened to you, I wonder. Something doesn't sit right with me. But I guess I'll never know.

I think about the story Father Comeaux told me—about what those boys said about you going into the woods. I should have talked with you about it then. I should have talked to those boys and their parents. It's still suspicious to me that they just happened to have been in the woods that night you died, that they were the only ones who saw anything of what happened to you. How I wish I could go back in time and have been with you there, at the edge of the water, under the arms of those moss-covered trees.

* * *

Right now, I want to think about you as you were when you were happy, especially in the year before you died. When we weren't thinking about a long life without you. I remember how much you loved feeding the chickens in the morning, the way you named each one, even though I knew we were going to have some of those birds for dinner, cooked in a gumbo or chicken fricassee. You never asked and I never told you what happened when one of the chickens disappeared from our flock. We just pretended it had gone off into the woods for a wild, new life.

You named them after flowers and plants, sometimes after things in the sky. Rosebud, Rosemary, Lavender. Star, Moonlight, Sunshine. They'd come running when you'd go outside, following you around like you were their mother, and you'd sit down in the dirt in the middle of them and hand-feed them worms and tiny bugs. I'd watch you through the window, thinking about how close you seemed to be to all of God's creations, the living ones and even the things without life in them, like the rocks and dirt around our house. You made me wonder if even those things had life in them, because things seemed to light up around you, Lily, as though you carried a lantern that turned things on that needed to feel the touch of something beautiful to come alive.

I remember how much you loved to go looking for berries, wild herbs growing in the woods. You even picked and brought home mushrooms once or twice, and knew not to taste them before you gave them to me to cook. We'd talked about how not everything that grows is safe to eat and I was so glad that you had good sense.

I don't know what happened to you that night you died, but I do know you had good sense about nature and being safe in it, which is why I still don't believe what the Benoit boys finally said about what happened, what they saw that night. It doesn't add up with what I know about you. I wish you could talk and tell me what happened, Lily. I wish you were here.

CHAPTER 25—ALICE

July 2019, Berkeley, California

Ronan knocked on Alice's door at exactly 2 p.m. Her body relaxed and she smiled when she opened it, seeing him standing next to her small garden of potted plants. He wore a crisp emerald-green cotton shirt and khaki shorts, the sunlight streaming behind him, creating a glow around his frame.

"Ready to head out? It's a gorgeous day." He leaned over and kissed her, surprising her with his ease in this simple gesture. She kissed him back, then pulled away gently.

"I'm ready." Grabbing her tote bag, she noticed how prompt he was. Reliable. Steady. She put her straw sunhat on and said goodbye to Isabella. They headed to his car, a blue hybrid with beach towels, a surfboard, and a wetsuit in the back seat.

"I thought I might surf for a bit after we leave the center, if you don't mind."

"I'd love that. You're braver than I am. Between sharks and the ice-cold water in this part of the ocean, getting in past my ankles is a big deal."

"I won't be in the water too long—we have dinner reservations at eight in Petaluma." He took her bag and opened the car door. She plopped her sunglasses on, smiling, as she got in. Yes, gorgeous day indeed.

* * *

The drive took them around the northern end of the San Francisco Bay, across the Richmond San Rafael Bridge. Seeing the bay sparkle, sailboats floating like kites that had been anchored to the water, sea birds in flight across the bright blue sky, Alice thought of how much she appreciated the beauty of where she lived. This part of the world was magical. Gulls, pelicans, and snowy plovers graced the scenery, some flying high, others skimming the water for food. Her mind went back to everything she'd seen in San Diego, thoughts about what human interactions were doing to the habitats of these magnificent creatures.

"My trip to San Diego was so great, and I got the article in. I have to say, though, that after what I observed there I can't shake the thought that so much of what we do is harming the homes of sea life and animals. It's strange, but I keep feeling like I'm supposed to do something with all this."

"The ocean environment is definitely precious." Ronan kept his eyes on the road as he took a hairpin turn around the mountain.

"After I saw the seal and then the sea lion, I started poking around on the internet." Alice stared out the window as she spoke, taking in the water and open sky. "It seems that sea mammals wash up in need of help much more often than I thought they did. I'm glad you're taking me out to see where you volunteer. Maybe it will give me a brighter outlook."

"I understand. I went into cartography because I thought that being part of a field that maps things would mean I could be part of solutions, but sometimes it feels like what I do is just extractive. Mapping things so big businesses can find resources to exploit."

"I never thought of it that way. I went into magazine writing so I could tell human stories that might make people be more understanding of each other. I'm not so sure that's what my work is about right now."

Ronan spoke softly.

"On my first visit here, I fell in love." He looked over at Alice, his face serious. "With a Pacific harbor seal." His mouth cracked open to a wide smile, eyes crinkling at the edges. "Her name was Millie and she'd been there for a few weeks after having been hit by a sea vessel. I fell in love with her spots and smile and the way she seemed to know me when I visited her, nudging my hand for treats. I was there every Saturday for a while, helping out with other tasks, but I always visited her. When she was released back to the ocean, I took the day off of work so I could be there. Magical sight—seeing her go back into the sea where she belongs."

The sunlight fell on his face as they turned another curve. He braked gently, and Alice noticed the muscles in his legs tense then release as he pushed on the pedals. Warmth flushed through her. She looked back out the passenger window and watched as a cyclist took the next hairpin turn with sharp precision.

It looked dangerous, the cyclist's moves. So fast. Things could so quickly spin out of control.

As though sensing her thoughts, Ronan reached to her with his right hand and took hers for a moment, then returned to steering the car with both hands. He had the car under control. Things were under control. At least for the moment.

They came to a slow stop behind a long line of cars as they approached the entry through a tunnel to the headlands.

"I've never actually been out here before," she said. She realized she wanted him to take her hand again.

"It's a one-way tunnel, so we have to wait until all of the cars coming this way get out before it's our turn. Kind of like waiting for a ride at an amusement park, but instead of going on a scary ride, we get to see an area that's cut off from the rest of the world, preserved out here away from busy cities."

They sat in silence until the line of cars in front of them began to move. As they entered the long tunnel, Alice did feel like they were on an amusement park ride. Everything closed in around them as they sped through the enclosed space. Closing her eyes, ocean waves washed through in her mind, the face of a turtle popping up momentarily, then receding back into the water. A seal appeared before her, its puppy-like face beckoning her, then the image faded away. As they emerged from the tunnel on the other side, she opened her eyes, taking in the breathtaking beauty of the hills around them. They continued around mountain curves, glimpses of the ocean peeking out in moments, then vanishing. They landed in a large parking lot filled with cars.

"Since it's Saturday, there will be a lot of people here. I scheduled a tour so you can learn about the center from one of the guides, but we can also peek around a bit since I'm a volunteer."

They were greeted by the squeal and laughter of children. Alice turned and saw a school bus with kids pouring out.

"Looks like we'll get to experience this with a group of kids," Ronan said, taking her hand as they walked toward the building. "They always have the best questions."

After checking in, Alice walked through the small gift shop. A large cotton beach blanket with a picture of a seal lying on a beach caught her attention. Its face mirrored the one she had seen as they drove through the tunnel. She purchased it along with a pair of earrings made of sea glass found on a nearby beach.

Ronan guided her out to the courtyard where the tour began. The swarm of children encircled them, and the guide welcomed them all.

"Meet our favorite friend," he said, waving toward a large sculpture. "He's a Northern Elephant Seal. Do you notice anything about him?"

The children started answering all at once.

"He's huge!"

"He looks like he can't walk very far."

"He has a funny smiling face that makes me laugh."

"You're all correct," the guide said. "These guys can grow to be sixteen feet long. As you can see, he doesn't have those flippers that look like feet like some types of seals do. These guys *palump* along on the sand. They're mammals, so they give birth to their babies and nurse them, just like people. They are also amphibious. Does anyone know what that means?

"It means they can live on land and in the sea." A small voice piped up from the middle of the crowd of children. "They're special because they connect the sea animals to the people."

Alice looked down at the child's smiling face. Young girl. White cotton dress. Her body swaying back and forth gently as she spoke.

"That's right," the guide said. "Do you know anything else about them?"

"If they could talk, maybe they could teach us what it's like to live underwater." The girl paused. "I've always wondered what that would be like."

Alice felt her stomach lurch. Images of the little girl at the park in Berkeley flashed before her.

"They could teach us a lot," the guide said. "And we have a lot to learn. Let's walk inside and I'll show you where we care for the ones that end up here. Seals, sea lions, and otters that come to us have all been hurt in some way, sometimes from being hit by ships, sometimes because they don't have enough to eat. Sometimes their parents are hurt and can't care for them. We'll start by seeing the kitchen where food is prepared."

He led the group toward a covered walkway between two buildings, both with large windows. In one building, a group of people in blue t-shirts stood cutting up fresh fish and putting it in buckets. As the guide led them to the window, Alice and Ronan stayed behind, allowing the school group to go ahead. The little girl hung at the back, standing near Alice. She continued to twirl back and forth as she watched the volunteers prepare a meal.

Dizziness hit Alice quickly as she watched the child. She didn't want Ronan to see her this way. As the guide began explaining the daily routine, she stepped back, leaning against a brick pillar. This wasn't the same little girl. Her dress was white, but it was decorated with blue edging—not exactly like the girl she'd seen at the park in Berkeley. None of these little girls were exactly the same. Of course they weren't. Coincidence. Just coincidences.

Ronan walked over and put his hand on her back. "Are you OK?"

"Just got a little dizzy. It happens sometimes. I'll be fine."

"Would you like to walk out and see the animals? It's just over here." He gestured toward an area on the other side of the walkway.

"Yes, that would be great," Alice said, taking his hand. She didn't want to admit that she needed it to steady herself.

They walked out to an area overlooking a large outdoor animal hospital. Black wired cages lined the pavement, side by side, each with a seal or sea lion inside. People moved from one to another, bringing buckets of fresh fish or playfully interacting with the animals. In one larger cage, two seals napped next to each other, snuggled closely together.

"I heard they just brought a pair in yesterday, a seal and a turtle, both found on the coast near here, just a mile apart. The seal is malnourished and the turtle was injured by a fisherman's hook. They named the turtle Orion and the seal Cassiopeia.

Orion shouldn't be up this far north. He'll be sent down to the Pacific Marine Mammal Center where Aunt Annie volunteers—the waters here are too cold for sea turtles."

"Can we see them?"

"I'll ask. But first, look up at the mountains. They remind me of Ireland. Gold, green, amber. We've had a lot of rain this year so everything is alive and beautiful. One of the reasons I feel so comfortable here is because it reminds me of my childhood home."

The mountains circling the center were majestic. Sunlight filtered down through clouds, the sky powderpuff blue. Trees dotted the landscape along with scattered sage bushes and brush. The sea was just visible around the corner, sea mist falling over everything, creating a magical aura. The salty air helped bring Alice back from the dizziness she'd been feeling, reminding her, too, of her childhood, visits to the beaches along the Gulf of Mexico, warm Southern waters.

"It's beautiful. Thank you for bringing me here." She squeezed his hand, aware that their bodies brushed against each other, mirroring the seals napping in their open-air cage.

They walked down the steps and Ronan found a staff member who brought them to visit Cassiopeia. She looked up at them with large brown eyes from where she lay.

"We can't bring you to see Orion because he's in a tank inside," the man said. "Hopefully he'll stay alive long enough for us to get him down south, where he belongs."

Alice leaned down and looked into Cassiopeia's eyes. *What are you thinking? What's happened to you? And what can we do to help you, help all of you?* The thoughts moved through her mind in a jumble, tears unexpectedly threatening to trickle down her face. The seal looked into her eyes, holding her with its gaze, as though trying to communicate with her. No words, only a warm sensation running through Alice as she stayed locked—eye to eye—with the majestic animal.

What was she seeing in those eyes? Grandmere Grace's words popped into her mind: *So much life is below the surface, and there is much to understand for those who have eyes to see and ears to hear.*

Alice stood, taking Ronan's hand, wondering if he, too, could see the seal's silent pleas or understand what she was trying to tell them.

* * *

Later, Alice perused the scene before her, her pink flip flops lying next to Ronan's brown ones on the beach blanket she'd purchased earlier. His surfboard and her sunhat perched together near a bottle of sunscreen. Remnants of crab claws that had drifted in earlier with the tide, now poking through the sand. Green-black seaweed stretching out as a fan-shaped tapestry, lapping gently at the spot where the waves fluttered over the shoreline, leaving creamy dollops of foam behind. They'd driven to Stinson Beach after leaving the center and taken a walk on the stretch where she'd first seen him standing against the shoreline.

She bumped her arm and shoulder lightly against his. "You've never told me about the song you were singing that day we met."

"You're right," he said, gently bumping her back. "Maybe that's a story for another time. For now, you can watch me surf." He smiled, kissed her gently on the lips, and walked toward the car to get his wetsuit. A slight sheen of sweat glistened on his back, the muscles in his calves bulging with each step.

Alice pulled her journal out of her backpack and stared at it. No words came. Ronan returned a few minutes later, picked up his surfboard, and moved out into the water, taking large leaps in the shallows, laughing.

He dove into the water full body then surfaced, his head popping up between waves, the surfboard floating beside him. He held it with one hand and waved to Alice with the other. *A seal. He looks like a seal. And I'm a turtle, afraid to pull myself out of my shell.*

She laid down on her belly, relishing the warm rays of the sun. Ronan's lithe body moved into standing position on the surfboard and he rode a wave close to the shore, then pushed back out into the sea, the light around him translucent.

He's beautiful. Sleek. Magnificent. And he likes me.

Her thoughts drifted away with the lulling sound of the waves, the edges of her body dissolving until she felt like she was one with the sand. Her eyes closed, the image of the seal she had seen sleeping on the beach faded in and out of her mind as she rested beneath the afternoon sun.

* * *

The drive from Stinson Beach to Petaluma took just under an hour. He drove them through the small hippie town of Bolinas and they stopped for coffee, enjoying people watching. A band was setting up for an outdoor concert that evening and a crowd was gathering. The air smelled like sea salt and Alice wondered if they should come over sometime and rent a place to stay, spend a weekend at the coast. Surprised by this thought—of spending a weekend away with him—she focused on the small stores along the tiny main street running through the town. Jewelry made of semiprecious gemstones, hand-crafted soap, cotton t-shirts with bright designs all for sale, hanging out of shop doors.

As they drove out of town, headed north, they passed a sign for St. Mary Magdalene Catholic Church. Alice turned her eyes toward the road when she saw it, distracting herself from the image it brought up. The church in Berkeley near her new apartment—another one dedicated to Mary Magdalene. How many of those could there be in such a small region? Berkeley was just across the bay. The memory of that day, of the little girl, the image of the small casket in the front of the church, the sounds of people crying, one woman's voice rising above the others . . .

"What are you thinking?" Ronan took her hand as he asked, gently breaking through her thoughts.

"Not much," she said. Should she tell him about the strange experiences she'd been having? Her haunting dreams? Not yet. *Things are going well. Keep it simple. Put your head back into the shell here.* She squeezed his hand, grateful for his kindness. She didn't want to break the beauty of the afternoon or bring something heavy to their dinner date. "Just enjoying the amazing ride."

"This is one of my favorite drives," he said, putting both hands back on the steering wheel, focusing on the road. They took sharp turns around curves, each one bringing new flashes of beauty. The sun was lower on the horizon now, painting the hillsides with shades of green, gold, yellow, and brown, wildflowers popping up everywhere. They passed eucalyptus trees with tall, willowy, pale trunks, their leaves hanging down like hair, reminding Alice of the curly gray moss that hung from oak trees.

"The trees look a little like women dancing along the side of the road, don't they?" She put her sunglasses on as she spoke, resting her head on the headrest of her seat, settling in for the remainder of the drive.

"They do," Ronan said, his voice soft. "If you look at things the right way, everything seems to be dancing, right?"

Alice smiled, then placed her hand on his knee. Silence settled over them, each with their own thoughts but together in the safe harbor of his car, moving down the road, dappled light shining on them through the trees.

CHAPTER 26—ALICE

July 2019, Berkeley, California

Basil, mozzarella . . . what else did she need? The recipe Madeline had given her for baked caprese chicken was simple and she had tomatoes. Wandering the aisles of the grocery store, her eye caught the wine section. Without thinking she pushed her cart toward the chardonnays. Maybe the one she'd bought when she was near Stinson Beach would be here?

Only one bottle of it was on the shelf and as she put it into her cart, a mix of feelings stirred.

What, exactly, was she doing with Ronan? Their dinner date had been amazing. He was gorgeous, kind, funny. And he had a good career and seemed interested in hers. Easy conversation, laughter, attraction. It was all there.

Crackers. She needed crackers and bread. Her hand reached to pull a fresh-baked loaf of French bread from the rack at the end of the wine aisle, and memories of dinner at the restaurant flashed before her.

Ronan's hand offering her a chunk of bread dipped in olive oil. Romantic. Playful. Wasn't that what she wanted in a guy? The date had been perfect.

Until the drive home. Until Cassiopeia's eyes kept appearing before her as they drove under the night sky. The whole hour as they drove from the restaurant in the wine country to Berkeley, the seal's plaintive eyes haunted her. What did she want? What was she saying?

When they pulled in front of her apartment, Ronan leaned over, kissing her, a quiet question. Should he come in? She kissed him back then stopped, putting her head on his shoulder. She was suddenly flooded with memories of her past relationships, most ending at this moment. When she had to decide whether to trust or pull inside. To open herself or close.

The words seemed to come from some place deep inside, instinctive. Reflexive.

"I'm really tired, but I had a great night. Thanks for everything today." She pulled herself out of his arms, leaning back against the seat.

"Maybe we can do it again next weekend? Or something like it?" He wrapped his hand around hers as he spoke.

"Sure. Let's talk sometime this week."

As she closed the door minutes later and his car pulled away, Cassiopeia's face returned, her spirit's presence seeming to fill the small apartment. Haunted, confused, Alice slept restlessly, hoping the young girl wouldn't appear in her dreams. She needed rest. It hadn't come.

"Are you ready to check out?" The words broke into Alice's thoughts. In line now at the checkout stand—how had she gotten here? Even simple things like walking through the grocery store seemed too much for her brain to handle.

"Yes. I'm ready."

After paying and settling into her car, she picked up her phone. A call to Sophia might help her feel more settled.

"Hi, Sophia." Alice said when her sister picked up. "Am I interrupting your Sunday?"

"Nope. We just finished lunch and we're running errands this afternoon. What are you up to?"

"I just finished grocery shopping. Resting up today before the work week starts."

"How was your trip to San Diego?"

Alice paused. "Good—um, great. It's beautiful, of course. Have you ever been?"

"No, but we've talked about going. Did you get to do a lot of high-end tourist things?"

"Yes. And . . . it was fun. And a little unsettling because we saw sea mammals washed up on shore, an injured seal and a sea lion that had died. Kind of put a reality lens on the whole *paradise* image of the trip. But I got the article in on time, and I think my editor is happy with it."

"Sorry to hear about that. I just read an article about harbor seals that spend part of the year on the coastline of New York. Fascinating story. Apparently, the males woo the females by singing to them in groups—their own little mating ritual."

Alice paused. Seals singing? Like whales? She thought of the boat ride the last day in San Diego, the mingling in her mind of the songs and sounds of animals and stars and people everywhere around the globe. Mental note—look up seal songs. "Wow. I didn't know that. Your story makes up for mine, thinking of the magic of the animal world instead of the destruction of it."

"Yeah. It's good to balance the hard stuff we hear with good news. If we don't look for the good, things can seem pretty bleak. Speaking of good, how are things going with that guy you met?"

"We spent the day together yesterday. He took me to the Marine Mammal Center on the coast where he volunteers, then we went to Stinson Beach and ended the day with a nice seafood dinner."

"Sounds like a pretty fabulous guy. How are you feeling about all this? Thinking of giving this one a try? Did he spend the night?"

"No, he didn't spend the night. I'm not really sure I want a relationship right now. My work is pretty full." Testing the words on herself as she shared this thought with her sister, she wondered if Sophia's response might help her make sense of things.

"But you like him? Maybe you should give him a chance?"

"I do like him. I'm just not sure it's a relationship I want to pursue, that's all." The lie—*what I think is happening isn't real*—appearing in a new form now.

"You told me about the carved turtle he gave you. Malachite shell, right?"

"Yes. It's on my dresser, next to the jewelry box Great Grandmere Grace gave me. Do you remember that?" Change the subject away from Ronan. Maybe Sophia could help her make sense of everything else that was happening.

"I do. I wished she had given it to me, but she must have thought you'd take care of it."

"You know, I called Grandmere Martha and asked her about it." Alice paused, unsure again how much she wanted to share.

"What did she tell you?"

"She didn't know much about it. When I open the lid, it still has a slight scent of Grandmere Grace's perfume. Can you believe that?"

"I can. When I work on estate sales here, sometimes the jewelry comes in old jewelry boxes, packed with all sorts of things. It's amazing how scents of the past can linger on in items that are kept hidden away. It's one of my favorite parts of the job—discovering new things that are really old things from the past, treasures that might be given a second or third life in a new generation."

“I love that thought, the image of what you do. I wish I felt that kind of magic with my job.”

“What do you mean? You have your dream job. You spend your days writing, and you just got back from a trip to San Diego.”

“Yes.” Alice was silent. She wasn’t ready to talk about the growing feeling that her career was pulling her in the wrong direction, even though she didn’t know what the right direction might be.

“I gotta run,” Sophia said, Camille’s voice now audible in the background. “Enjoy the rest of your Sunday and let me know how things go.”

“I will. I love you, sis.”

“You too, Alice.”

* * *

The gift came in a large manila envelope, Alice’s name and address written in Grandmere Martha’s unmistakable shaky handwriting. Alice pulled it out of the mailbox on the way in to her apartment, juggling her keys as she opened the door and dodged Isabella trying to squeeze her way outside.

“Stay inside,” Alice said to the cat. “Looks like we have something to open.”

The envelope was padded. Alice plopped on the couch, eyeing the small white printed label with the return address. Magnolias surrounded her grandmother’s name. The heady scent of magnolia bushes in her family’s yard came to mind, their white flowers like bright stars in a sea of green leaves.

Alice opened the envelope and slid her hand inside, immediately feeling the soft leather covering of a small book. She slipped it out then reached back in to see what else was there. Rose petals and a card, sealed up in an envelope. She poured the rose petals on her coffee table, picturing her grandmother cutting roses in her yard, carefully arranging them in vases, and decorating her house with them throughout the spring and summer.

She opened the card first.

Dear Alice,

I found this journal after we talked on the phone. Our conversation got me thinking, and I went to the closet and pulled out a few boxes that had been there for decades. Going through them brought back so many memories. This journal was in a box of old books my mother had, and somehow, I never saw it before. She must have taped this box up herself before she died.

I thought you should read it. I thought about copying the pages for you and keeping the journal, but I think she may have wanted you to be able to read this in her handwriting. I read it cover to cover and the words are now etched in my mind, which is all I need. Thank you for asking me the questions that got me looking for this. That was a gift you didn't know you were giving me, and I'm grateful.

Je t'aime, Alice.

Grandmere Grace

Alice opened the cover of the green journal, noting the year written on the first page—1934. The card in the jewelry box she had been given had the date June 21, 1934. This journal was written the same year. She turned to the first page and melted into the couch as she began reading.

The world split open the day you were born.

* * *

Alice read the first sections without stopping, riveted by the echo of her great-grandmother's voice on the pages. Isabella had given up on trying to get outside and was napping on the windowsill. After reading about Lily's funeral, Alice stopped and closed her eyes, an unnamable grief threatening to overtake her.

The little girls in white nightgowns and dresses appearing everywhere.

The acorn the little girl had given Alice. *Her name is Martha.*

The image of the small coffin in the church, the aching wail of a woman mired in grief.

The dreams—of being pulled into water, of vague images that floated in front of her then receded before she could make sense of them.

And what of the images of the shotgun? Was it all connected?

And—was it possible that all of these things that had been a part of her great-grandmother's life were now seeping into her own, through the cracks of her psyche? And even finding their way into her daytime reality? How was this possible?

The jewelry box, now displayed in the middle of her bookshelf, caught her attention. She walked over, opened the lid, picked up the scarf that was nestled inside. She put it on her neck, the faint scent of gardenias floating up to tickle her nose, bringing back more memories of gardens from her childhood. She picked up the river rock, nestled it into her palm. Warmth pulsed through her hand again. What was its message? What was she supposed to do?

She turned back to the couch, looked at the journal, and decided to leave it for now. She had read as much as she could process for the day. Tomorrow she would read more.

The last words she had read haunted her. She opened the journal and read them again, before closing the book.

The world opened when you were born and closed when you died and now you are everywhere, like the air wrapping around us after a thunderstorm, thick and pure and hanging with the deep scent of water from the heavens.

CHAPTER 27—GRACE

July 1934, Richarme, Louisiana

We went out one Saturday to pick blackberries for pie late last summer. My mind keeps going back to that day. We wandered down the road to a patch just near the church and I saw Father Comeaux standing on the steps and decided to go over and talk to him. I left you alone for a few minutes picking honeysuckle, trusting you'd be fine. I was only away from you for ten minutes or so, and when I came back to find you near those honeysuckle bushes, I could see that something had frightened you. I asked what was wrong but you wouldn't tell me. Your eyes had a look that let me know you were far away again, wherever it was you used to go. Round and wide open with a hazy glaze over them—that look came over you either when you were seeing into those other worlds or when something scared you into going there on your own, taking your spirit to a place that must have seemed safer to you.

I saw those boys walking away from you just before I walked over, so I knew they had something to do with whatever happened. Rather than talk to them directly about it, I decided I'd follow them a little way and see if I could hear them talk, hoping they'd say something. I walked down the dirt path as though I was looking for a good patch of honeysuckle and I caught up close enough to them to hear them snickering and talking about you.

"That girl ain't right."

"She acts like she ain't from around here."

"Like she's from outer space, the way she acts."

"She oughta go back to wherever she's from. She ain't one of us. She don't belong here."

"Did you hear her talking to the bushes, asking the honeysuckle if it wanted to go home with her? Same way she talks to that tree in the woods and to those otters in the river. She's crazier than an old hen."

"She knows we're on to her, though. Did you see how wide her eyes opened when I asked her what the moss says? I'll laugh about that look on her face all day. Crazy girl."

I turned around to walk back toward you, my mind running through with so many thoughts. Of course you talked to trees and all kinds of things. For you, they were alive and deserving of God's love just like people. Something in me got nervous hearing them, Lily Mae, and I did what I always did then. I pushed it down and decided it wasn't anything more than two boys with nothing much to do, making up stories to amuse themselves. I didn't like what they said about you or how they seemed to upset you, but I told myself that you'd have to find a way to live in this world and deal with people like that, so the best thing for me to do was to love you and let you work some of these things out on your own.

I think about that day a lot, Lily. If I'd gone up and shaken those boys up a little by letting them know that I was on to *them*, maybe they'd have stopped bothering you. Maybe things would be different.

But *maybe* and *what ifs* aren't bringing you back. I know that.

* * *

The morning I woke up to find you gone started with the same sound that brought you into the world. Lightning struck a nearby tree and jolted me out of bed. The first light of dawn had just started creeping into our room and I was in the middle of a dream. When the lightning struck, I was struggling with an octopus that had wrapped itself around me, trying to pull its tentacles off my arms. I was breathing fast, my chest stretched tight with fear as I tried to peel those spiny arms off. I was suffocating, Lily, before I even woke up, that first day of my learning to live without you in this world.

I pushed the bed covers away and tried not to wake your daddy. He can sleep through anything, as you know. I crawled out of bed and headed to the kitchen to get some water, hoping to quiet my mind and shake off the feeling of being strangled. When I walked by your bedroom door, I saw Martha, awake, looking over at me as though she had something she didn't want to tell me.

I think I knew before I even set one foot into that room that our lives were changed, that a dark veil had come over any happiness in our home. I saw right away that your bed was empty.

"She's been gone a while, Maman. I woke up when the storm started and she wasn't here. I kept thinking she'd be back. I'm sorry Maman. I'm sorry I didn't stop her from going out. I've tried before, but she never listens to me. I'm sorry I've never told you."

I knew in that moment that I'd given her a heavy burden to carry. She'd known that you'd been going outside in the middle of the night but didn't want to tell me. She'd been carrying the weight of keeping your secret and I never helped her with that when I had a chance. In that moment, some part of me knew I should have asked more questions about what Father Comeaux had said about you being in the woods late at night. My own fear had pushed me back into hiding from the truth, and your sister had to hold it on her own.

Later, after the funeral and after the relatives had gone and we were all trying to fill up the horrible emptiness in the house, she told me that she'd thought about telling me but didn't because she thought you never went far. She said she tried to talk you out of it, but you always told her it was fine because Mamou was with you, watching over you wherever you went. Martha hoped that was true, but realized too late that Mamou couldn't save you from whatever happened that night. She told me you'd crawl out of the window and come back in late, your feet wet from mud, your hair decorated with leaves.

Martha said you were always smiling when you came back in, so she thought that whatever you did, it must have been alright. You were always braver than Martha—although she'd hate to know I think that—but I think she knew that part of why she never stopped you was because she was too afraid herself of going out and doing something like what you did. I think she felt that she should have been the one to lead you to do things, not the other way around. In one way or another, Martha and I both suffered from our own fears, and we let you down because of it. I pray Martha can let go of any feelings she has about that, because I know that in the end, I'm the one who holds all the blame.

You were the brave shining star among us, Lily. Shining on still, I imagine, wherever you are in the heavens. I look up sometimes, hoping I can figure out which one of those lights is you, which one might be the one for me to follow when I feel like I'm losing my way in this life.

* * *

There are moments that are frozen like a memory held in time, unchanging, etched in the very cells of your being. They can come back to us in a flash, as a gift or a warning, a blessing or a curse. And if we stop what we're doing and let them wash over us, we can slip through the folds of time and be there again. We can live those moments over and over, each time getting something new. Each time settling a little more deeply into whatever we're meant to learn or experience or understand.

The moment I saw you lying near the bank of the stream that morning is one of those for me. I still don't know how I knew where to find you. After I left Martha's room, I walked out to the front porch and stood still for a moment. I said a little prayer, asking Mamou to help me. She may have been the one to direct me toward you, out the back and through the trail that led to that place in the woods you loved so much. I saw moss hanging from a big oak and it pulled me, as though the ends of that moss had hands that reached out through the silent air and drew me toward it. The tree is so big that I couldn't see around the trunk of it until I got up close. When I did, I heard the sounds of the river nearby and walked toward the gurgling.

I took a step around the tree, dipping my head below the moss, and the first thing that greeted me was the sight of your bare feet, coming out from below your nightgown.

I remember how they looked, Lily. For just a moment, I flashed back to the day you were born, the moment I saw your tiny feet for the first time. That morning at the water, your toes looked as perfect as they did when you were born into this world, soft and still, the color of polished ivory. My gaze fixed there on your feet, something in me not wanting to look beyond the edge of your nightgown, up to where your body and beautiful face told me that you were no longer with us. No longer with *me*.

The sun was slowly peeking through the trees. The rain had stopped—suddenly—as though it had come only to wash your spirit to heaven, with that one lightning bolt a short time earlier to wake me up so I could find you, there, that moment, at the river.

I held my breath, hoping I'd hear some sound come from you, something that would let me believe that if we could just get you moving, you and I could walk back to the house together. I felt in my bones, though, that your sweet body was just that, a body, no longer holding your spirit. It was just you and me for that short amount of time before I called for help, and even though you weren't in your body anymore, I know you were in the air and the trees and clouds above me. You were in the dirt below my feet and the water gently swishing by in that stream.

I dream about that moment sometimes—when your brightness was all around me. I couldn't see it in that moment, but I know it was there. In my dreams, I'm standing before a river of silver, flowing slowly by me, flickering light off in every direction like diamonds setting off the sunlight. And then I feel it, something warm and lovely coming up from the ground, up through my bare feet—like yours were that morning—softening and brightening everything inside me until I can't hold it all anymore, can't contain the bursts of love pulsing through every vein in my body. I wake up trembling from the feeling and it always takes me half a day to pull myself back into this world around me.

I know those dreams are showing me what was happening on another level, Lily, one I couldn't see that morning. You were shining all around me, free from the ties of your life here, loving me bigger than anything I could imagine. But I didn't see or feel it then because my own shock and grief filled me and halted me into a kind of blind numbness. My life will always be drawn by the line of that morning, before and after the moment I picked up your body and cradled it in my arms, my tears washing over you with a prayer that you'd come back to life, that you'd move your arm or open your eyes and look at me. The first time I held you, your eyes were wide open, taking in everything around you, most of all my face shining down on you with love. That morning, your eyes were closed, Lily, and mine were so wet from tears that I could barely see you, lifeless in my arms.

* * *

What I don't want to remember from that day, Lily, was the bruise, the gouge on your face, the place where the jagged rock cut into your head and took your life away. I want to remember your face as beautiful as it was when you were alive, with sparks of light coming out of your eyes, your cheeks red from being outside. The cut on your head was deep and your face was covered in blood, and later the doctor who looked over you said you'd sprained your ankle when you fell. Bruises covered your legs.

What happened, Lily? What were you doing out there that night? You were holding Mamou's river rock, her healing stone, when you died. It was still there when I found you. What were you doing out there? Were you visiting her? Later I learned how that stone had been important to you, but that day, it only added to the mystery of how you died, of what happened to you.

How could you have fallen and hurt yourself so badly that it ended your life, when you knew those woods so well? I will never understand, and I just can't believe what the Benoit boys finally said about it. They're the only ones who seemed to have known anything, and I know as certain as I know my own name that they'll never tell the truth about it. Never.

This is what they said—that they saw you throw yourself into the water like a crazed person. They told that to their parents, according to Father Comeaux, after it came out that they'd been out hunting in the woods the same night you died. I know they didn't want to say a thing to anyone, but when word got out about what happened, people started to talk, everyone wondering how you could have been out there that night, Lily, and what it was that made you fall on those rocks. The boys' parents kept it to themselves for as long as they could, not telling anyone they knew those two had been out there and may have been the only ones to see you. I think they may have been afraid that someone else was out that night too, someone who might do harm to Robbie and Ricky, and maybe that's why they finally talked to those boys and then told Father Comeaux what they said.

How could they have seen you fall like that and then gone back home as though nothing had happened? They told their parents they were "awful sorry"—as though that would ever be enough. That they were so scared by watching you throw yourself into the water that they ran away before they saw what happened to you. Repentant, they were, to their parents and the priest, for running away like that, at least that's what Father Comeaux said. They were sorry, he said, that they didn't go over and help you. But I know they wouldn't have done that after what I heard them say about you, and their repentance was about as real as a snake's after it bites you and leaves you for dead.

I'm sorry to say and think that, Lily, but it is what I feel. Snake venom. That's what their repentance seems like to me.

CHAPTER 28–ALICE

July 2019, Berkeley, California

Amanda was waiting for Alice when she walked into her office, still groggy from sleeplessness and hazy dreams of funerals, marshy bayous, women moving in and out of the water, sometimes changing shape as they moved between the worlds.

"Great work on the San Diego article," Amanda said. "We'll run it next month. We just need a few more photos, so if you can reach out to the tour guides and ask them for some showing sunsets on the beach, that would be great. I love how you ended your article with the line about the green flash at sunset. I doubt they can send us a photo of that, but if they can, it would be perfect."

"I'll email Kaitlyn this morning."

"We liked it so much we have another assignment for you. Up for another trip?"

Another trip? Foggy thoughts and exhaustion weighed heavily on any excitement she might feel. Amanda jumped in with details before she could answer.

"Hawaii. Isn't that a great surprise? We'll send you to the Big Island. We want this article to follow up on what you wrote about the sea life on the beaches. We'd like to focus this on ocean-based vacations—more whale watching, swimming with turtles—that sort of thing. Show people the magic of being so close to animals in the sea."

Magic. That wasn't the thought surfacing in Alice's mind. The sea lion that had washed ashore, lifeless, filled her thoughts. How could she do another story about sea life without getting pulled down even deeper into the issues related to tourism, human behaviors, and the ways it all impacted the ocean environment? But how could she turn it down?

"Sounds great. I've never been to Hawaii. But I met someone from there in San Diego." Alice wondered what Tutu Amelia would think of this assignment.

"Maybe that's a great place to start researching. We're sending you in two weeks. I'll give you more details later, but I wanted to tell you now." Amanda tapped Alice's desk, smiling as she walked back to her office.

* * *

Early evening light cascaded over the houses in Alice's neighborhood, creating a glow around bright splashes of flowers in gardens: daisies, petunias, ranunculus, roses, lavender, and iris. Flowering trees, lemon trees, and camellia bushes burst with color in yards, and flowering weeds that Alice couldn't identify poked their tiny heads through the slats of picket fences, bowing to the sidewalk as though passersby were worthy of adoration.

The beauty eased her thoughts, allowing her to enjoy the graceful simplicity of the natural world. She needed to think. The work assignment in Hawaii was tempting—who wouldn't want to go? At the same time, the growing sense of being part of the problem tugged at her, a knotted rope pulling at her thoughts. Could she go and write about sea life from a different angle? Would they be open to that? Could it be more of an environmental piece, reflecting on the way human actions are impacting the homes of these magnificent sea creatures?

No. The magazine depended on ads from the tourist industry to survive. An article that pointed out the flaws of the world of high-end travel wouldn't do much for ad sales and the relationships with companies that had come to see the magazine as a perfect place to attract new customers. The job at the magazine was perfect on so many levels—good pay, flexibility, great co-workers. Most importantly, it offered the chance for high-profile bylines that could help her get the type of job she'd always wanted—writing for a national magazine with a focus on human interest stories. Stories that mattered. Stories that might change the world.

The park was quiet today, only a few families playing in the grass. The children's theater was empty. Alice walked to the oak tree where she'd met the little girl. The image of her standing there, talking about acorns, brought on a momentary wish to see her. Alice quickly pushed the thought away. She didn't need more distractions or interactions that muddled her thinking. She needed quiet.

She sat on the warm ground, leaning her back against the tree trunk, settling her body between roots. Maybe research would help her decide how to handle this assignment. That always worked—getting the facts straight. She pulled her phone from her pocket and clicked on the link for the tourist company Amanda had sent her as the focus of the article. Several options for tours popped up, including one that said "Visit ancient sites and see hidden places not usually open to tourists. Swim side-by-side with dolphins. We'll always get you closer than any other company!"

How close should you get to dolphins? And what sacred sites were they visiting? She typed in "ethics of swimming with dolphins" and found articles that set out guidelines. Swimming at least fifty feet away and not seeking them out seemed to be the minimum. How could she take this assignment on?

Curious about other types of sea life in the islands, she typed in "sea mammals in Hawaii." Stories popped up about Hawaiian monk seals, humpback whales, and northern elephant seals. Alice clicked on the image of the elephant seal. It was one of the types of seals treated at the Marine Mammal Center. The first article that popped up was a story of an adolescent seal that had eaten a plastic bag, mistaking it for food. It had died slowly and painfully, its body unable to process the man-made materials designed to last forever.

Alice's stomach turned, her body tightening, almost as though she had ingested plastic herself. She typed in "monk seal," hoping to see something more hopeful. Weren't people doing things to revive their population? She opened a story that talked about their history, where they had lived before becoming so close to extinction. She was surprised to learn that one had even been sighted in the Gulf of Mexico many years earlier, swimming up from the Caribbean before becoming extinct in that area of the world. The waters Alice had spent summers swimming as a child, where Grandmere Grace had loved to visit.

Bring the jewelry box to the ocean and you will find me there.

Alice thought of the stories she'd read about the shoreline of the Gulf coast states washing away, year by year, the water rising from global warming. *Grandmere Grace, the ocean is changing.* Everywhere, it seemed to be in trouble, signs of it washing up on every shore. The monk seals seemed even more like ancient messengers now, their slow journey toward extinction a very real sign of what was being lost.

At the bottom of the article, Alice saw a link to another story about monk seals being killed on the Big Island. She clicked on the link and immediately regretted it, her body reeling from the photo that popped up. A monk seal lying on a beach, shot in the head, a gaping hole where its right eye should have been. She skimmed the story quickly, unable to take in the details too deeply without feeling sick. A fisherman had done it, fighting for his own livelihood. Warming of the oceans was causing the food chain to diminish and monk seals were seen as competitors for the fish local people depended on to feed their families. The issue was splitting communities, some wanting to protect the monk seals, others wanting them kept away from the areas where they fished. Some of the fishermen ran businesses which had been in their families for generations.

Alice closed the browser. She closed her eyes, hoping to push out the images she'd seen,

The seals tied up in nets.

The elephant seal that died from eating a plastic bag.

The monk seal in Hawaii, shot in the head.

Then the image of the little girl at the river, her white-clad body limp, blood spooling from her head, overlaying itself on the image of the monk seal, their faces becoming one . . .

Everything began to spin. Alice pulled herself to standing, blinking her eyes, hoping that she could shake it all off, if she could just find a safe space between the worlds, the one that seeped into her mind through dreams and images and the real world of animals dying.

Orion and Cassiopeia. The seal and turtle at the Marine Mammal Center that had just arrived. How were they? Were they alive? The memory of Cassiopeia's eyes boring into Alice's held her. What had the seal been trying to say?

Alice needed to know. She had to see them. Walking quickly down the sidewalk now, she didn't see the flowers or the trees that had graced her walk to the park. Tears running down her face blinded her to any beauty around her. She had to drive out and see Orion and Cassiopeia. She couldn't do anything for the animals she'd seen suffering so badly online, and she couldn't do anything about the bigger problem of what was causing it all. But she could check on Orion and Cassiopeia. She had to see Cassiopeia's eyes—maybe that would give her some sense of peace and settle the whirlwind inside her.

CHAPTER 29—ALICE

July 2019, Berkeley, California

She drove with her body gripped in grief, in a slowly increasing panic, her chest constricting. Everything blurred—dreams, day visions, animals seeming to speak to her. Turtles beckoning, calling her. Seals dying on beaches, the otter family in the stream in Berkeley. Her grandmother's journals. A flash of Ronan swimming in the ocean, his head popping up above the waves like a seal himself.

As she drove through the tunnel toward the headlands, time seemed to fall in on itself, everything collapsing into this moment, bringing her to this place, this time, transporting her physically from the world behind to the protected world ahead, the place where sea mammals were cared for. The Marine headlands, which were federally protected to maintain a healthy habitat for marine life and birds and the small creatures that called this area home. Everything pulled her forward, tugged at her, carrying her to . . . what?

She wanted to see Cassiopeia and hear about Orion. To know that at least these two animals were healing, that they would be able to go back into the ocean where they belonged. She pushed out thoughts about growing dangers—rising sea levels, dwindling food chains, ice caps melting and changing the entire pattern of sea tides.

She couldn't think about that now. Only on seeing the seal alive, on maybe being able to understand what she was trying to say as her eyes bore into Alice's.

Her mind spinning, she rolled her windows down so she could smell the salty ocean air. A line of cars was exiting the parking lot. The center closed soon and she had to make it inside before visitors weren't allowed. Without looking, she took a quick left turn, dodging a car that was pulling out. Her body jerked and the sound of a crash exploded in her ears before her mind registered what was happening. Her car banged into a pole in front of her with such force that her body was thrust forward. Her head hit the steering wheel and bright lights flashed in front of her eyes. She slumped onto the steering wheel, everything around her going dark.

A dream-like hand reached toward her. Hazy faces appeared before her—three of them, Grandmere Grace, another woman whose smile mirrored that of her great grandmother, and a small child. All looking at her from above, bright sunlight shining around them.

Alice, we're always here. It's your time to do what you were born to do. One day, you will be with us. We'll always be watching over you, helping as we can.

"Are you OK?"

The man's voice jarred Alice, pulling her out of the haze. Disoriented, she lifted her head, which throbbed from what would surely be a large bruise. She looked left, her neck stiff and achy. A man and a woman with concerned looks on their faces stood beside her car.

"Can you move? You ran into the pole. Can we help you?"

Alice sat back. Lights still flashed in front of her eyes. Breathing slowly, she pulled her thoughts together. What had just happened?

"I . . . think I'm OK. I just didn't see the pole."

Opening the door, the man reached in and gently touched her arm. “Can you move? You have a little bump on your forehead. Is anything else hurt?”

“I feel a little in shock, but I think I can move.”

She slowly climbed out of the car, gently moving her body.

“I can move your car if you'd like,” the man offered. Alice nodded, grateful for his offer. She wasn't sure if she could do more than take a few steps without falling. He got in and maneuvered it into an open parking spot. The woman led Alice to a low wall, helping her sit down.

“We're volunteers here,” she said. “We'll call someone for you if you'd like.”

“I'll be OK. I'm just in shock.”

“It looks like you'll need a new bumper, and your head will probably have a little lump for a while.”

“I'm feeling more stable now. Thank you for your kindness.”

“Do you want something to drink? I have a water bottle in our car.”

“OK.” Alice thought of Cassiopeia. “Do you know how the new seal and turtle are, the ones that came in over the weekend? Cassiopeia and Orion?” Her voice trailed off, realizing that she may have sounded crazy, driving so wildly, getting to the center just as it was closing. All to see the two animals.

“I'm sorry to share this,” the woman said. “Cassiopeia didn't make it. She died this morning. They found a plastic bag in her body in addition to the malnutrition. Between those two things, she just couldn't pull through.”

Alice looked into her lap, her hands tightening into a clasp. She squeezed them together, the pulsing feeling helping to give her a sense of grounding as her head went light.

“Orion is doing fine, though,” the woman said. “He's headed down south to the Pacific Marine Mammal Center tomorrow. We're all hopeful for him. I'm sorry about Cassiopeia. We're heartbroken.”

Alice kept her head down. Unable to look up at the woman without risking breaking into tears, she let her breath slowly quiet the shaking in her body. Slow breath. She finally looked up. The man was walking toward them, holding Alice's car keys out.

"I think your car will drive fine. You'll just need to take it into a body shop. Do you think you're alright to drive?"

"Yes. I'll just sit here for a few more minutes and catch my breath."

The woman retrieved a bottle of water. "Drink this. It will help." She handed it to Alice.

Alice forced a smile. She was grateful for their help. And ready to be alone. "I'll be fine," she said again, as though to convince herself.

"Take care of yourself now," the man said. He took his wife's hand and they smiled at her and turned away, walking toward their car, bodies bumping up against each other in the way of couples who've been together a long time. Easy. Comforting.

Alice thought of Ronan, their walk on the beach over the weekend. She wanted to see him, have him wrap his arms around her. Ease the rising tide of emotion inside her. Help her sort all of this out—all of it.

But she couldn't call him, not now, when everything was crashing in on her, the visions happening constantly. She was barely holding herself together. A mess. A vulnerable, shaky mess.

She dropped her head and wept silently, her body shaking in cascading waves she could not control. The parking lot was mostly empty. The distant sound of the ocean washed through the high grasses around her, its gentle rhythm holding her as she allowed herself to finally let go, the tears dissolving everything going through her mind. The melody of a seagull calling out like a trumpeter, its low call filling the air around her, was the only other sound, a guardian above her as her body drained itself of emotion. Alone with the grasses and birds, the ocean and all the animals that lived there just over the hill, she had no sense of how much time passed before the tears finally subsided, her body slowly quieting.

No more thoughts. At last, only a still center point holding her, her arms wrapped tightly around her body.

CHAPTER 30—GRACE

July 1934, Richarme, Louisiana

At the funeral, everyone was so quiet it was as though the Earth had closed itself up, sucking out the sound along with your precious life. Martha stood next to me the whole time, holding my hand, as though she was afraid that if she didn't hold onto me, I might follow you into that grave. Losing two sisters in such a short time has changed them both forever, your sister and your brother, and I pray that they can find a way to heal and move on. Martha lives her life now afraid of everything, I'm sorry to say. And I don't think I'm much good to her. In a different way, I think I'm losing all of my children in one big wave washing over our family. I don't know how to change it, Lily, or how to undo what's happening and what continues to happen with you gone from us and no answers about why it happened. Father Comcaux prayed at the graveside, saying it's not for us to question God's ways, and that sometimes God takes the brightest and purest souls from this Earth when they are young. He said it to try to comfort us, I guess, but there is no comfort.

There was one moment that day that brought a bit of peace, though. It was a gray, rainy day when we buried you, raindrops coming down on us as we said our prayers and held to each other, trying to keep each other standing up through it all. We ended the service at your gravesite by singing "Amazing Grace," and just as we started on the verse about being there ten thousand years, bright shining like the sun, the clouds parted just a bit and let the sun peek through. A golden light shone down on us as we sang those words, putting a little spotlight on your headstone. I was holding Mamou's stone in my hand—your stone—and felt a warmth flood my whole body. I hold that moment close to me now, that sunlight shining down and the healing warmth moving through me as we sang. It made me think that song and the stone bridged the space between us, parting the waters from the sky and connecting us to you where you are in the heavens now.

After everyone left our house the day of your funeral, I pulled the quilt Mamou gave you out from the cedar chest. I hung it from the branches of the magnolia tree in front of the house. I think I wanted to leave a sign for you, something to guide you back home to us if your spirit needed it. I looked at it there with all of those patches, each one stitched by Mamou's hands, each one with a story behind the cloth it came from—a torn dress, a piece of an old blanket, a cut of material that grabbed her eye—and prayed that you two were together someplace, watching down over all of us. Watching over us like angels in the sky, holding all of the threads of our stories together until we can be with you there. I'm holding on to that picture in my mind until I can see what you two can see, and I can finally understand everything that happened.

* * *

I will stop writing now, Lily. My story ends here, with you far away from me and my soul looking up to find you. I don't think I can ever make sense of what happened, but I'm trying to make amends for anything that I did or didn't do that brought us to this place. I'm telling this story as a way to heal my own hurt, and maybe to make sure your story is told.

One thing I understand now is that we owe something to the past, and maybe we owe something even more to the future. We are born of the actual cells of the past—our mothers and grandmothers and great-grandmothers. All they lived, all they loved. All they did and didn't do. And the future comes from our own bodies. Our words and choices in each moment.

Lily, did I do enough? You died—left us like a monarch butterfly taking flight without anyone watching—and I wonder what I could have done to keep you here.

But maybe you were meant to go when you did. Young, innocent, beautiful. Still pure of heart, an angel of heaven sent here to bless our lives. What can I do, now that you're gone? I failed in whatever my responsibility was to you, at least while you were alive. What can I do now for whoever will come after us?

I know this, Lily, that all of our stories are woven together, like the threads and squares on the quilt Mamou made. We are all at the end of a whole set of strands of stories, and if we lose our connection to what came before us, to how we came to be who we are in this world, we can feel lost. Wandering souls, that's what we become. We can wander our whole lives not knowing what we're looking for, when what we need is to reconnect to what came before us. Weave ourselves into the quilt of stories and wrap ourselves in it, until we know our own place in the tapestry.

Your soul wandered away from me and I can't help but think that I could have helped you stay tethered to this Earth if I'd just known how to hold you tighter. I'm writing all of this down now so that one day, maybe another beautiful soul like you will find their way back and know where they belong, a part of our quilt, our family story.

And our quilt is part of the whole big story of this world. I think about the endless waves of the gulf stretching to the horizon and up to the stars—up to the sky paintings, where I think you are—and I can see that we're all strands in this great big universe of stories. We're all connected. We all belong here. We just have to find our place in the great big story that holds us together.

Your song goes on, Lily, and I will listen for it every day of my life, carrying me through until my day comes to join you and Haydee, wherever you are now.

Mamou

We are all part of one big story, Grace. And our individual stories are bigger than we understand.

There's more to the story of how Lily came to us.

Those boys did see her. They saw her that night Father Comeaux told you about and they saw her the night she died, the night she joined me—and little Haydee—in our world. They were out hunting in the woods, like they often did, looking for anything they could shoot with those guns. They were looking for the little family of otters Lily loved so much, I think. They came to the spot at the river where they usually were and saw Lily under the oak tree talking to us, her face shining and happy. You should know that, Grace. She was so happy just before it all happened. Bright shining like the sun, as the song goes.

She had come to see the otter family. They knew her and came out when she went to the river bank, calling out to them with her sweet sing-song voice. After she said hello to them, she came to the tree next to the bank and looked up, talking to those of us who are always here, always watching over.

When the boys saw her near the tree, they decided to get closer. I'm not sure what they were thinking, but they got near enough that they could see the whites of her eyes when they pointed their guns, aiming at her like she was one of the small animals they liked to kill. They were laughing, saying they weren't going to shoot her, just scare her a little.

She froze for a moment and everything began to spiral. I could see Billy aiming his gun at Antoine, Billy's face and the faces of those boys mixing together, and Lily's face blending together with Antoine's and Samuel's, all together in that moment, all of us. It was as though what had happened with Lily's great-grandfather was coming around to circle back to her, completing itself in that moment, mirroring the spiral on my healing stone that she held in her hand, but in a way that would bring only grief, not healing.

And from where I was, there was nothing I could do.

When the shots rang out, birds flew out of the trees. Nothing touched Lily, but the sound frightened her so badly that she ran away from the oak tree, tripping on the roots and falling into that stream of water, her body so terrorized that she didn't put her hands out to protect herself. Her head split open on the rocks and she died quickly, Grace. Know that. Haydee and I were there, lifting her out of that body, leaving it far away, taking her from any suffering that she might feel. She didn't suffer. She went quickly.

The mother otter swam up close to her, as though to honor that moment of her passing. Lily had named her Luna—like the moon—and in that moment, she gave Lily a blessing to carry her on her way to us, up to the heavens.

The boys had come to hunt those otters, and Lily had died instead. One small life given in place of another.

Now Lily is here with us, watching over you and everyone else, still the same bright light that she has always been, Grace.

Now she is a light in the firmament and you can look up and see her here with us. Shining over everything. One with everything.

CHAPTER 31–ALICE

July 2019, Berkeley, California

Ronan's face, softened with concern, was all she saw when she opened the door to her apartment. She'd broken down and called him before heading back to Berkeley, knowing that seeing him was the only thing that might ease the grief she felt. Now he stood in front of her, a bag of take-out dinner in one hand, his other reaching out to gently pull her into his arms.

"I'm glad you called, Alice." His voice was soothing. Isabella came up behind her, rubbing against her legs as she let her body rest in Ronan's arms. The cat purred, her body vibrating against Alice's ankles.

"Come in," Alice said. "I can make tea."

"I brought some Irish tea. I thought we might need something that comes from near the sea. My grandparents swear it can get a person through anything."

They walked into her apartment and sat on her couch, Isabella joining them, curling up next to Alice.

"I'm not sure what happened today, Ronan. I was offered another assignment, this one in Hawaii. They want me to write more about travel tours where people can get close up to sea animals. I said yes, of course, because what choice do I have? And why wouldn't I want to go to Hawaii? But I'm just not sure how I can do it. Everything I keep seeing, everything that seems to be happening . . ." Her words trailed off.

He took her hand, pulled her into his arms again.

"You see what others don't always see, Alice. You can sense the layers between and beneath everything, which not many people can do. You're sensitive, and it isn't easy living in the world when you can see and feel so much. Don't shut it down. It's part of who you are. And, I suspect, it's part of what makes you so good at your work."

"I don't know, Ronan. I've always tried to hide it, even from myself. Why can't I just write what they ask me to write? Why can't I push all these other things out of the way and live like normal people do, without everything seeming to wash its way inside me? Sometimes I'm afraid I won't be able to function in this world if things keep going as they have." Alice melted into his arms, remnants of her fear of getting too close to him dissolving.

Her defenses were gone.

"Not being able to push things away means you have a gift the world needs. You can be one of the people who does something. Can you ask if they'll let you write the story from an ecotourism approach?"

"I don't think so. And, honestly, I don't want to ask. I'm not up to hearing them say no and then having to face whatever that means for me."

"I understand. I feel the same way at my job a lot of the time. Even with all of the science we have available to us, people don't seem to want to face the fact that the world we grew up in, the environment we all love so much, is changing. And it's because of what we're doing. Nothing we do can buy back what we're destroying unless we make big changes soon."

"The sea animals that are coming ashore are showing us that. Have you read the articles about the whales beaching themselves all over the planet? It's almost like they're sacrificing themselves to tell us something. We can't see what's happening in their world under the surface of the water, so they're trying to show us."

"Yes. But we can't seem to see it. Or maybe we don't want to."

Ronan leaned forward, looking at the envelope from Grandmere Grace on the coffee table, the journal sitting next to it.

"What's this? I don't want to pry, but the journal looks old."

Alice turned toward him, grateful for a change in subject. It had been a long day.

"It is. My grandmother sent it to me. It was written by her mother, my Great Grandmere Grace." This was it, the moment to tell him everything. The time to open up and not hold it all alone. But . . . what if he decided she was too much of a mess?

"That's amazing. I'd love to receive something like that from my family." He touched the journal, running his hand over the cover.

"How about if we make a pot of that great tea you brought over?" Alice stood up. Tea would help.

"Tea heals everything. I'm not sure if it can heal that bump on your head from what happened today, but maybe it can help heal a little of the sadness about Cassiopeia."

"I can't stop thinking about her. When we saw her, I felt like she was looking right into me, trying to tell me something. It seems crazy, but I really felt that. And now she's gone and I still feel at a loss about what she seemed to want from me."

"I feel that all the time when I'm there. I think they just want us to see them, to see what's happening. And we can do whatever is in front of us to do, at least as a start. As a start here, how about if I put on the kettle? I think I can find my way around your kitchen."

"I'll help." Alice leaned over and kissed him. "Then I'll tell you more about this journal and maybe we can read it together. There's a lot here—things I never knew about my family."

It was time. She was finally ready to tell him about all of it.

* * *

Early morning light flowed into her bedroom through the window. Alice stood in front of the windowpane, peering out at the neighborhood slowly awakening, a cup of coffee in her hand. She looked over at Ronan, asleep on her bed, still in his jeans and t-shirt. They had stayed awake until late into the night, reading the journal, talking, connecting dots between the stories and histories of their families.

And she had told him everything. About her visitations by the little girl dressed in white that started in her childhood, the recurring images of turtles and seals. The sights and terrifying sounds of shotguns in her dreams.

They'd read the journal together, poring over each page as they drank tea, curled up together on her couch, then finally moving to her bedroom where he'd fallen asleep only an hour before.

She couldn't sleep and had finally gotten up and made coffee. As she looked out of the window, thoughts ran through her mind as waves, one after the other, each leaving imprints she tried to piece together.

They'd talked about their grandmothers and what they remembered about them. She shared with him memories of French music on Saturday nights, the fais do-dos—dances until early in the morning with aunts and uncles and cousins and grandparents all laughing, eating what her grandmother had cooked for the evening, cousins and uncles playing music on their accordions and guitars. When they read about Mamou's Irish heritage, Ronan told her of the Irish dances his aunts taught him when he was a child, of their days at the ocean shore fishing and telling stories—of seals turning into women, of men falling in love with them and their lives changing forever. Of magic and beauty.

Grandmere Grace's journal had answered some of the

mystery around what Alice had been experiencing. It gave her a new sense of her great-grandmother, as a woman grieving, a young mother—a woman Alice had not imagined. Now she understood more about Lily's life, about her own grandmother's life. Martha as a young girl losing two sisters in a few short years. Losing a part of her mother with these deaths.

And how had Lily died? What had really happened? How was Alice to make sense of it all?

Sunshine was beginning to shine down on the roses in the yard across the street from Alice's house and she thought of the ones her grandmother had grown when she was a child. The roses in front of her seemed to connect her to memories of that time, as though she was back in New Orleans, barefoot and playing in the sun on the grass in her family's yard.

Was time even real? Alice rubbed her hands over her coffee cup. *If time is so slippery, can I actually be having memories that aren't mine? That are—were—Grandmere Grace's? Or even going before that, all the way back to Mamou?*

She walked to the kitchen, put on another pot of coffee, thoughts continuing to wash through like the tide. Stories pulsed through her. The story of Lily, of her death at the river's edge connected now in her mind with the death of Cassiopeia. With the seals and turtles. With everything she had been seeing and experiencing, all of it circling in her mind, like the spiral-shaped wind chime outside her kitchen window, now reflecting the early morning light as it gently twirled in a circle.

Stories moving through families, growing and deepening with each generation, tragedies and joy, side by side. Only now the tragedies seemed to be spiraling outward too, with far-reaching impacts beyond what anyone could predict.

She was a writer. What was she to do with all of this? How was it connected?

Cassiopeia's face emerged. Eyes wide open, with a message, sent silently.

The message from the letter in the jewelry box came to her.

Use your gifts to protect what you love and create what you desire.

The coffee pot made short popping sounds as the nutty smell of chicory filled her kitchen.

Alice looked over at her bookshelf, the jewelry box now taking center stage in the middle, the river rock on top of it, the spiral and stars seeming brighter than usual in the early morning light. An image from her dreams—a turtle peering at her then turning back toward the ocean—rose in her mind.

Follow me, it seemed to say.

The memory of talking with Ronan about Cassiopeia: *I think they just want us to see them, to see what's happening.*

An idea slowly began to form in her mind, emerging from her muddled thoughts like a seal poking its head above the waves.

A small one, percolating with the coffee that now announced itself with a final whooshing sound, one final puff of steam sending up a signal that it was ready.

PART 5

Belonging

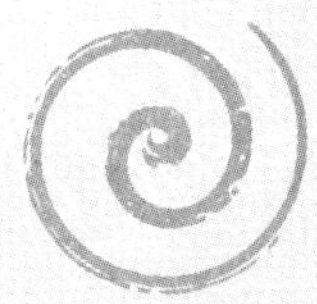

CHAPTER 32–ALICE

July 2019, New Orleans, Louisiana

The funeral took place on a Saturday. Only a week had passed since the night reading the journal with Ronan. Now, standing in the church in her grandmother's neighborhood with her sisters and mother, Alice wished he were with her, holding her hand.

Grandmere Martha's passing had been sudden. She died in her sleep, apparently from a stroke that released her from her body quickly.

What had she been thinking as she went to sleep the night before? Could she have known this would be the last time she would close her eyes, the last time she would look at her African violets, sitting in small pots in the same window ledge where her mother had tended her African violets before she died? Alice wondered these things as she stood to sing "Amazing Grace" with the rest of the congregation, the church full of people who loved her grandmother. Could Grandmere Martha hear them? The song rang through the church, all voices distilled into this single sound, a serenade to a life that had been completed.

"Alice," Madeline whispered as the song finished. "Look, Francois is here." She pointed toward the other side of the church. "The older he gets, the more he looks like Uncle Pierre. The genes are strong in this family."

"Looks like all the cousins are here," Alice whispered back as they sat down. Grateful that she had been able to get a few days off to fly to New Orleans for the funeral, she realized that if she hadn't, she would have been the only grandchild to miss it. Amanda had been kind, offering her the time off, but it had put a hold on the article about Hawaii and Alice knew her trip for the funeral was putting a strain on deadlines for the magazine. She couldn't miss this, though. Especially after receiving Grandmere Grace's journal from Grandmere Martha.

Grandmere, can you hear me now? Thank you for sending it to me. And thank you, Grandmere Grace, for writing it.

The church in Berkeley rose in her mind, the image of the small coffin—Lily's—clear in her vision, the sound of crying still palpable. The coffin was similar to the one in the church where she now sat, this one for Lily's sister, Martha. Alice smiled thinking of them being together again, with Haydee, their mother Grace, their father and brother. And maybe others? Maybe Mamou and Antoine and others who came before them? How far back did it go, the connections between family members? How many might be with them all now, in the church, watching over them?

Alice opened her eyes, looked up at the stained-glass windows surrounding her, each one bringing in fractals of colored light reflecting off the pews, the people, the candles. The church was quiet now, the only sound that of footsteps as the priest walked down from the altar toward the casket and blessed it with a sprinkling of holy water.

Water. River water. Ocean water. Holy water. All of it coming into one in Alice's mind. Water washing over everything, washing away the past, making things clean again.

She watched as her mother stood, walked to the casket, leaned over, and kissed it. A quiet, simple gesture, saying goodbye to her own mother. Sophia and Madeline stood, Alice following them, ready to walk behind their mother and Grandmere Martha's casket, her aunt, uncle, and cousins standing on the other side of the aisle.

As she walked out of the pew, following behind Madeline, a beam of sunlight broke through one of the windows above the altar, casting a glow around Alice and her sisters. She stood in place for a moment before moving, looking up toward the window, listening. Was there a message with the light beam?

Grandmere Martha, Grandmere Grace, is there something you want me to know? Is there something you still want me to do?

No words came to her. Only the sound of walking, her family members taking slow, steady steps, clicking sounds on the stone floor as they followed the priest and the pallbearers carrying Grandmere Martha's casket down the aisle.

* * *

"Sophia, I'm sorry Camille couldn't make it." Alice handed her sister a glass of wine from the dining room table set with a large bowl of floating magnolias, the white crocheted tablecloth barely visible with all the food people had brought to the house.

"She was sorry too. In some ways, though, it's nice to have just the three of us together."

"I'll take a glass of that wine," Madeline chimed in, walking toward them with a basket of cards in her hand. "Mom asked me to put this on the table, all the notes from everyone who came by today. Is there a spot there with all the food?"

Alice moved a dish with remnants of red beans and rice, a few pieces of spicy sausage poking out of the mix, to the side, pushing it next to a platter with a few slices of ham left. "Put it here. I don't think anyone is going to eat anymore. We can probably start taking these dishes to the kitchen."

"It was good to see so many cousins and friends here," Madeline said, placing the basket on the table. "Grandmere Martha was definitely loved."

"Yes, just like Grandmere Grace. Do either of you remember her funeral?" Sophia looked at Madeline then at Alice. "I remember people crying and eating a lot at the house later, and Grandmere Martha kept herself busy, never stopping through the whole thing. I remember her cooking and serving everyone all weekend. Her usual self. Never showing much outward emotion, but I could tell even then that she was trying to keep her feelings at bay by not stopping. I kept wanting her to just sit down and let people do things for her, but that was never her way."

"No, it wasn't. She was definitely a caretaker," Madeline said, picking up a thin slice of ham and rolling it around a piece of cheese. "Mom's just like her."

Alice paused, thinking about the journal. How had Grandmere Martha felt after her sister died and her mother was washed through with such deep grief? Did she just pull into herself, never letting anyone in? Thoughts of the turtle shell came to mind, the malachite one carved by an Irish craftsperson. Her own tendency to pull into her shell, safe and protected, not showing emotion. Maybe she was like her grandmother?

"Alice, what are you thinking?" Sophia's voice broke through her musings. "You look a little lost. But I guess we all are."

"I was actually thinking about Grandmere Martha and how stoic she was," Alice said. "Not ever really showing emotion. I wonder if she felt more than she let us know."

"It's kind of the family way, isn't it?" Madeline said, popping the ham and cheese into her mouth.

"I guess so." Alice paused. She hadn't told her sisters about the journal, about any of what she'd learned about their grandmothers. Suddenly feeling guilty, as though—again—she had been given a secret to hold, she wondered if this was the time to tell them everything about Lily, about the grief that Grandmere Grace must have carried until she died. Before she could come up with the words to start, their mother walked over, carrying a vase of flowers.

"Hi, girls. I'm glad you're all together. I have a few things to give you. Let's go into my room."

"Mom, the flowers are beautiful. Who are they from?" Sophia touched the purple glass vase with one hand and put her other hand on her mother's shoulder.

"Father Ardoin. He couldn't come to the house, but he had them sent over. I'll leave them here with the food and we can find a place to put them after we clean everything up. But now, I want to give you the things your grandmother left for each of you."

They walked down the hall, past photos hanging on the walls of family members over many decades, a line of guardians watching over them as they went into their mother's bedroom. On the bed were three bright-colored paper bags, each with a name on it.

"My mother planned this ahead of time. She put your names on the bags and had them in her closet for me to give you when she finally passed away. We talked just last week and she told me she'd done this, what she was leaving for each of you. I just didn't think the time would come so quickly. Go ahead and take a look."

Madeline walked over first and picked up the bag with her name on it. She pulled out a cookbook with pages falling out of it, the cover embroidered with roses and lavender. "Mom, she left me the book with all of her recipes!"

"Of course, honey. Who else would she leave it to? Take care of it. Some of those recipes go back many generations."

Sophia stepped up toward the bed next, picking up the small bag with her name on it. She reached in and pulled out a tiny black box and opened it. "It's her wishbone broach, the one with tiny emeralds. It's beautiful."

"She knew you'd appreciate it. I remember her wearing it to church every Sunday. She never wore it for regular occasions, just for Mass and special parties. It was given to her by Mamou, and before that, it belonged to Mamou's mother, who brought it with her when she came from Ireland. No one really knows how she had something with emeralds in it when they were so poor. It's amazing they didn't sell it when they needed money for food, but somehow it's stayed in the family all these years."

"It's beautiful. I'll cherish it." Sophia turned to Alice. "Your turn."

Alice walked to the bed and looked inside the last bag. A quilt, faded from years of being washed and loved, was folded up, filling most of the bag. She pulled it out gently.

"Is this the one Mamou made?" Alice could hardly believe she was holding the quilt that had been at Lily's funeral, the one they'd covered her with when she was so sick as a young girl, the one Grandmere Grace had hung in the oak tree after her funeral.

"Yes. She said she thought you'd understand it and that you might have your own stories to add to it. I'm not sure what she meant by that, but she wanted it to go to you."

Alice draped the quilt around her shoulders, wrapping it around her body. Time seemed to seep off the faded fabric, stories woven into each square. Gifts that women in her family held, some hidden, some unable to be kept hidden or held in a box. The quilt holding all of them, gifts from her grandmothers now wrapping around her, creating a sense of safety she hadn't felt since she'd opened the jewelry box in her Berkeley apartment. Sophia and Madeline wrapped themselves around her, then their mother joined them, putting her arms around all three of her daughters.

No one spoke as they held each other, each with their own thoughts, the photos of family members watching over from silver and pearl-colored frames on the oak dresser.

* * *

The drive to the river where Lily died took Alice along the marshes and close to the coastline. Highway 90 was still much as it had been for decades, small towns dotted along the waterways that defined the way of life in this part of the state for generations of families. The home where Grace had raised her children was still there, repainted by the current owners but recognizable by the large oak tree in front, the one where Grace had hung the quilt after Lily's death, its arms reaching far out across the yard.

Alice turned off the road, headed for the river nearby. Having visited this area a few times as a child, she hoped her memory—and possibly her grandmothers—would lead her to the spot she needed to visit.

The place where Lily died. The place where the curse—or at least the darkness—that had hung over their family for so long had been deepened by grief that started at this spot and that had never left her grandmother.

The dark cloud had started earlier, of course, with what had happened during Mamou's time. Her decision to shut down her healing and intuitive gifts. Samuel's death began what hung over them, and now Alice believed she understood what the letter meant.

Protect what you love.

Create what you desire.

Wispy moss danced in the breeze as Alice drove, creating a backdrop to her thoughts, as though ancient spirits were guiding her along, bringing her back to the place where she could make things right. End the grief. Begin something new in her family's lineage.

A small grove of oak trees lined the bank of the river at the end of the road, one large tree standing in the center, a guardian over the rest. Alice picked up the jewelry box, touched the scarf around her neck, and approached it, wondering if she would feel the presence of her grandmothers, of Lily.

The only sound was of a bird calling out as she walked toward the tree. High in the tallest oak tree, a cardinal—bright red with a black beak—whistled then trilled, calling her toward the large trunk. The river bank lay just beyond it and as she walked toward the water, a faint glow seemed to rise from the ground around her, lighting up the trees for a moment. Was that imagination?

It didn't matter anymore. Real, imagined—all of it was part of her reality now. This world and those beyond the veils. The physical and the spirit world. She was ready to accept all of it, and she belonged wherever her journey took her.

It had taken her here now, to the place where Lily died. A grouping of rocks at the bank created a comfortable place to sit, to open the jewelry box. She pulled the doll out first, sitting it beside her, then placed the hair pins on the small rock below where she sat, the small carvings of the sea creatures close to the water. The river rock came last, and as she picked it up, the warmth she now expected moved through her hand, running up her arm, until she felt it pulsing through her whole body.

The gift of healing. Of connections with the spirits and the ancestors. With the Earth and water and stars. All of it. No longer afraid, she held up the stone with a silent promise to her grandmothers.

Protect what you love.

Create what you desire.

She finally understood. Her path was connected to theirs, and she would continue the work Mamou had begun. She no longer needed the stone to guide her.

She placed it gently at the water's edge, tracing the spiral one last time with her finger, her soft whisper rising into the air, "Thank you, Mamou and Lily. Thank you, Grandmere Grace, Grandmere Martha. Merci . . ."

CHAPTER 33–ALICE

November 2019, Berkeley, California

Isabella's tail swished across Alice's face.

"Come on, off my laptop." Alice scooped up the cat and put her on the couch. "I know it's time for dinner, but you can't keep walking on my computer."

She scrolled up to read what she'd just written, one hand rubbing Isabella's head to keep her still. A knock at the door let her know Ronan had arrived with dinner. She popped up and let him in, greeting him with a kiss.

"Let me help you. I can open the wine. You brought one of my favorite syrahs. Perfect for finishing up the text for our website."

"The pasta dish will probably help too. Let's get this food served so you can show me what you've done so far."

They walked into the kitchen and he served the steaming food onto plates while she poured them each a glass of wine. A small vase of camellias she'd placed on the dining room table that morning caught her eye, bringing to mind all the women in her family and the ways their stories were impacting everything that was happening in her life. Before she could share her thoughts, Ronan walked over, picked them up, and put them on the coffee table with their wine glasses.

"Might as well have a pretty centerpiece here while we work on the website, right?"

"We should definitely have a beautiful work space." Alice smiled. He'd put the vase on their makeshift table without her having to ask. She could get used to this. "Let me feed Isabella before we start."

She opened a can of cat food and dished some up as Ronan carried their dishes to the couch and sat down. Alice looked over at him, realizing how comfortable she was with him in her home. *He belongs here.* The words popped into her mind unedited, and she smiled. The thought didn't scare her. *Yes. He belongs here with me.*

"So, the name is Cassiopeia's Constellation, right? That's what we're settling on?" Ronan asked, handing her a glass of wine.

"Yes, I think so. Cassiopeia was the reason I couldn't stop thinking about what's happening with the ocean. I know the full name is a mouthful, but it fits. It ties together the ocean and the sky, the constellations above and around us, the whole thing. I just finished the description that will go on the home page to let people know what we're doing and why we gave it this name. Take a look."

She turned her laptop toward him.

Join us on a journey along with the beautiful creatures of the sea that share our planet. The ocean environment they call home is changing quickly in ways that are putting many of them at risk of extinction. As caretakers of the environment, we can all do things that turn that around. Cassiopeia was a seal who lost her life due to human behaviors. She led us to create this platform where you can join us in raising funds and awareness about what's happening to our oceans and the amazing animals that live there. Join our community by choosing one of the seals, turtles, sea lions, or sea otters below to sponsor. As their sponsor, you'll be able to learn about their journey in the sea, and your sponsorship will go toward ocean research and conservation, helping to save their habitat. You'll have a front row seat as we feature stories of these amazing sea beings and what is being done to preserve their home.

"It's perfect, Alice. I think Cassiopeia would be happy with this."

"We can get photos of the animals that come to the different centers along the West Coast to start, then maybe we'll be able to expand. I know there's a lot we still have to figure out, but we can start small and let it grow. I'd love to connect with marine hospitals in Ireland at some point. Wouldn't that be great?"

"We'd have to visit, of course," Ronan said. "We couldn't do it without research."

"Of course." Alice smiled. Visiting Ireland with Ronan, meeting his family there—it seemed natural, almost inevitable. How could things have changed so quickly, bringing so many surprises?

"I'm glad we were able to talk with Aunt Annie and hear how Orion is doing. It's amazing that she and Tutu Amelia were able to watch him swim back out to sea after the center there got him back to health."

"Yes. Full circle in some way. We were here when he landed, and they were there to watch him swim back out to his home. And somehow, I feel like Grandmere Martha is with us on this, with her help in getting our project started."

"Are you sure you want to use the money from your grandmother on it? I know you've gotten some good freelance writing work since you quit your job, but maybe you should save it? We could probably start the project without going too big at first."

"I'm sure. I have some savings of my own that will last a while and freelance work lined up for several months. She left each of us a small amount, and I'd like to use it for something that will last, something that will help turn things around. Somehow it feels like this is a way to make up for what happened to Lily, to my grandmother and her mother and their whole family when Lily died. I keep thinking that the reason Lily died was because she was pulled toward something that no one understood. Maybe she didn't even understand it. She was so young. And the Benoit boys, whatever they had to do with it, it's clear they didn't put much value on her life. They were only boys, but from what we read, they seemed pretty hateful. This is about the opposite of that—the opposite of hate and the opposite of looking away from things we don't understand."

Her voice drifted off and they sat in silence as Isabella jumped up into her lap. She placed her hand on the cat's back, rubbing it gently. Isabella leaned into Alice and purred, her ribcage vibrating next to Alice's heart.

Alice turned to look at Ronan and spoke softly. "I'm not going to turn away from the things I see anymore, the ones I see in the world right in front of me or the ones I see from the other worlds that seem to call to me. Mamou turned away from her gift after Samuel died, and I think that's when something in my family closed up." She reached her hand out, touching Ronan's arm. "I used to tell myself that what I saw wasn't real, that if others couldn't see it, then I was making it up. I'm not going to do that anymore. It's time for the gifts in my family to open again, and I know now I want to be a protector of the water, of the beautiful life that lives in the oceans and rivers, just as Mamou was. I'm finally ready. And I'm so grateful you came into my life to help me get to this place."

She leaned toward him and he kissed her, slowly at first, then more deeply. Isabella jumped off her lap and Ronan wrapped his arms around Alice. Her body melted against his, all thoughts leaving her mind.

She belonged here with him. This is what she desired—a life with a man who could break through the walls she'd built and accept her fully as she was.

That was all she knew, all she needed to know for now. The rest would unfold in time.

CHAPTER 34—GRACE

May 1999, New Orleans, Louisiana

She is old now, close to the time when she will fly with the angels, escorting her far beyond the clouds and this limited world of men and their petty angers.

Her face is relaxed, softened with a certainty that she has done the best she could with this life she was given. She understands she must choose her last tasks carefully, with precision. She has little time left and almost no time for mistakes, so she must move slowly. Already the angel stands waiting at her door. She has no time to re-do this.

She has already chosen how she will do it. No one suspects she is still carrying the burden of guilt for her daughter's death. They only see a four-foot ten-inch woman whose body looks like that of a preteen. The wrinkles on her hands and face and her thin, white hair show her age. That and the cotton gingham dress that hangs loosely on her frame. It is the dress of a woman born at a much earlier time, one whose long life has left her many memories.

She wants to tell some of her story, leave some of what she remembers behind.

She has chosen the perfect place to leave gifts for her great-granddaughter, the one whose gifts mirror Lily's—in the sea-green jewelry box her mother gave her when she turned eighteen. And she has chosen what will go in it. Lily's favorite doll, a swath of fabric matching the quilt from Mamou, four hairpins with animals from the sea to lead Alice to the ocean—to the place of water where all stories begin. And, of course, the river rock, Mamou's healing stone, painted with the spiral and stars to light Alice's way.

In the jewelry box she would also leave a note, leaving her love behind and words she wished she had been able to say to Lily. That time was gone now, but there was still hope for Alice.

She turned to see if the angel was still there. The angel nodded, giving her time to complete her task. This was often the way of moments like this, when a life is closed up, leaving behind whatever remnants are necessary for those left with the pieces.

She turned back to write the note. She couldn't say everything she wanted to say—that would be too much for a seven-year-old child. She would just give a message of love and enough clues to help the child unravel what she needed to know when she was older. She had to trust that the most important truths would be told to the girl in the space between words, in the dreamtime, in the whispers of memory. One day, maybe Alice would also read the journals, and she would understand more. For now, she would leave this note.

She knew she had no time left to do anything more. She had only enough time to begin unburdening her soul of the weight of all that had happened, of all she remembered. She knew her great-granddaughter had the gift of seeing, and one day she would grow into knowing how to use it.

It had started so many generations ago, a family lineage of dark and light, shadows and secrets mingled with the gifts of the mystics and seers. Yes, her great-granddaughter would be up to the task one day.

And she would be with her, from her place in the clouds. Her great-granddaughter would hear her whisperings and nudges. She hoped Alice would untangle the truth, be brave enough to open to her gifts and use them for good, and maybe, just maybe, finally set them all free.

EPILOGUE

ALICE AND RONAN

June 21, 2023—Arch Rock Beach, Oregon

The sun was setting on the horizon, barely visible as it began its descent into the ocean.

"Watch now, it will happen so quickly you can miss it." Ronan reached over to Alice and put his hand on her growing belly. "Little one," he whispered, "one day you'll be able to watch this with us."

Alice put her hand over his. "Do you think she can hear us?"

"Of course. I'm sure she hears everything we say. She comes from a long line of women who hear what others may not, right?" He grinned as he spoke. Alice looked at him and laughed, wondering if their daughter would have his smile.

"She does. She also comes from your family, a long line of Irish people who believe in magic, so between those two things, I think we're going to have a pretty special child on our hands."

"She'll be special because she's our daughter." Ronan leaned over and kissed Alice just as she felt a little kick right where he had his hand.

"See, she's listening now."

"And look—the sun just set below the sea line. The stars will start appearing soon."

"Do you think we can stay awake until the meteor shower? If I fall asleep, you'll have to wake me up. We drove all this way. I don't want to miss it." Alice pulled the quilt from her grandmothers out of their backpack and wrapped it around her legs. "And I'm excited about our drive tomorrow up to Otter Rock Sanctuary. Our baby's first big trip is a drive up the coast of our favorite ocean. Perfect."

Ronan poured them each a glass of sparkling cider and opened the picnic basket, pulling out chocolate and strawberries.

"Here," he said, offering her one. "Remember when you offered me strawberries the first day we met? Exactly four years ago today. They've been my favorite fruit ever since."

Alice picked one up and took a bite, its juice sprinkling on her chin as she bit into it.

"Mine too. I'm making pies with the ones we picked up at the market yesterday. Maybe I'll make an extra one and send it to Aunt Annie. I've been thinking about her a lot lately."

"Me too. I know she misses Tutu Amelia."

"We all do." Alice reached over and put her hand in Ronan's. "Did you read about what the city council in La Jolla is considering? Apparently, they close off a portion of the beach there every year for a few months to let the sea lions give birth on shore without human interference, but now they're considering having it be closed to the public for several years to give them time to re-populate and have a space that's just theirs, with no humans messing things up. I'm sure Aunt Annie will be happy about that."

"Tutu Amelia would have been happy about it. I wish she could have been here to see it."

"I have to believe she's still with us, along with all of the others." Alice looked up and saw the first star appear in the early evening sky.

"Yes, I'm sure she is. She was never one to miss a party."

"And this is a great one tonight. I hope the water around Arch Rock lights up again tonight during the meteor shower. The blue light rising off of it was so was amazing, other-worldly, this afternoon. What is it again that makes it happen?"

"The plankton in the ocean. Scientists still aren't sure what causes it, but they think it has something to do with warning off predators. I love that they warn them off with something so beautiful."

"It gives me reason to hope. It's a message to predators but it's also a message to all of us on the shore how much life is below the surface. How intelligent it is."

"Cassiopeia's Constellation has been getting so many views and sponsors lately that I'm feeling more hopeful about humanity too. And next year we'll finally get to Ireland and see the center we've been working with there. Our baby girl will get her first international trip before she's even a year old."

"I'm excited about the trip. I hope we can travel a lot with this little girl and let her see the ocean in lots of places."

"I just read something about research that's happening in the Caribbean. Some scientists are setting up shop to study the songs of the whales off a few islands to see if they can decode it, possibly understand what the sounds mean. Maybe we'll finally be able to communicate with them in a shared language."

"That would be pretty amazing. Closing the gap between our worlds more."

"And speaking of connecting worlds, I also just read an article about scientists finding gravitational waves coming from all parts of the universe that are connected. They say the waves create one big song that we're all a part of. It made me think of what you wrote last week, Alice, the article for the magazine. You captured it all so perfectly there."

"Which one? The article for the environmental magazine? I didn't realize you'd read that. It hasn't been published yet."

"You left your browser open after you wrote it and I happened to see it. You usually let me read them before you send them off, so I thought you wouldn't mind. I loved it so much I took a snapshot of it with my phone and saved it."

"You didn't!"

"I did. Can I read some of it to you now? Or to our daughter? I think she'd love hearing her mother's writing." Ronan pulled his phone out of the pocket of his shorts and clicked on his photos. "Listen up, little one. Here are a few thoughts from your mother." He leaned in closer to Alice and began reading, his quiet voice a lullaby.

"Scientists and mystics are all searching for the same thing—the song that weaves us all together, the rhythm that gives our existence some sense of meaning. It's in our own heartbeat, in the sound of the cicadas at night, in the flutter of butterfly wings our ears are too undeveloped to hear. It's in the music of the galaxies collapsing and rising, reverberating across the heavens. All around us, all the time, the song is moving waves through the universe. It's the song we all belong to—you, me, the earthworms digging in the deep Earth, the bamboo and reeds growing by the river, the whales singing in the ocean depths."

Alice let out a sigh as he finished reading and turned to her. "You really took a photo of that?"

"I did. It's beautiful, Alice, and one of the reasons I love you so much. You're an artist at heart."

"You are too. You're a musician." Alice paused, remembering their first day together on the beach. She leaned toward him, placed her hand on his leg. "Tell me again about the song you sang on the beach the day we first met. Tell our daughter. I think she'd also like to hear the story."

Ronan laughed, his curly hair softly glowing from the light of the rising moon. He placed his hand on top of Alice's and leaned toward her. "The song is a love story. It's about a selkie, of course. She was both a seal and a woman, able to change shape as she moved between the sea and the land. She swam in the ocean near a small island south of Ireland and came ashore only when the moon was full, only near the time of the equinox or the solstice. One night she came ashore and a young man caught sight of her. He was captivated by her beauty and knew that if he lost her, he would never be able to find his way in the world. He began to sing a song that captured her attention. She was so spellbound by his song that she agreed to marry him and stay in the body of a woman. They lived happily together for the rest of their lives and had children, but she never stopped visiting the ocean at night, and sometimes she would disappear for a few days, perhaps to visit her ocean family. It's a song of love that my mother used to sing to me when I was a boy."

"That's such a beautiful story, Ronan. So much love and longing in that. I can almost imagine it's true, hearing you tell it."

"Some say," Ronan said, leaning over and rubbing her belly, "that the selkie was my great-great grandmother." He looked up and grinned, then leaned down and kissed the place where his hand was on her stomach. "And who knows what's really true? Today is the solstice. A day to believe in the magic of what we can't always see."

The baby kicked, poking at Alice's stomach. She smiled and ran her hand over his head, her fingers running through the curls in his hair. Ronan was only telling her a story, of course, and she loved the way his culture and hers were connected by the ocean and waters, but she realized that she wouldn't mind if the legend were true. If her daughter was a child of both the land and the sea. The thought brought back the memory of a dream she'd had early that morning.

"I had a dream about our baby . . ." Alice hesitated before saying more, allowing the memory to return slowly. "I was standing in front of the ocean and a woman swam up from the water, rising up from the foam, appearing almost like a mirage at first, but then she came into focus, her body clearly taking shape just a few feet from where I stood. She held out her arms and handed me a baby girl, wrapped in a sea-green blanket. I looked at the baby first, then at the woman, and suddenly she had the face of my Grandmere Martha. I looked at the baby again, staring at me with wide open eyes, and when I looked back at the woman, she had the face of my Great Grandmere Grace. After that, her face started changing, into faces I don't know, each one looking a little like the one before it, but with small changes. Slightly different eye color. Different smile, or face shape. And it was as if I knew all of them, or at least they knew me, even though I didn't recognize them. I stood there feeling unable to move, then suddenly the woman transformed into a pillar of water that rushed up into the sky, the stars. It was if she just expanded until she was part of everything around her."

Alice turned to Ronan, his eyes reminding her of the color of the blanket swaddling the baby in her dream. "I'm not sure why I didn't tell you about the dream earlier today. It engulfed me so fully that I think I needed time to let it settle inside me."

Ronan leaned over and kissed her. "Beautiful dream. Maybe it's time we decide on a name for our beautiful baby girl who is coming to us so soon. What if we name her after one of the constellations?"

They looked up at the sky, stars poking through the inky blackness one at a time.

"Which one are you thinking?"

"How about something most people know about, the Big Dipper? It's part of the constellation called Ursa Major, so we could name her Ursula. The Big Dipper has seven stars, just like the Pleiades, the constellation also called the Seven Sisters. Lots of mythology and folklore connect those two sets of stars, but who knows what's true. The universe is so much bigger than we understand."

Star sisters. Alice thought of Martha, Lily, Haydee. Of her own sisters, Madeline and Sophia. "Does the name Ursula have any other meanings?"

"It means 'little bear' which would mean she's not only connected to the stars, but also to the Earth. A protector."

Alice thought of her grandmothers—Martha, Grace, and all those who came before. "Could we name her Ursula Claire, after my great-great-grandmother Mamou?"

"That's a perfect name. Ursula Claire. Claire is an Irish name, so she'll bring both of our families together."

Ronan picked up the quilt and wrapped it around Alice, bringing the other side around himself. Cocooned together, they looked up at the sky. Alice rubbed her hands across the soft cotton of the quilt, thinking about the stories it held of her grandmothers. She had just started making a new quilt, one for Ursula, from the squares of fabric Grandmere Grace had left for her in the jewelry box. Time to start a new chapter in their family's story.

Alice looked up and noticed the patterns between the stars, wondered how far away they all were. Wondered if her ancestors, Ronan's ancestors, were there, watching over them. A star blazed across the skyline and dimmed to nothing, leaving behind a palette of lights twinkling in scattered, perfect patterns. She spoke softly, almost inaudibly, gently rubbing her stomach, lulling Ursula to sleep.

"It looks like a sky painting, doesn't it?"

Our stories start in the water
birth and death
and birth again
like the stars and planets
swirling
we are water and Earth
we are fire and air

Our stories end in the water
returning to the primal source
which births us
endless flowing
back to the source
the song which reminds us,
endlessly:

You belong.
You belong.

BOOK CLUB DISCUSSION QUESTIONS

1. One of the major themes of *Song of Belonging* is learning to listen to the wisdom of our ancestors as we navigate the challenges we face in an uncertain world. Have you ever had an experience of feeling as if one of your ancestors had a message for you? Do you believe these types of experiences are possible?

2. Grace's story is mired in grief. At one point she writes in her journal: *The world opened when you were born and closed when you died and now you are everywhere, like the air wrapping around us after a thunderstorm, thick and pure and hanging with the deep scent of water from the heavens.* How did you respond to the levels of grief in her story? How does the way she speaks of her grief impact your experience of it?

3. Lily seems to have had an easy relationship with the natural world and with "seeing" into other worlds. She is connected to the otter family and wants to care for them. Does she remind you of anyone you know who

has a similar connection to nature? Do you relate to Lily's experience of the world?

4. We learn about several acts of cruelty that happen where no one is held responsible, beginning with the death of the deer that Mamou finds. Later, we learn of the deaths of Emile, Samuel, and Lily. In some parts of the story, cruelty seems almost casual, with no one seeming to care. How do you feel in these scenes? Does it make you think about other ways cruelty happens without anyone being held accountable?

5. Alice's story begins with her opening the jewelry box from her great-grandmother and looking at all of the gifts inside. What did you think of the items that were in the box? Did any stand out to you? Have you ever received a gift that impacted you the way the jewelry box and its contents impacted Alice?

6. In the beginning of the book, Alice copes with her experiences of seeing into other worlds by denying that they are happening. On the day she opens the jewelry box after many years of it being put away, she begins having frequent experiences of seeing and hearing things she cannot explain. Eventually, she acknowledges her abilities and chooses to use them to *protect what she loves and create what she desires*, as her great-grandmother wanted her to do. Have you ever had experiences like Alice's? What do you think of the message left to her in the letter by her great-grandmother?

7. At one point, Alice sees Ronan as a seal in the ocean when he is surfing, and herself as a turtle, hiding in her shell. Do you see this as symbolic of their relationship? Do you

feel more aligned with Ronan or with Alice in this way? Or with Lily, who may be seen as living her life like the otters from the story, playful and comfortable in the water and on the shore?

8. Alice learns that she comes from a lineage of women who see themselves as caretakers of the waters. Mamou was a healer in the French Acadian tradition, but she closed down her gifts after the death of Antoine. This lineage is finally reopened when Alice understands her family's history and connects it with things happening in her own life. Auntie Annie and Tutu Amelia appear in her life at a time when she needs help coming to terms with what she is learning, and they are able to help her accept and understand her experiences, even though they come from different cultures. What do you think of the role the grandmothers play in this story? Do you have anyone like this in your life?

9. The story covers many generations of Alice's family, ending with Alice pregnant with Ursula, who will begin a new chapter in their lineage. Do you see connections between the women in each generation? Do you see connections between Mamou, Tutu Amelia, and Aunt Annie, or between Lily and Alice?

10. In between pieces of Grace's journal, the ancestors "speak" and share their perspective and wisdom. Grace does not hear them, but at times she wonders if they are connected to what is happening. How do the messages from the spirit world impact your experience of the story?

11. *Song of Belonging* carries a message about our responsibility to care for the environment—the oceans and rivers

and the habitats of animals. At times, animals seem to be messengers of the need for humans to notice and take care of the planet. The otter family Lily loved, Orion, and Cassiopeia in particular play this role. How does this impact you? How do you see the relationships between humans, animals, and the natural environments we share?

12. This story begins with a prologue that sets a mythological tone, with a woman rising from the ocean. In the epilogue, Alice and Ronan are on the beach and Alice is pregnant with Ursula, whose name comes from a constellation of stars in the sky. Imagery of water runs throughout the story, with connections to the sky and stars. Does this imagery bring up anything for you? What is your relationship with the oceans, rivers, and stars?

13. What does the title *Song of Belonging* mean to you? How do you see the themes it brings up emerging in the story? How do you see these themes in your own life?

A FEW WORDS OF GRATITUDE

This story began in my mind when I was seven years old and was given a green jewelry box from my great-grandmother upon her passing. She and others who have come before me whispered stories to me for decades before I finally began to write what is now *Song of Belonging.* It has come into being through the generosity of many.

First, thank you to my family of origin, particularly my great-grandmother, Haydee Richarme, and her sisters, Aunt Martha and Aunt Lily. Thank you too, to my grandmother, Alice Lester, her sister, Ursula Barrios, and my cousin Haydee Blanchard, for being the link to our ancestors and their stories. While *Song of Belonging* is entirely a work of fiction, it was inspired by the rich fabric of our family and the French Louisiana culture.

All my thanks go to my mother, Ursula St. Romain, for nurturing and supporting my love of books, writing, and stories from the time I could hold a book and crayon. I am grateful to my siblings, in-laws, nieces, and nephews, and to all of my French Louisiana family—with more aunts, uncles, and cousins than I can count. You have taught me the gift of living with laughter and gratitude no matter what life offers, the joy of cooking with fresh ingredients and then enjoying great food with those we love, and the power of generations of family and community to remind us of our strength and place of belonging in this world.

The book wouldn't have been completed without the support of my writing friends along the way: Kathy Williams, Jennifer Wolfe, Alma Rosa Alvarez, and my Bookgardan cohort—Tara Badstubner, Lorene Garrett, Ann Mullen, and Meg Lamme. How could I have done this without you? Thanks to my current writing group for keeping me connected to the page every day: Julie Wurth, Anita Burke, Lois Schlegel, and Cathy Noah. I am also deeply appreciative of the Women Write community, those who participate in my writing workshops and continue to inspire me as we move through cycles of creativity together.

Thank you to Kate Moses of Birds and Muses Literary who took me under her wing when I wasn't sure if I could finish the first draft. The Bookgardan program helped this novel become all that I wanted it to be. Thank you for nurturing each of us through our writing projects. I am also grateful to Craigardan for offering the most amazing place at the top of a mountain in the Adirondacks for our writing residencies.

I appreciate all of the early readers who helped this book become much better than what I could have created alone: Jennifer Wolfe, Kathy Williams, Julie Wurth, Anita Burke, Liz Bahl, Anne Devane, and Priscilla St. Romain. Special thanks to Áine Galach for helping me with the Irish characters in the book and to the Marine Mammal Center in Sausalito, California, for education on marine mammals and their habitats. I am also grateful to Kathleen Furin and Maressa Garner for their support during the revision process of the novel.

Mahalo nui loa to Laura Kealoha Yardley, my long-time teacher and friend, whose love and guidance have supported me for decades on more levels than I can say. Thank you for being the inspiration for Tutu Amelia, for generously sharing the wisdom of your Hawaiian culture and ancestors, and for being a chosen grandmother to my children. I am also deeply grateful to Denise Elizabeth Byron whose ongoing friendship and support have helped me stay connected to the true source of this story.

A special note of gratitude goes to my brother Dan St. Romain, whose friendship and support through every stage of our lives continues to be a great gift.

Thank you to the Poetry Phone Line Project of the Oregon Humanities, *The Rapids* literary journal, Jefferson Public Radio, Ashland Community Radio, Rebel Heart Books, and Bloomsbury Books for featuring my work and giving me the inspiration to keep writing and sharing my words with others.

I am deeply grateful to Brooke Warner for believing in this story from its early days and choosing to publish it, and to everyone at She Writes Press, Simon and Schuster, and Books Forward for bringing *Song of Belonging* into the world in such a beautiful way. Special thanks to Shannon Green for shepherding it through each phase of this publishing journey, to Tabitha Lahr for interior design, and to Lindsey Cleworth for such a gorgeous cover. It takes a village!

I also want to thank my dear friends, Sara McLeod Judson, CEO of the Community Foundation of Southwest Louisiana, and Pam Breaux, president and CEO of the National Assembly of State Arts Agencies, for helping to share this story with such a large audience. Our high school English teachers would be proud of us!

Thank you more than I will ever be able to express to my family. Reid, you have changed and blessed my life profoundly from the moment you were placed in my arms, and you continue to carry a part of my own heart out into the world. You are making your ancestors proud. Evan and Charlotte, you are the children who were given to me as an unexpected gift, and you have brought untold amounts of joy and love to my life. You, too, are making your ancestors proud. And Ellen. I cannot imagine my life without you. You are the steady guiding light for me when I need it, the rock of support beside me, and the best playmate I could ask for. In case it isn't clear, we all belong to each other, and that was written in the stars long ago.

Finally, thank you to the oceans, rivers, and beautiful areas of this planet that have nurtured me over my life. May we learn to give back to you and to the animals of the waters, land, and sky as you so generously give to us.

ABOUT THE AUTHOR

Michelle St. Romain has been writing since she was a child. The co-author of two poetry books, *Promised Fruit* and *Water's Edge*, she holds a BA in English from Loyola University, New Orleans, and an MA in Creative Writing from California State University, Sacramento. Her work has been featured in the Poetry Phone Line Project of the Oregon Humanities, *The Rapids* literary magazine, and on Jefferson Public Radio and Ashland Community Radio. Michelle grew up in Louisiana and has lived in California and Hawaii. She leads writing workshops, reads voraciously, and enjoys learning life lessons from two spaniels and a wise, aging cat. She currently lives in Oregon with her family.

To learn more about Michelle's books, events, and ways to connect, visit **www.michellestromain.com**.

Looking for your next great read?

We can help!

Visit www.shewritespress.com/next-read
or scan the QR code below for a list
of our recommended titles.